Hailey Edwards writes about questionable applications of otherwise perfectly good magic, the transformative power of love, the family you choose for yourself, and blowing stuff up. Not necessarily all at once. That could get messy. She lives in Alabama with her husband, their daughter, and a herd of dachshunds.

Visit her website at www.haileyedwards.net

Pleas
Service

By *Hailey Edwards*

The Foundling Series

Bayou Born
Bone Driven
Death Knell
Rise Against
End Game

END GAME

HAILEY EDWARDS

piatkus

PIATKUS

First published in Great Britain in 2020 by Piatkus

1 3 5 7 9 10 8 6 4 2

A CIP catalogue record for this book
is available from the British Library.

ISBN 978-0-349-42338-8

Typeset in Goudy by M Rules
Printed and bound in Great Britain by
Clays Ltd, Elcograf S.p.A.

Papers used by Piatkus are from well-managed forests
and other responsible sources.

Piatkus
An imprint of
Little, Brown Book Group
Carmelite House
50 Victoria Embankment
London EC4Y 0DZ

An Hachette UK Company
www.hachette.co.uk

www.littlebrown.co.uk

I'm going to miss you guys.

CHAPTER ONE

———◆———

Warm blood stuck my fingers together, but there was no point in cleaning my hands. I twisted the blade, a quick snap of my wrist growing smoother with practice, and the bone popped out of its joint.

An unmistakable trill of interest rose over my shoulder, and I wasted no time flinging the chicken thigh in the air, feathers and all.

A slender bolt of white scales shot past my ear, crimson eyes fixed on her target, and I clapped when Phoebe caught the snack between her needlelike teeth. Dragon young, I was learning, didn't waste time with pointless activities like chewing their food. They gulped it down whole and came back for more.

"You're spoiling her," Cole rumbled from behind me. "She can hunt for herself."

An incredulous squawk rang out overhead as Phoebe flattened her round ears against her skull and dove at her father. She pulled up at the last second, kicking out to scratch his shoulder through the fabric of his White Horse polo before landing on my lap, as light as a feather. She cuddled me, already sucking up to get out of the trouble she was in.

"You hurt him," I scolded, hardening my heart against the pitiful expression widening her liquid eyes. "Look." I brought her attention to the dark stain spreading beneath the ruined fabric. "He's bleeding."

A whining noise made for the weakest apology in the history of children apologizing to their parents.

Phoebe was lucky she was so stinking cute. And we were doomed because she knew she was too.

The scratch itself was hardly life-threatening. Cole probably viewed it as being on par with a mosquito bite. That wasn't the issue. The problem was behaviors we found cute and mostly harmless coming from a baby would turn lethal as she matured into a full-fledged dragon. We had to correct her behavior now or suffer the consequences later.

First things first, though. Phoebe had to learn she couldn't play her parents against each other, and that she couldn't lash out in a fit of pique when her dad schooled me on how best to raise her.

I had no memories of his world, his culture, our past. I had to lean on him for guidance. I didn't want to raise her like a spoiled pet. I wanted her to grow up to be a strong and independent woman.

Starting right after we finished playing catch. The chicken was already dead. It might as well be put to good use.

"Thom caught a few Silkies on the neighbor's farm. This was our cut of the spoils." I made a mental note to put a check in the mail to cover the cost of purchasing more chicks. "It would be wasteful not to eat it."

Usually, the most feline member of the coterie brought me a mouse or the occasional snake. Pretty sure the mice were food, and the snakes were meant as a *look what I killed to protect you* gesture. Either way, I had always buried the bodies so he wouldn't know his thoughtful gifts went uneaten. These days, I didn't have that problem.

"You mean you decided to feed the evidence to Phoebe and save yourself from digging."

Busted.

"I helped Dad clean deer, so I ought to be able to figure out how to pluck and clean a chicken too, but . . ."

Cole strode over and sat on the grass next to me, the bond between us a live wire that tingled, electric without him laying a finger on me. "You couldn't resist."

The fact we had moved back to the battered farmhouse where I grew up in order to accommodate her was further proof none of us were great at telling her *no.*

"She's adorable." Unable to resist touching him when he sat so close, I rested my head on his shoulder. Rocks made more comfortable pillows, but he was worth the discomfort. He was mine. All mine. In all ways. And there was an unspeakable joy in that which I intended to savor for as long as I had left. "Just look at that face."

Phoebe hammed it up, fluttering her gossamer wings, twitching her slender tail. She licked my fingers clean while staring pointedly at what remained of the chicken.

"And to think I worried you two might not bond." He scratched under her chin, and she purred the littlest purr, melting my heart into a puddle of goo. "You two are as thick as thieves."

Had Phoebe emerged from stasis as a child, human in shape if not in genetics, I might have struggled more. That she was a dragon didn't change the fact she was Cole's child with another woman. Even if that other woman was, well, me.

Sheesh.

This amnesiac harbinger of doom gig was tough.

"It's go time," Santiago announced as he burst through the front door we had to replace to make the place inhabitable again after the Malakhim skirmish that sent Death into mourning over the children she lost. "We've got another Malakhim sighting near Canton."

The cold place tickled the edges of my senses, eager to rise up and swallow me whole.

I clamped my left hand over the rose gold bangle encircling my right wrist and tightened my grip like I might prevent Conquest from rising if I squeezed hard enough. The bangles had done their job well, and they still kept me *me*, but these episodes kept coming, with shorter breaks between them.

Only the worried trill of the dragon in my lap and the solidness of my mate cushioning my head yanked me back into my skin. With Cole beside me, it was too much to hope he hadn't noticed my struggle. At least he hadn't called me out on it. I was doing my best to throttle Conquest, and he was helpless to do more than watch.

"You have to stay with Uncle Thom." I tasted frost, and my voice crackled. "And you have to behave."

Snapping her tail against my thigh, Phoebe flattened her ears and growled at me this time.

"Uncle Thom can't come with us," I reminded her. "He can't fight. He's still healing, remember?"

Thom could and would fight if I let him, but I couldn't bear putting him in the path of danger when I had other options. The time would come when I couldn't spare him, but it wasn't here yet. Until then, I was grateful to have a trusted babysitter, one who could keep up with this little monster when she went on a tear.

Phoebe grunted, clearly unhappy, but her annoyance dimmed a few watts.

She had a wide protective streak that had stretched to encompass the coterie within days of meeting them. It gave me hope she would turn out more like her father than her mother. Me? Whoever.

"I need you to protect him for me," I murmured softly enough only she and Cole would hear, and I kept my tone as earnest as possible. Kids picked up on deceit far quicker than adults. "You have to keep him safe until I get back. Can you do that?"

Puffing out her chest, she fluffed her wings and stood her mane on end. Classic posturing behavior. So why did I have to fight the urge to whip out my phone and snap a dozen photos?

"Good girl." I bent down and kissed the top of her head. "Make sure you keep him in the house." As I stood, she climbed up my side to perch on my shoulder. "If anyone comes to the door, make him run. Make him hide. Bite him if you have to. We'll find you when we get back."

Phoebe bobbed her head once, following along or faking it, I still wasn't sure most of the time. She slitted her eyes when she spotted Thom sunning on the porch in a peeling rocking chair and growled.

Quick as a shot, she leapt down. I was still grasping for thin air when she hit the ground. She raced to him, nipped at his ankles until he jumped up, then cracked her tail until she herded him indoors.

"She doesn't grasp the concept of *me* space," he hissed from the doorway. "And she bites."

"She's a baby." I wiggled my fingers at them as I backed away. "She's just teething."

Fine, so she came with a full set of chompers. I wasn't about to tell him she was the one on babysitting detail in her book. It would embarrass him, and I couldn't bear to injure him, or his feelings.

"Why are we stuck with Junior again?" Santiago huffed with annoyance. "This is no place for a kid."

No surprise, Santiago was not a fan of having a baby dragon underfoot. I wasn't dancing in the streets about it either, but I didn't have much choice but to make it work. The least he could do was pitch in, but that was about as likely as a pig sprouting wings and flying into a barbecue pit.

Which reminded me, I hadn't eaten lunch yet.

"Believe me, this is the last place I want her to be, but she keeps escaping from Haven." Dad had tried his best, but she was a prodigy when it came to invisibility. She would hide near the door to whatever room he attempted to keep her in, wait on him to open it, then skitter her way to freedom. While Dad was the first to admit it was a neat trick, after she almost gave him a heart attack the first time, it also made keeping tabs on his granddaughter next to impossible. "We can't allow someone to follow her there, and I won't risk her being captured or killed."

Cole wasn't much help on the escape artist front. According to him, Convallarian youth learned to camouflage themselves early in order to escape predation. He was thrilled she was adept, and he had different views than I did on what constituted a safe environment for raising children.

"Can't we put her back to sleep?" Santiago tore his gaze from the screen of a tablet, one of many he kept on or around him. "I'm sure Death wouldn't mind."

"Why don't we put *you* to sleep?" I countered sweetly. "I wouldn't mind that."

Pretty sure if we put it to a vote the motion would pass unanimously.

"You'd miss me," he said absently, certain I would actually care if I never saw him again which, to be fair, I would. If for no other reason than he was the keeper of the Wi-Fi code. "Besides, you need me. You don't need her. She's a distraction. Distractions get people killed."

So did being a smartass, but so far he had beaten the statistics.

"The Malakhim?" Cole hauled us back on track. "Where are they?"

"About two miles east of town." He checked a map app with glowing dots. "They've made no move to enter the city limits. They're waiting for something."

"Or someone," I said, dread coating the back of my throat.

Ezra, the real one, had yet to put in an appearance. It was only a matter of time before he kicked off this war in earnest, and he was too bloodthirsty not to lead the charge. He wasn't the sit back and watch type. More the kind who threw Malakhim at us until exhaustion made lifting weapons against him impossible. Then he could strut onto the battlefield, probably sporting gilded armor buffed to a high shine, and run us through while a crowd chanted his name.

Lately, I had been putting a lot of thought into envisioning my final moments. The scenarios just kept getting more intricate and ridiculous. Who knows? Maybe my brain was trying to convince me the worst was in my head so that when I faced the reality I would be relieved. Or maybe I had watched films like *Gladiator* and *300* one too many times when it was Santiago's turn to pick the flick on movie night.

Tracing a line from his elbow to his wrist, I asked Cole, "Can I bum a lift?"

Between one breath and the next, a preview of Phoebe in another few years shimmered into being where Cole had been standing. The dragon wrapped his whiplike tail around my ankle three times then gave a gentle tug. I laughed and let him topple me against his side. Still smiling, I scratched behind his ears when he ducked his head, careful to avoid his antlers, and he blew warm air in my face.

"Coming with?" I checked with Santiago after climbing on Cole's back. "Or are you driving?"

"You need me to play GPS." He secured the tablet to his hand with an elastic strap. "I'll come with."

As usual, I occupied the first-class seat on Air Cole, the most secure position for dragon riding. Anyone else would have cozied up to me, but Santiago would rather fall to his death than admit he needed a handhold. His thigh muscles must be ridiculous if he held on with those alone. That, or he was devout and one of his god's personal favorites.

Face glued to the screen, Santiago guided us to the outskirts of town, to a field littered with white dots that resembled tents if I squinted hard enough against the sharp wind making my eyes water.

"Are you sure this is right?" I called back to him. "This doesn't look like a Malakhim host to me."

Malakhim hated being on the ground. It put them at a disadvantage. They must sleep sometime, somewhere, but I doubted it would be in an area exposed to flyovers. None of this added up, and I didn't like when the numbers didn't work in our favor.

A lone figure strolled out of the largest tent as if he sensed our arrival through Cole's invisibility, and when I saw the three sets of golden-brown wings unfurl from either side of his spine, I knew what he had sensed wasn't Cole but me.

Adam Wu, Ezra's son and heir, my partner with the NSB charun taskforce, mate, and all-around ginormous pain in our asses, made his presence known.

"This ought to be good." Santiago passed a fluttering dollar bill over my shoulder. "I would like to purchase a front row seat for the ass kicking he's about to receive. I'll take popcorn if you have it, with extra butter."

I took his money because — hey, free money — but I would have preferred to turn tail and run home rather than engage him.

Wu reminded me I came with an expiration date I hadn't

shared with the coterie, Cole, or my dad. He made it impossible to pretend this war could end any other way than with my death. The rest was trickle down fear.

Would Cole, as my chosen mate, die with me? Or only Wu, the mate who selected me without my permission? Thom? Miller? Portia and Maggie with her? As much as he annoyed me, I didn't want Santiago paying for Wu's machinations with his life either.

I wanted my coterie spared. I wanted them to have a life beyond what Conquest had shown them. I wanted them free, safe, and happy. I was willing to trade my life for theirs, but the reverse ... I couldn't let them pay for Conquest's nature or Wu's hubris or his father's ego.

The last man I wanted to see, missing Ezra by a narrow margin, rocketed into the sky, narrowly avoiding Cole biting him in half. The dragon was joking around. Probably. But Wu shot higher, almost out of hearing range, just in case the mate I had claimed for myself hadn't forgiven him for leaving his mark on me.

"What is all this?" I yelled as he struggled to keep pace with Cole while also staying clear of his teeth and tail, a conundrum I had limited pity for, given all he had done to me. "Who are these people?"

"Malakhim who have defected. They wish to meet with you and join your cause."

Suspicion honed my voice to a razor when I cut Santiago a glare over my shoulder. "You knew about this."

He found joy in the most annoying places, such as arranging for me to meet with various charun factions who may or may not want to join us without me unleashing my inner dragon on them. He knew it bothered me, the adoration, the worship, the mouth-breathing, so he kept the nature of those meetings under wraps until it was too late.

"I suspected they were up to something when they didn't attack

Canton," he said dryly. "They could have wiped your hometown off the map before we arrived if they wanted, but they didn't, so I figured they had an agenda that wasn't the usual doom and gloom." He shrugged. "Plus, lover boy here was with them. I figured that meant they wouldn't kill us on sight."

Meaning Santiago was still tracking Wu. No surprise there, except that meant Wu hadn't removed the tracker Santiago planted in him. Granted, he would have to cut himself open and dig around in his thigh to find it, but still. I figured he would grit his teeth and put in the effort. That he was allowing us to monitor him made me suspicious, probably the exact opposite of what he hoped to accomplish. Any olive branch Wu attempted to extend at this point ought to be snapped in half and then used to beat him.

"I didn't wash my hands before we left." The skin pulled tight when I made a fist. "They're coated in chicken blood."

"They don't need to know it's chicken blood," Santiago added helpfully.

Worst campaign manager *ever*.

"These are seasoned soldiers," Wu reasoned. "They could make or break your campaign."

Plus, they were identical to the enemy. That might come in handy down the line too.

"You're the one who started this war," I reminded him. "How come you're giving me the credit all of a sudden?"

"They need a figurehead, and yours is the one on the chopping block."

"Great motivational speech." I tightened my fingers in the dragon's mane. "You really know how to get the juices pumping."

A smile threatened to overbalance his mouth, his full upper lip curving, but he suppressed the urge to walk through the door I had left open. As much as I wanted to believe he was smart enough not to rile up Cole, I worried I was giving him too much credit. Likely, he was aware his current odds for getting eaten were at an all-time high if he pissed Cole off one more time.

The encampment drew my eye, and I had to admit my curiosity. "When and why did these guys defect?"

"After The Hole," he said, and that was answer enough on both parts.

His father had activated emergency protocols and imploded the charun prison facility where Famine was being held. All the guards and inmates, including my sister, had been killed. The news of his father's ruthless disregard for life had rocked Wu, and it was clear ripples of doubt had spread from that point throughout the ranks.

How Ezra's brutality had shocked them, I couldn't begin to imagine, but I was cadre. The charun on this terrene accepted my sisters and I would be hunted down like dogs and/or experimented on like lab rats. They also expected the punishment to stop there. With us.

The death toll at The Hole alone was staggering, the act one of pointless violence. Perhaps that was what this terrene needed to be shocked out of their complacency.

And what breed of monster was I to even think that?

"How do you know we can trust them?"

Heartache flooded his expression before he smoothed it into an indifferent mask, but I saw and guessed at the cause.

Kimora, the latest casualty on our side, had been dead only a matter of days. By the time we killed her, she had already been taken over by a Drosera and was following Sariah's orders to infiltrate the enclave. That didn't change the fact the last time Wu and Knox saw her alive, she was being gutted by Cole.

Intellectually, they might understand she had ceased to exist before that point, but emotionally, I feared they might never be able to look at him without hostility, without seeing her final moments replay in their heads, but he wasn't the only one to blame. Taking her down had been a group effort.

"They were all born in the enclave. Knox and I handpicked them to join Father's cause because they could pass for full-blooded Malakhim. Some have been embedded in Ezra's ranks for a century or more."

The news they were Wu's kin didn't comfort as much as it might have once, but it explained why they were flexible enough in their beliefs to join with us, and why The Hole's destruction hit them so hard. "Why pull them out now?"

Wu was big on reminding me the world would keep on spinning long after we were gone. He never let small things, like mass murder, derail his vision. The man possessed more contingency plans than I owned long-sleeved shirts.

"This is the best chance we're ever going to get to end this. I'm pooling my resources."

Never had I wished more for Deland Bruster and his particular skillset, but he was one of a kind on this terrene, and he was dead. Sariah killed him. There would be no soul-deep probes to determine motives or authenticity. We had to rely on our guts and hope for the best. "Can we trust them?"

Double agent was a dangerous game to play, and quitting wasn't always an option.

"Yes." Wu kept the emotion out of his voice, which only served to emphasize the lack. "I vetted them myself."

The endorsement wasn't as much of a gold standard as he must have thought, not as far as we were concerned. We didn't know his agenda beyond deposing his father, and that was troubling. His life was forfeit if his plan to seal this world from the ones above and below it succeeded, and his death, on the heels of Ezra's, would leave a gaping hole in the charun hierarchy of this world. Wu had his own end game in mind, but he hadn't shared his vision with me.

Done with the conversation, or his inability to participate in it, Cole dove for the widest clear space available, leaving Wu to hover alone while he carved a downward path toward the waiting Malakhim.

"Trained Malakhim might come in handy," Santiago mused. "They could protect Canton from another attack until we need them for active duty."

The idea gave me chills. "I don't want Malakhim anywhere near town."

Again, I tasted frost and had to shove down the cold place to stay present. I shook my wrists, and the bangles slid over my skin, cool to the touch. Forget a ticking clock, the temperature of these acted as a barometer for Conquest.

The first attack on Canton had leveled the police station where Dad, Uncle Harold, and I used to work. We might have all moved on from the department, through tragedy or necessity, but that didn't make the loss any easier to stomach. Especially since officers had been inside the building when it burned to the ground. Those men and women had died because of me, and I would never forget that.

Canton was a weakness of mine, and it was too late to avoid its exposure. I had done my best to keep Dad and the Rixtons safe, but the rest of the town was still a glaring target. As much as I wanted to believe they would have suffered with or without me, since the breach site was in nearby Cypress Swamp, I couldn't discount the simple truth that wherever I went, destruction followed in my wake. And that by the time this was done, I would have far worse than chicken blood on my hands.

CHAPTER TWO

⬤

The Malakhim, or however they self-identified, met us with curiosity rather than outright hatred and general disgust for our existence, which was a nice change. They stood golden-haired and blue-eyed, dressed in the simple white garb I remembered from our last encounter with their kind.

This was the first time I had a chance to study the species without an entire host attempting to kill me, and I wasn't convinced I could tell them apart in a lineup. There was something deeply troubling about that total absence of self, the utter lack of identity.

Ezra disdained other species of charun, found their differences abhorrent, but here was proof he demanded uniformity even among his own kind.

His army was cookie cutter, and while the lack of individuality saddened me on one level, it also gave me hope. This was a peek inside the enemy's head, and what I saw told me these men — because they were all male — would fight the same way, using identical strategies, with no embellishments. A personality was a requirement for personal style, and this crowd had none that I could distinguish.

One of them stepped forward, his stride sure, his expression tight. "I'm David."

The temptation to crack a Goliath joke almost overwhelmed me, but I managed to resist. Uncle Harold would have been proud.

"I'm Luce." I didn't offer my hand since he withheld his. "I didn't get the memo about this meeting, so why don't you catch me up to speed?"

"Adam called, and we came."

I waited, but that seemed to be the whole of his explanation. Short and to the point. I liked it. Except for the implication they were in Wu's pocket and deep. I had expected it, but it sucked hearing it. That meant we could only trust them so far.

"Well, that's great." I laced my fingers at my navel. "Do you have any feelings about joining up?"

A line appeared between his eyebrows. "No."

"You're cool with being drafted for Team Conquest, no questions asked?"

Back on solid ground, he relaxed his features. "Yes."

Desperate for numbers I might be, but I couldn't stomach sending these guys to their deaths on a whim. It wasn't right. Maybe that was stupid of me, or short-sighted. They were definitely warm bodies, and I needed plenty of those. The fact they leapt to take orders didn't hurt either, but most of them would die. That was the hard truth. I wasn't willing to soften it by playing the good solider card. I wanted active participants, not cannon fodder.

"I can't do this." I could barely stand to look at Wu. "He's an automaton."

Cole hadn't shifted back, so I sought out the dragon, ready to head back to the farmhouse.

"I told you," Wu addressed the host. "Didn't I tell you?"

Puzzled, I frowned at him. "Tell who what?"

"That you're not Conquest, not as they've known her."

A second Malakhim jogged over, clasped David on the shoulder, and dismissed him.

"I'm Able." He flashed a quick grin. "You'll have to forgive David. He stayed under too long."

"They brainwashed him," I realized. "That's why he's so . . ."

"Yes." He cut me off before I could put a name to the condition. "He's a good man, and a loyal soldier. He'll follow the orders he's been given to the letter, but he won't deviate from them. Not by an inch."

Since Able appeared to be the Malakhim in charge, I asked him, "How do you feel about joining up with me?"

"This is what we've trained for," he said, and an eager light entered his eyes that told me he hadn't been under long at all to have retained his spark. I recognized it from every rookie who had ever come to work for the PD. Some kept it, some dimmed, and some extinguished. He struck me as the type to keep his shine, and I hoped he lived long enough to prove me right. "We're ready to serve, ma'am."

Ma'am.

Well, I couldn't fault his manners. Even if they made me feel old.

"Coordinate with Santiago." I turned to locate him. "You're point man with Able."

"Here you go." He passed over the tablet he had been using, or maybe it was a different one. He kept them in his pockets and handed them out like other people offered mints. "You can contact us through this app." He indicated the correct icon. "It's video and audio, so you've been warned."

"Put on pants first," Able joked. "Gotcha."

I wished I hadn't liked him. I wished he wasn't as bright as a new penny. I wished liking him didn't mean agreeing they could join us, for better or worse.

The dragon, always keyed into my moods, nuzzled my cheek with his velvety soft muzzle.

"Impressive beast," Able said. "He lets you ride him?"

Cole and the dragon were one and the same, but the dragon had a wicked sense of humor, and he lipped my ear, causing a flush to rise into my cheeks and ignite across my face.

"Yes." I patted his neck with the force of a slap. "He's a mighty steed."

The dragon wound his tail around my ankle and tugged hard enough I would have landed on my butt if Wu hadn't caught me against him.

Despite the fact Cole only had himself to blame for my current predicament, he growled a warning at Wu, who turned me loose before the antlers rising over my shoulder pierced him through the eye.

"Knock it off." I elbowed the dragon in the chest. "You started it."

Huffing his annoyance, Cole subsided, but Able was reevaluating his opinion of my *impressive beast* if the line gathering across his forehead was any indication.

"We were about to eat lunch." Able smiled in invitation. "Would you like to join us?"

"Sure," I said in the spirit of cooperation.

"Not really," Santiago countered with a put-upon sigh, as if this whole situation wasn't entirely his fault.

"Cole?" I gave him the deciding vote. "Are you hungry?"

A shimmer in the air announced his intention to dine with our newest allies, and I had to fight a smirk off my mouth before Santiago saw it. He really did bring out the brat in me. Thank God I was an only child.

When Cole stood before him on two legs, Able turned a shade of red tomatoes would envy. Poor guy must have been replaying his earlier comments, and my responses. As much as I wanted to place the blame solely on Santiago, I had trouble behaving myself around Cole too. For very different reasons.

"What's on the menu?" I spared Able more embarrassment before Santiago zeroed in on an easy mark. "I hope nothing morally objectionable."

"We've all got human in us," Able said, glad to drop the previous topic. "We're not cannibals."

"Good to know." I linked fingers with Cole. "This is my mate, by the way. Cole Heaton."

"I should have realized." Able kept stealing glances at him from the corner of his eye. "I was told you mated a Convallarian, but I've never seen one."

"No worries," I assured him. "We're all learning as we go."

Every time we met new potential allies, I got introduced to a species I hadn't known existed. He could hardly be faulted for not recognizing one on sight. At least he had known Convallarians existed. That put him miles ahead of me.

Able led us to the big tent Wu had emerged from, and we found a dozen Malakhim — make that Malakhim lite — sitting with their legs crossed and cradling small bowls in their hands. They looked up in unison, which wasn't creepy at all, but the tension released from their shoulders when Wu walked in behind us.

One thing about Wu. I might not trust him, but his people did, and that might be the only reason why I hadn't tempted fate by letting Cole maul him a little. There must be some basis for their allegiance, right? If they wanted to follow someone blindly, they would have stuck with his father.

The Malakhim in charge of rations scooped us each a bowl full of —

"This is birdseed." Santiago pushed the food around with his finger. "Is this a joke?"

"It's not birdseed." I stomped on his instep while stepping forward to claim my portion. "It's more like trail mix."

"Nuts, seeds, and dried fruit. I could buy this by the bag at the local dollar store. This is not food." He glanced around the room. "Unless you're half bird."

"How did you end up in charge of diplomatic relations?" I doubted he could have landed the job unless it was self-appointed. "Literally anyone else in the coterie would be more suited to the role of ambassador."

"You're just lucky." He took a spoon and scooped up a big mouthful. "Mmm. Seedy."

"I'm sorry," I told the server. "He was raised by wolves. Rabid ones."

Cole stepped up and accepted his bowl, and Wu did too. The four of us found an empty corner and sat.

All eyes were on me when I took my first bite, but I was sold. "Homemade granola?"

"Yes." Able munched away. "We used to sneak milk when we could. This stuff makes amazing cereal."

"I bet." Milk would have helped it go down easier, but it was delicious. "You'll have to give me the recipe." I took another bite. "My aunt ..."

My aunt Nancy loved this kind of thing. She would have bribed me for his notes with chocolate chip cookies or cake, and then she would have whipped up a batch large enough for the congregation at her church, me, and small baggies for anyone who happened to drop by for a visit.

God, I missed her. She was the closest thing I'd had to a mother figure, and she was gone. It still didn't feel real.

"I'm sorry about your aunt," Able said softly. "We heard about her death, and your uncle's."

No doubt Wu had illuminated them in order to cast me in a better light.

"I haven't had time to process," I admitted. "Little things, like this — a recipe she would have liked — remind me of her. It takes a minute, sometimes, to remember I can't pick up the phone and call her or drop in for a visit."

The room blurred around the edges as memories of her brought Uncle Harold to mind, and fresh grief threatened to overwhelm me, a tight fist clenching around my throat until I couldn't suck down enough air.

"I lost my brother during a mission two years ago," he said gently. "I wish I could tell you it gets easier, but it doesn't. Or it hasn't, not for me. It just becomes ... different. You go days or sometimes weeks without thinking about your loss instead of counting the time in minutes or hours."

"I'm sorry," I rasped and wished I had a more original condolence to offer. You would think someone, somewhere would have dreamed up a better way to say *I wish loss hadn't broken your heart, but one day the pieces might fit together again if you're lucky.* "I want to end this cycle so that more families like ours aren't ripped apart. I'm not sure we'll win, the odds are pretty long, but I know the cost of doing nothing has already been too high."

Charun like Conquest, like *me*, should be contained to their own terrene. That was an impossible wish, given our powers, and a criminally selfish one too. Earth was no more or less worthy of salvation than any other terrene between here and Otilla. The only difference was ... me. I was here, and I was willing to fight. And maybe it was all for nothing. Maybe the next cadre would find another way in, or the one after that, or the one after that. But what mattered to me was that I tried, that I gave my all to end this. To give my goddaughter the potential to lead a normal, happy life unscarred by violence. To give my dad a chance to enjoy the retirement he had earned ten times over through service to his community. To give the coterie the freedom they deserved after giving so much to a cause that wasn't their own.

"I believe you."

We fell into silence after that, but I felt the weight of every pair of eyes in the room on me. For once, I didn't mind the scrutiny. Let them see my tears, let them understand my pain, let them believe that I mourned my dead the same as them, thirsted for vengeance the same as them, wanted to dismantle Ezra, feather by feather, and crumble his regime to dust I would scatter to the four winds.

Back at the farmhouse, I lagged behind the others, emotionally drained from sharing my pain so publicly. I was happy to be rid of Santiago, who swaggered into the house mumbling about pork rinds, but I was equally glad that Cole remained with me. He was my rock, and I couldn't imagine doing this without him.

"I want this to be over," I said with my back to him. "I want to wake up and not have this hanging over me."

He encircled me with his strong arms, locked his wide hands around my waist, and rested his chin on top of my head.

"All we do is talk and talk and talk," I vented. "We've gathered all the forces we're likely to recruit, unless Wu has more tricks up his sleeve."

And I had no doubt he did since he was forever vanishing and returning with useful tidbits of intel or new allies eager to join the cause. Why he kept it at a steady trickle instead of instigating one huge recruitment drive, I had no idea. Unless, like Santiago, he ultimately expected me to shake hands with each new addition to the cause in order to give them a glimpse of what they were fighting for, and with.

"When does it kick off?" Terror danced down my spine whenever I pictured the form the final battle would take, but anxiety chased it. I wanted it done as much as I never wanted it to begin. "When does the final battle start so it can be over?"

Gently, Cole turned me in his arms until I could bury my face against his broad chest. "The anticipation is hard, almost worse than when the moment finally arrives."

A text chime had me digging out my phone, and I breathed a sigh of relief at its message.

"Rixton says Haven is secure." I had volunteered him for a task that let him visit with his family in the hopes he would elect to stay put with them. "There are no signs of anyone lying in wait for Phoebe, and no indication anyone has followed her."

The invisibility trick came instinctive to Convallarians, especially sneaky kids disobeying direct orders from their parents, so a slim chance existed that she had enjoyed her rebellion without consequences. But she had escaped from Dad several times, and the more often she visited us, the less likely it was her antics would go undetected.

None of our enemies knew to look for her at Haven, but she unerringly found us, no matter where we went, like Cole and I had homing beacons in us she could key into, and that was the problem. We were under surveillance. Heavy surveillance. Each of her arrivals at the farmhouse would have been remarked upon, and one of our people could easily have been tracked dropping her back with her grandfather.

"Haven is no longer secure." Cole took the words right out of my mouth. "We need to relocate your father and the Rixtons."

"The staff too." I massaged my forehead. "Rixton is buying us time, but he won't stay put forever."

Rixton wasn't the wait and see type. He understood the stakes, and he was willing to go all-in with us if it meant preserving a future for his wife and daughter.

Another text chime rang out, but this one came from Cole's

back pocket. I was tempted to slide my hands around and help myself — to the phone and his buns — but I didn't want to be the kind of mate who acted like either belonged to me.

"You can check if you want," he said, amused. "I'll only tell you what it says anyway."

It took a minute for me to frame the issue, but I finally pegged what bothered me about my first instinct.

"I don't want to start taking liberties with you." I thumbed one of the bangles. "It feels like a slippery slope, given how present Conquest is these days."

"There are some liberties I don't mind." He guided my hand around his hip to his pocket, the one opposite his phone. "Is that what you wanted?"

"Maybe." Heat prickled in my cheeks. "Last I heard, it's not a crime to have the hots for my mate."

Mate.

My mate.

Nope. Still not tired of hearing that.

The message forgotten, Cole leaned down and brushed his warm lips over mine.

Rough fingers brushed where I cupped Cole's butt, and I jolted to find Santiago fishing out the phone.

Craning my neck, I glared at him around Cole's side. "Do you mind?"

"Do you?" He used his thumbprint to access the phone, telling me nothing was sacred with him, which, honestly, I should have figured out by now. "I just ate, and yet there you two are, making smacking noises and groping each other in public."

"I'm so sorry," I said, not sorry at all. "I should probably wait to get my fill of Cole until after this is over."

The bitter tightness there at the end caused Cole to tense in my arms, but he couldn't have known the reason. Wu wouldn't still have his head attached to his neck if he knew the truth. For that matter, neither would I.

Fine, so he probably wouldn't lop off my head. He would duct tape me to a chair in a basement with one exit he could padlock. Odds were good he would stand guard over it himself, in his dragon form, in case anyone got ideas about helping me escape to fulfil my apparent destiny. While I might be willing to explore the tied-to-a-chair thing with him, I wasn't onboard with him protecting me. Conquest didn't deserve his consideration, and . . . she and I were a package deal.

God, it hurt keeping this secret when all I wanted was to curl against him and pretend his arms were safe, that he could make it go away, but only I had the power to end this.

"That would be great," Santiago agreed absently then gave us an update. "Maggie and Miller have secured supplies for our allies. They estimate six months' worth of food and water have been delivered to each encampment. That doesn't take into consideration the game they can hunt on their own. Most have chosen areas where clean water and wildlife are plentiful in the event this drags on longer than anticipated."

All at once the reason for his grabby hands became clear to me.

Maggie, and therefore Portia, hadn't checked in for over twenty-four hours.

He was worried about his BFF and obnoxious with it.

"That is good news." I disentangled from Cole. "The least we can do is make sure they have a tent over their heads and food in their bellies."

Thom was seeing to the medical supplies, another necessity. Most camps employed their own healers, thankfully, who specialized in their species' biology. That cut Thom's prep work in half.

"They're bringing the rest here to the farmhouse," Santiago

read off a new screen. "They'll be here in thirty minutes or so with the surplus. Be thinking on where you want to stock it."

Thumbs flying over the screen, he chuckled under his breath, a wholly evil laugh then tossed the phone back to Cole.

Whatever Santiago sent Portia via Maggie shot Cole's eyebrows straight into his hairline.

I didn't ask him.

I was better off not knowing.

As I turned, a snout struck me in the spine with the force of a bullet, and I hit my knees.

"Phoebe," I grunted, bracing a hand on my back. "Was that really necessary?"

A happy trill answered me with a resounding *yes*, and she curled her tail around my throat to steady herself while she perched on my shoulder. Good thing oxygen was optional. This kid wasn't big on giving me breathers.

One of my favorite people in this world or any other stalked into the yard behind her. Had he been in his cat form, he would have twitched his nubby tail.

"She refused a bath." He folded his arms over his chest. "She tastes like mud and chicken blood, but she won't hold still long enough for me to clean her."

The mental picture his complaint summoned rendered me mute.

Thom was the most feline member of the coterie, more in tune with his true nature, and I could respect that. I thought it was cute most of the time. But I had trouble wrapping my head around the idea that he might have tried to lick Phoebe clean the way a mother cat might care for her kitten.

As was the case with most charun culture, I wasn't sure what I could say that wouldn't cause offense.

"I'll give her a bath." I looked to Cole for help, but he was too amused to offer any. "Thank you for letting me know she needs one."

Mollified, Thom crossed to me and rubbed his cheek against mine. "You could use a bath too."

"Oh." I jerked back before he got the chance to lick me too. "I, uh, will get right on that."

I showered yesterday, with Cole, which was an adventure since he took up the whole tub, and I was forced — forced, mind you — to rub all over him in order to get clean. But there was a difference between human levels of cleanliness and catlike charun ideas on personal hygiene.

"Do you want to get in some practice while we wait?"

Eager for an excuse to escape a possible tongue-bath, I blurted, "Yes."

Hand in hand, we walked into woods to practice the art of shifting and gliding while not eating people.

CHAPTER THREE

Farhan rode the wind, wings outstretched, and completed a lazy circle that encompassed Haven. Rixton was doing his best to keep the area secure, but he wasn't charun. He didn't have the hearing or sight of one. Otherwise, he would have noticed the small contingent camped out five miles from their doorstep.

The Malakhim had been hunting Heaton's daughter, he was sure, but they hadn't stumbled across Haven yet, and he aimed to keep it that way.

Adam requested he remain in his room, but Farhan was twitchy with the need to spread his wings, and the perfect distraction had just fallen into his lap. He would get in some exercise then return before he was missed.

Adjusting his flight pattern, Farhan sailed for the patch of woods where the handful of Malakhim rested in the trees. They were hidden well, and they would have spotted the baby dragon with ease from their location had she not been clever enough to use her glamour.

The sword in his hand felt odd after having retired from his position as janitor, but it also felt right. Righter than anything since Ezra stabbed him in the gut in his own damn office.

Just the thought of him was enough to make Farhan see red, for his grip to tighten on the hilt.

Ezra had done things to him. Horrible things. Terrible things. And the rage wouldn't stop.

A cry went up when he landed on the topmost limb of a spiky tree where three males slept, but it was too late. He slit their throats, watched their bodies fall, then leapt to the next tree and the next until there were none left.

The blood marring his blade wasn't enough. He wiped it clean on the shirt of a male slumped against the trunk, then sheathed it and patted down the Malakhim until he found the golden dagger they each carried as a sign of their fealty to Ezra.

The next time he killed, he wanted it slower, closer, so he could watch as the light went out of their eyes.

"He will kill you for this," the Malakhim rasped, his voice a thready whistle.

"He was going to kill me anyway." Farhan stabbed him through the eye. "I might as well take as many of you with me as I can before that happens."

The wrongness in him twisted until his gut cramped, and he purged over the side of the limb.

And that's when he saw what he had done.

These weren't Malakhim. They were Oncas, loyal to Luce.

As he replayed the dying male's last words, he realized he had said *she* and not *he*.

Luce was going to kill him for this, slaughtering her allies. But he hadn't meant to do it. He hadn't known he was doing it. He thought they were Malakhim. They had been Malakhim, hadn't they?

The dagger trembled in his hand, and it was a plain blade, nothing gilded or branded by Ezra.

"What have I done?" He turned his blurry gaze skyward. "What have you done to me?"

Ezra was nowhere in sight, but Farhan was terrified the silky laughter he heard was real.

Sweat pouring down his spine, he hurled the dagger away and set out for the farmhouse in Canton, too afraid of what he might do if he returned to Haven, too afraid of what he might have already done.

Adam might not welcome Farhan's arrival after he told Luce what sacrifice was required of her, but he would see that he was too well informed to be left unsupervised if his mind was going.

Farhan never expected to outlive the apocalypse, but he refused to help bring it about, even if that meant he spent it chained to a chair in a bunker.

CHAPTER FOUR

———◆———

Thanks to Cole and a week of downtime, I had mastered summoning my dragon aspect on command, as well as tucking her away when I was done. I could glide without puncturing a wing, which I had done a few times now, but I couldn't lift off and fly like Cole. Invisibility was also out of my reach, which sucked. Even Phoebe, a child, had mastered it. I wanted to have a stealth mode too, damn it.

Muscles aching in a pleasant way, if you were into masochism, I was ready to call it a day on the practice field. I had been spending my mornings with Cole, but the coterie spent evenings scattered across the floor in the living room strategizing until dinner arrived, usually in the form of pizza.

Thoughts keyed on food, I started for the house with Cole.

That's when I spotted Kapoor on the lawn, a sword drooping in his hand.

Charun were really, really into carrying them. And, well, sticking them through people.

"I didn't expect to see you so soon," I called. "What's up?"

The blank expression he wore shot chills up my arms. He hadn't been right since we rescued him from Ezra, to the point I wasn't sure if we had saved him. The human guise he used to wear no longer fit him. He kept to his natural form, and it was disconcerting to say the least. Wu had checked him in to Haven, so I was surprised to see him out and about — and armed — this soon.

Massive black wings twitched along his spine, pronounced veins filled with ichor crisscrossed his face, and sharp horns sprouted from his forehead and cheeks.

Funnily enough, he still wore suits like he was on the job with the National Security Branch of the FBI. For all I knew, those were the only clothes he owned since his life, as far as I could tell, was the job. Or it had been. I wasn't sure where he stood on that front either. Job security hadn't ranked high on my priority list lately.

The NSB was like a distant dream to me, a barely recalled series of events that I sometimes doubted had ever happened. I hadn't gotten much mileage out of that promotion to Fed from local cop before I had to ditch the badge Wu never bothered issuing me and step into the role of Conquest full time.

I still collected paychecks, though. There were definite benefits to working with Wu. His familiarity with the system, and his ability to manipulate it, were big ones.

Without meaning to, I pictured a future where I could pin on a badge and get back to the work I loved, the job that was as much a family tradition as fireworks on the Fourth of July. But I saw no path available to me where that was a possible future.

Kapoor didn't blink, and that made his reappearance all the more eerie. "Where is Adam?"

"He's at the Malakhim lite encampment near Canton." I edged in front of Cole. "Can I help you?"

Because it was clear he needed help, had come in search of it, and left Haven behind in the process. I had been fooled until he opened his mouth, but yeah. He still wasn't right. In fact, he might be more wrong than the last time I saw him.

"I'm tired," he said on an exhale, and then his legs buckled, crumpling him to the dirt with his wings mashed beneath him in a feathery tangle.

I rushed over, dropped to my knees, and pressed my fingers under his jaw. "Pulse is strong and steady."

"I'll scout the area, make sure no one followed him."

Cole gave himself over to his dragon and left me with the mystery of Kapoor.

"Thom," I yelled. "We got a man down out here. Bring your kit."

He shoved through the front door, pinpointed my location, and ran to me.

"You're all right?" He raked his gaze over me. "He didn't hurt you?"

Moved by his concern, I tossed him a smile. "I'm fine."

With a brisk nod, he turned his attention to Kapoor. "What happened to him?"

"I'm not sure. Whatever is wrong with him was wrong with him when he got here."

"I will examine him." Thom leaned down, sniffed Kapoor's breath. "Hmm." He licked the underside of Kapoor's chin then paid special attention to the other man's hands and fingers, which he licked too. "There's blood under his nails, but it's not his. There are multiple flavors."

"More than one person?"

"Yes." He compared his findings to the gore on the sword. "The matter under his nails is consistent with the blood on his weapon."

"I don't get why he left Haven." I owed Rixton a text to

check and see if he was aware Kapoor had fled or if Kapoor had slipped out while he was on patrol. Either way, he would want to know where Kapoor ended up and that he was okay. "He was safe there."

"He might have a message for you," he theorized. "Did he say anything before he passed out?"

Dread tickled my hindbrain, imagining the worst-case scenarios. What if Haven had been breached? What if the Rixtons hadn't survived? What if the Malakhim had taken Dad hostage? What if that was why Rixton hadn't called to report Kapoor's absence? What if Kapoor was the lone survivor?

Skin crawling, I couldn't ask Thom if his palate was developed enough for him to tell if the blood belonged to humans or charun. If Kapoor had hurt the Rixtons . . . or my dad . . .

"He asked for Wu." Ice crackled on my tongue, crunched between my teeth, and I shoved Conquest down until my ears stopped ringing. "He said he was tired, then he dropped where he stood."

"Hmm." Thom bit his palm and sampled the welling blood. "He hasn't been poisoned. I don't smell fresh blood, so he has no new injuries. He doesn't smell sick." His nostrils flared in a rapid flutter as he breathed in over Kapoor. "He smells afraid." A frown gathered across his brow. "Terrified."

As much as I feared the answer, I had to ask, "Can you identify the blood under his nails?"

"Yes." He wet his lips, sat back. "It belongs to an Onca."

This just kept getting better and better. "Great."

The Oncas were hard-won allies, hardcore Conquest loyalists who followed me out of devotion to her. Their clan had saved our bacon after we blew the enclave bunker, and several Malakhim, sky high to prevent them from locating the enclave's inhabitants until we could relocate them to safer territory. Their intervention after the fact had quite possibly saved Wu's life, not to mention Miller's and Portia's.

"When Cole gets back, we'll go check in with Noel and Franklin, make sure everything is okay."

Dominance fights and interspecies scuffles were common, but an outright attack from one of our people on theirs would be bad news for us. For me, in particular, since I won their allegiance by biting the hand off one of their dissenters. I didn't enjoy knowing there had been body parts floating in my stomach when I changed back, even if the magic that made it possible also kept fingers, elbows, and other pointy ends from protruding out of my midriff.

I had a recurring nightmare where I woke with an upset stomach and yanked off the covers to find I had fallen asleep nude — and hands were clawing across my abdomen, from the inside, trying to tear their way out of me to freedom.

A shudder rippled through me, but the warm sunlight helped thaw the chill settling over me.

"I'll help you get Kapoor settled." I checked to see if Santiago had made an appearance, but he was MIA. That happened a lot when a nontechnical problem reared its ugly head. He was ten times faster to lend a screwdriver than a hand to someone in need. "Do you want him upstairs or down?"

"Down." Thom gave a decisive nod. "There are a few cots in the dining room."

The enclave left a few of their supplies behind when they fled across the sea to a more secure safehouse in the event we could put them to use. For that, I was grateful. We wouldn't have had enough soft places to sleep otherwise.

Before Thom could lift the heavy end, I hooked my hands under Kapoor's armpits, leaving Thom to hold his legs. I tried for smooth so he wouldn't notice what I was doing, but he was much older than me, and luckily, he seemed more amused by my coddling than offended. That must be the healer in him.

Together, we carried Kapoor into the dining room turned bunkroom and laid him out on a cot.

"What do you think is wrong with him?" I ducked into the next room and returned with a pair of kitchen scissors to cut him out of his clothes. One thing I had learned about charun was they hated exposing their weaknesses to others. His clothes stank of fear sweat and our allies' blood. With other factions checking in at regular intervals, we couldn't risk leaving him in his present condition. The clothes had to go before they lured someone more predatory and less self-controlled than my coterie to him. "I don't see any marks of any kind on him."

"Perhaps they aren't visible." He helped me strip Kapoor down to his underwear. As it happened, he was a boxer brief kind of guy. "We know Ezra is a terrible power. We have no idea what Kapoor endured at his hands, what lasting effects he might suffer, and Kapoor is in no shape to tell us."

The whole reason for leaving him behind had been to give him time and space to heal, more in soul than in body, but it must not have done the job for him to show up in this condition. Selfish as it made me, I was grateful the blood hadn't belonged to anyone at Haven. I only wished I could say the same for our allies and their encampments, who would be calling in with missing persons reports I would have to field. Before they started calling for his head on a pike, I had to get to the bottom of this.

The Oncas had rebelled against me in Virginia City and required a brutal demonstration. Noel and Franklin swore they had culled dissenters from their ranks, but they must have assumed that prior to my arrival as well. Until I spoke with them, and heard Kapoor's side, I had no way of knowing where to cast the blame.

Heavy footsteps as familiar as my heartbeat set the old

floorboards on the porch creaking, and I craned my neck in search of Cole, who must have detoured through the kitchen.

"We're in here," I called. "What did you find?"

"Nothing." He took a long pull from the bottle of water in his hand then flicked a glance at Kapoor. "How is he?"

"Stable." Thom lifted Kapoor's hand and bit down hard in the meaty webbing between his thumb and index finger. "That ought to keep him sedated long enough for Wu to arrive."

Since I had yet to reach out to him, what with Kapoor's fainting act, I texted him now.

"Where is Santiago?" Their noses would tell them quicker than I could locate him. "Upstairs?"

"He's taken over your old room," Thom informed me. "He installed a new lock."

Claiming territory was a very charun thing to do, so I couldn't fault him there, but did the instincts he chose to listen to have to be so freaking annoying?

"Of course he did," I grumbled. "He can stay here with you."

Cole didn't hesitate. "Where are we going?"

We. Yeah. I liked the sound of that.

"Kapoor has Onca blood under his nails." I glanced up the stairs but decided I had had enough Santiago to last me. He could keep my room and the dust bunnies that came with it. "We need to check in with Noel and Franklin, see if they're missing any people."

Nodding agreement, he still asked, "Did Santiago mention a disruption in the feed?"

One of Santiago's pet projects had been wiring the area where each of our allies awaited our signal with video and sound. The leaders of each camp had a tablet with an app that allowed them to video chat with him at the push of a button. It made tracking them, and any moves against us, much easier.

Though I would never tell him out of fear his head would swell to Hindenburg size, Santiago's skills might very well be what tipped the balance in our favor.

"The tablet he left with Noel and Franklin is for their use in the main encampment. There's been no action on that front, or we would have seen or heard about it." I blew out a sigh. "They'll have scouting parties keeping the area secure. The scouts won't have any tech on them, except maybe personal cellphones, and we don't have access to those. That's my bet."

"All right."

"I hope it's not a wasted trip." I looked down at Kapoor and couldn't help seeing the beginning of the end of my human life. "But I think it's worth a look."

"I'm not questioning your instincts," Cole assured me. "I'm considering the angles."

"That makes two of us." I crossed to him, breathed in his scent, how it mingled with mine, and settled. "Drive or fly?"

"Fly," he said without missing a beat. "Both of us."

I smothered a groan against his chest, my shoulders ready to cry uncle before we even began.

"The Oncas have always responded best to displays of power. They will be soothed by your dragon."

"They'll probably line up virgin sacrifices for me to munch on."

Laughter shook him, but I wasn't joking. Oncas had weird — no, very *charun* — ideas about things.

"You're forgetting something. I can't manage vertical takeoffs yet." I felt a smile blooming. "Guess you're out of luck." Rearing back, I patted him on the chest. "Good plan, though."

"Oh, I do have a plan." His answering smile caused heat to swoop through my middle. "Come with me."

Unable to resist following him anywhere, I let him lead me to what promised to be my doom.

*

As it turned out, my doom wasn't all that bad. Cole shifted and let me climb on his back. He shot into the sky, and relief loosened the knots in my shoulders. Guess he changed his mind about the flying thing.

He really does love me.

Basking in the glow of that thought, I didn't grasp the change in altitude immediately. But I did notice when he executed a series of barrel rolls without any warning whatsoever.

Howling in terror, I clung to him, but the dragon only laughed.

He doesn't love me.

Not at all.

Not even a little.

I stuck to him like a tick on a hound dog, but he kept going and going until I was dizzy and sick with it and starting to think I had chosen wrong. Maybe Wu was a better alternative to this. Clearly, the dragon was a sadist.

The silk of his mane slipped through my damp fingers, and I didn't have the same thigh power as Santiago. I couldn't hold on. One more rotation, and he flung me off screaming into thin air.

The change was instinctive. Within seconds, I embraced my inner dragon. But I was still too drunk to tell up from down, and I was falling too fast to open my wings.

A guttural trumpeting cut through the whistling noise in my ears, and I grunted on impact. Not with the ground, as expected, but with Cole.

While saving me was a nice gesture and all, it meant he couldn't operate his wings. He was gliding, but we were going down unless I got my scaly butt in gear.

A rumbled apology from him vibrated through my chest where it rested against his back, and I was tempted, so tempted, to change and give him an earful. But he was only pushing a baby bird from its comfy nest. It no doubt made sense to him.

Just like it would make sense to me to never have sex with him again. Pretty sure this little stunt had shriveled my lady bits beyond reviving.

With a groaned prayer, I stretched my wings to their fullest, then rolled off his left side.

I yelped when I dropped faster than anticipated, instinctively searching out Cole, but a few slow wingbeats steadied me.

After a good ten minutes where I didn't fall out of the sky, I couldn't help the teasing call I yelled to Cole, who followed behind me like a parent ready to catch their kid riding a bike without training wheels for the first time.

I was maintaining altitude, gaining even. This wasn't gliding. I was *flying*.

Flying.

Now that I wasn't in danger of going *splat*, I could embrace the thrill of riding the winds.

Driving was so much better than playing passenger. I could get used to this.

About the time I was ready to forgive Cole, he tapped my shoulder with his tail.

Oh crap.

The thing about flying, or even gliding, is you have to land sometime. And while I was decent at it when coming down from a solid glide, I had never tried it from this height or this speed.

Whatever Cole hoped to show the Oncas, I worried might get undermined if I landed in a tangled heap of wings and tail that required immediate medical attention.

No one wanted to follow a general into battle who might fall out of the sky and smush you at any given moment.

Surging ahead of me, Cole stopped pumping his wings and eased into a simple glide. I did the same, watching him for instruction. He made graceful circles I struggled to mimic, dipping lower and lower, slower and slower, until I felt confident if I bungled this I wouldn't die on impact.

Our arrival was drawing attention, and the Oncas were gathering, which gave me performance anxiety. I wished harder than ever that the invisibility trick worked for me, but I hadn't figured out how to trigger it yet. And thanks to the bangles, Conquest couldn't give me any tips.

Cole cut his current loop short, flared his wings behind him, and sailed into a gentle landing.

I mimicked him as best I could, but the ground rose up crazy fast, and I was trying to put on the brakes, but there were no brakes, and oh God I was going to faceplant or flip ass over teakettle.

A cool flavor hit the back of my tongue, and my body corrected itself in time to give me one of my top five best landings.

An inquisitive rumble filled Cole's chest, and my victory high sank to an all-time low.

The coterie could scent Conquest on me when she rose to the surface, and he must have caught a whiff, no matter how faint. The bangles had been a stopgap measure at a time when I needed to be leashed, but it was never meant to last forever. Though I had hoped it would last longer than this.

We shifted in tandem, which was a cool trick, and Noel and Franklin shoved through the crowd to greet us.

"Mistress." Noel bowed. "What an unexpected delight."

"How may we be of service?" Her mate, Franklin, hit his knees. "You have only to ask, and it will be done."

Their adoration made my skin crawl, but I was getting used to it. No, that's not exactly true. I was growing more accepting of it. Tolerant even. I don't think I would ever get used to people so willing to follow me to their deaths. As a former cop, I got the *serve your community* mentality, and that's how I had started thinking of our charun allies. The alternatives were too grim for me to stomach.

Offering them each a hand up, I asked them both, "How many patrols do you have in the field?"

"Two," Noel said. "There's been no trouble in the area. We didn't see the need to increase our presence."

"You haven't done anything wrong," I was quick to assure them. "I was just curious if you're missing any people." Hope threatened to surface, but I crushed it before it took root. "But if there's been no trouble, I apologize for alarming you."

Not all Oncas were aligned with us or even willing to participate. The largest clan, yes. But there must be outliers. Kapoor could have come across a hostile clan. Somewhere. Somehow. It was possible, right?

"One of our patrols hasn't checked in yet," Noel said slowly. "They aren't scheduled to return until tomorrow."

"Do you know the area where they were assigned?" The smidgen of hope curled up and died. "A general direction works."

"They were southeast of here," Franklin said, "about ten miles out."

"Get a headcount of your people." I exchanged a look with Cole. "We'll check in with the scouts and then report back."

The couple bowed low and stayed that way, which made our exit easier, if more uncomfortable.

"Cole," I said softly, "you are evil and cruel."

"And you can fly."

"Try that stunt again, mister, and I will tie your tail in so many knots, you'll never unwind it again."

"Fair enough." Amusement tickled the corner of his mouth. "Do you want to fly or be flown?"

"It depends." I gave him room to shift. "Can you behave?"

Without answering, he traded one skin for another and stood before me in all his majestic glory.

"You didn't win this argument just because you can no longer speak."

He nudged me with his muzzle, lipping my shirt until his teeth made purchase. He hauled me closer and rubbed his head against my chest, asking for scratches behind his adorably round ears.

"Payment comes *after* services rendered," I informed him in my best hard ass cop voice.

Grumbling amiably, he let me climb on, the perfect gentleman, and launched us in the direction Franklin had indicated. We didn't have to go the full ten miles before the dragon went stiff beneath me, and a rumble of caution rolled through him.

The bad feeling I hadn't been able to shake since Kapoor collapsed in the driveway kicked up several notches.

I didn't have a charun sense of smell, but the rank odor hit me not long after Cole veered off to do a circuit of the area, and I tasted bile.

Eyes on the horizon, I kept watch in the event whatever took down Kapoor was responsible for what awaited us, but nothing materialized, and it made the anticipation that much worse.

Once certain the site was secure, Cole angled toward the strongest concentration of rancidness and set down on the grass near a copse of trees in a wedge formation that blended into the wider forest.

"This isn't going to be good." I hopped off his back and started walking. "Bodies get ripe fast in the heat, but not this fast."

Kapoor couldn't have left this massacre and come straight to the farmhouse. Either he hadn't been here, and we had a whole host of new problems on our hands, or he had flown around dazed for a least a day afterward before stumbling back to the farmhouse.

"Look there." Cole, back on two legs, caught up to me within a few strides. "Bodies."

I adjusted my course and headed for what had appeared to be gnarled roots to my weaker vision, but I didn't have to get much closer to smell he was right. "Can you tell if they belong to Noel and Franklin?"

"They share the clan scent marker."

So much for hoping these weren't the scouts due in tomorrow.

"Two here." I tipped back my head. "Three more still in the trees."

I squatted next to the first corpse and examined it for cause of death, not that I had to look hard to tell.

"Her throat was slit." I closed her eyes with a grimace. "The blade was long, at least a foot." For charun, that generally meant a sword. "It was wicked sharp too. There's no tearing. She wasn't hacked open. This was done in one smooth arc with a weapon sharp enough to cut flesh like butter."

"Kapoor didn't have a scratch on him," Cole said what I was thinking.

This was a massacre, but Kapoor hadn't gotten a scratch on him.

"He was also the janitor for the NSB for God only knows how long." I stood and moved to the next body. "He's a killer, and a damn good one, or he wouldn't have kept his job long."

The argument didn't settle my nerves. That strand of logic might tie Kapoor to this scene, but it would also form a noose of guilt to hang him. I preferred to hope he had witnessed a skirmish in progress and thrown his weight in with the Oncas. That fit more with his personality. For him to swoop down on the Oncas and do this ... without provocation ... Ezra would have had to well and truly break him.

"We need to get back to the farmhouse. There's not enough evidence here to tell us who is responsible beyond the shadow of a doubt, but there's enough to make me nervous about leaving Kapoor with —" I almost named Thom before I caught myself, "— Phoebe."

Cole didn't call me out on the slip, his expression tightening as he ran probabilities.

Without another word, he changed, and the dragon cracked its tail with impatience.

He didn't play where his daughter was concerned, and I could respect that. I climbed on, and we returned to the farmhouse without so much as a dip, let alone a dive or roll. That didn't help my gut unclench. When it came to aerial acrobatics, I had trust issues with the dragon.

About the time Cole decreased his altitude, I spotted a pair of large moving trucks in front of the house.

Portia, Maggie, and Miller were back. Good thing too. Thom might have put Kapoor under, but it didn't mean he would stay that way. Charun biology being what it was, Thom would have to learn through trial and error how fast Kapoor processed any medications he was given since his species was unknown.

Cole touched down, and I dismounted, happy to find my stomach contents settling after so much abuse.

A whistle blasted through his teeth, an earsplitting summons that brought Phoebe shooting out of the house and straight toward us. She struck Cole in the center of his chest, and he staggered back while she chattered her nonsense update to us.

Portia strode out the door next and lifted her hand in a wave. "Hey, Mom and Dad are home."

"Well?" Santiago bumped her out of the way. "What did you find?"

Pretending their juvenile shoving match to see who got off the porch first wasn't happening, I waited for an opening to check on our guest. "Kapoor still out?"

"Yeah." Santiago quit acting like a two-year-old and awarded me his full attention. "Thom is with him."

Confirmation Thom was alone with Kapoor sent my gaze zipping toward the front door. "Any word from Wu?"

"He should be here in a few hours."

"So ..." Portia twisted left and dipped enough to sweep his legs out from under him while he was distracted. He dropped like a ton of bricks and came up growling, but we both ignored him. "What did we miss? What happened to Kapoor? Where did you guys come from?"

The questions kept coming, and I couldn't decide which to answer first. "You must have just arrived."

"What did you find?" Santiago repeated himself. "Talk, or I give the baby a piece of candy. The sugar will have her bouncing off the walls all night."

Sugar and kids don't mix. Even I, with my limited experience, knew that much thanks to Maggie. One year, she took off the day after Halloween just to avoid the fallout from a night of parent-approved debauchery. If you considered shoving chocolate bars, lollipops, and taffy down your throat debauching.

"Five Onca scouts are dead." I held his gaze. "They weren't reported missing because they weren't expected to check in until tomorrow."

The playfulness drained away and left Portia sobered. "How did they die?"

"Someone cut their throats with a long blade. My vote is a sword given how popular they are among charun."

"That narrows it down," Santiago snarked. "Anything else?"

"We need to wake up Kapoor so he can tell us what happened, but we need Wu before we try it."

Kapoor might come out of sedation swinging, and I would prefer Wu take the hits over us.

"Do you think he's responsible?" Portia shifted her weight like she might go back in to check on Thom, and I was glad not to be the only one worried about him. "Why target our allies?"

"He's got Onca blood under his nails." The evidence didn't add up yet, but we were piecing it together in fits and stops. "We don't know that he didn't spot them in a scuffle and lend help. That might explain why he showed up in this condition."

"There was a sword by the cot," Santiago noted. "I've never seen him carry one. He's more of a click-click-boom kind of guy."

Thanks to Kapoor's position within the NSB, he carried a fire-arm at all times, but it seemed to me that all charun kept a sword or two in their closet. I had no idea it was a must-have accessory until I rejoined the coterie.

"Cole and I will wait on Wu to arrive." I glanced over my shoulder. "We'll start unloading the supplies."

Portia picked up on the drift of my thoughts first. "What are we doing?"

"You and Santiago are going to inform Noel and Franklin of their loss. We'll text you the coordinates. You can help them retrieve their dead, or not. Whatever their customs demand." I paid Santiago special attention. "Be on your best behavior. These people have suffered a loss, possibly at the hands of their allies, and we need to be respectful of that. Assure them we're investi-gating the incident, but do not implicate Kapoor. Until we have more evidence, we can't afford to risk the Oncas taking their grief out on him."

Checking with Cole was instinctive, but he didn't offer his two cents. He was content to let me lead my own way, which was terrifying when you considered all the ways I could screw up if left unsupervised.

After Santiago and Portia left in the White Horse SUV we kept stashed behind the house, I ducked my head in the front door and called, "Miller, you got a minute?"

"Sure." He came in from the back porch with a screwdriver in one hand and a manual in another. "I'm installing some new freezers. Thought they might come in handy. It requires some rewiring, though."

"That sounds great." The kitchen wasn't all that big, and the supplies in the truck had to go somewhere. "I wanted to ask you about your trip. Did you guys have any trouble?"

"No." He set aside his tool and booklet and grabbed a bottle of water. "Everyone was on their best behavior. The various clans seemed pleased we had done our research and brought them supplies that fit their dietary needs."

"No one was missing any scouts or civilians? Nothing like that?"

"Now that you mention it, there was a dust up when a pregnant female couldn't be located. She was part of a recon team, but she was on light duty until she delivered. Her mate brought it up to the elder in charge as we were leaving, so I didn't hear the outcome. I assumed the team had been delayed, possibly by her if she needed to rest. I didn't give it much thought past that. We had too many stops left, and no one else seemed overly concerned."

"Can you do me a huge favor and check in with them while Cole and I start unloading the trucks?"

"Sure." He wiped his hands clean. "It won't take but a minute."

While he dialed them up, Cole and I got serious about tucking away our rainy-day supplies. Most of the items, I recognized. Some I had no guess as to their purpose. Others appeared to be military surplus. Overall, the boxes, cans, and jars gave me a great sense of emergency preparedness. As if I could reach into the storage building and pull out anything, like a magician doing a hat trick.

Miller caught up to us fifteen minutes later, and he didn't look happy.

"The scouts never checked in." He tapped the phone against his palm. "They sent out a search party. We ought to hear back soon."

"This keeps getting better and better." I waved him off. "Get back to work. We'll finish up out here."

Another thirty minutes lapsed before Wu graced us with his

presence, and I drafted Miller to help Cole with the last truck while I escorted Wu to meet with Thom about Kapoor's condition.

Once I caught Wu up to speed, he gave the impression he would rather be anywhere other than here, leaving me to believe he must know something we didn't — big surprise. Personally, I was stunned. Stunned, I tell you, to learn he was keeping more secrets.

"Bring him around." Wu dragged a hand down his face. "We owe him a chance to defend himself."

Ominous as that sounded, I had to agree. "Thom, can you wake him?"

"Of course." He produced a syringe I assumed was filled with another of his bodily fluids, but I didn't ask which. In some cases, ignorance truly was bliss. "It will take a few minutes to go into effect."

The opportunity to grill Wu proved irresistible. "What aren't you telling us?"

"Kapoor spent an undetermined amount of time in Father's presence." Wu made it sound like exposure to his father equaled a death sentence. "Father has been known to . . ."

"Brainwash?" He startled, and at any other time I would have laughed. "The Malakhim are drones. They have no independent thought or identity. They're a host, a mass, a *thing*. They're not individuals. It stands to reason if Ezra can reduce the masses to bees working for the good of the hive, then he could do the same to Kapoor."

The emotions firing behind his eyes were too complex for me to single out more than the dominant one: regret.

As with The Hole, I got the feeling Wu was continually surprised to discover the depths to which his father had sunk or was willing to sink. I wasn't sure if he held out a child's hope that his father could be reasoned with, that their differences could be overcome, or if it was merely a coping mechanism.

Since I was a champion coper with multiple mechanisms to avoid tuning in to the persistent voice screaming in the back of my head that monsters existed, that I was one, that all of this was my fault, I could sympathize up to a point. But Wu had to get his ducks in a row. I wasn't asking that he smile while we murder his father for the good of the world, but I did expect him to follow through without any of those messy, muddled emotions freezing him.

Chagrinned by the harshness of my outlook, I checked the bangles, but they remained warmed by my skin, not chilled from Conquest's influence. I couldn't blame her for the ugly thought, and that was enough for me to dial back my temper where Wu was concerned. For now.

"It's possible," he allowed with the enthusiasm of someone whose worst nightmare was coming true.

"Adam," Kapoor whispered. "Adam."

Shocking me with the humanity of the gesture, Wu grasped Kapoor's hand. The prickle of energies on the back of my neck told me he was funneling some of his healing powers into Kapoor. The fact he and I were so in tune left me grinding my molars. I still experienced a disconnect when looking at him now, and not just because the bangles suppressed our mate bond. I kept seeing the Ezra he had invented rather than himself or his father. Like I needed more confusion in my life.

"I'm here." Wu leaned in, his voice as gentle as the grip on his friend. "What happened?"

"Dead." Eyes screwed tight, Kapoor sobbed, "All dead."

A migraine set up shop in my left temple, throbbing in time to my heart.

"Who's dead?" I pressed when Wu made no effort to clarify.

"All dead." Tears rolled down his cheeks. "I ... I ... killed them."

Slashing me with a glare, Wu tightened his grip on Kapoor. "Who did you kill?"

"The Malakhim. They were Malakhim." Kapoor's eyes flung opened, black from edge to edge. "I thought ... I thought ... " Confusion knit his brow. "But I was wrong." He wet his lips. "I was trying to help. Haven was in danger. They were all in danger." Kapoor tightened his fingers, and I heard one of Wu's knuckles pop. "I was wrong."

"You killed the Onca scouts," I said gently, "because you thought they were Malakhim."

"Yes," he hissed, spittle flecking his lips. "They were Malakhim."

"Thom, put him under." Oblivion was the only mercy available to him. "You tried to do the right thing. It's okay. Just rest now."

Once Kapoor was out cold, I exhaled through my teeth. "Can Ezra do that? Plant a suggestion that doesn't take immediate effect? Could that be why he allowed us to retrieve Kapoor?"

With mines planted in his subconscious, and us none the wiser, any small thing could have set them off and resulted in mass casualties. We got lucky the inhabitants at Haven weren't the ones targeted. This time. But Kapoor's meltdown was the cherry on top of my apocalyptic sundae.

"Yes." Wu hung his head. "There would be a trigger word or event that caused it to kick in."

"I don't want to come off as insensitive, but this can't be news to you." I twisted to face him. "You're taking this pretty hard, considering none of it should exactly be a shock. You just admitted you knew it was a possibility, one you didn't bother sharing with us — as usual. We left him with our vulnerable when you knew the potential was there, that he might be compromised."

"I'm well aware of what Father is capable of, and if I had forgotten how ruthless he could be, he reminded me with The Hole's destruction." He realized he still held Kapoor's hand and placed it gently beside him on the cot. "Malakhim can't be deprogrammed. They simply are, and that's all. I've tried. Many times. A few recover for a while, but they self-terminate if they're kept apart from the host. Their relationship becomes symbiotic, they can't survive apart."

"Are you saying Kapoor might kill himself?"

"I'm saying what's wrong with him can't be fixed." Misery crashed over his face. "I'm saying we might have to kill him before he kills us."

CHAPTER FIVE

———◆———

Santiago and Portia didn't make it back to the farmhouse before I called them up and rerouted them to visit the clan Miller confirmed was missing a scouting party. It was important for our allies to understand that we mourned with them, and that each of their losses were felt across the alliance. Otherwise, I might as well be Conquest.

The problem became that they wanted blood in payment for their blood, and they expected us to find the person responsible. They wanted us to turn Kapoor over to them, though they didn't realize we had already heard his confession, and I couldn't make the punishment fit the crime.

Yes, Kapoor was a murderer. Yes, he had done terrible things in his work as a janitor. Yes, he ought to be held accountable for what he had done of his own volition. But he hadn't chosen to commit these acts. He was innocent of these crimes, even if he had committed them, and it wasn't fair to write it off as justice served when he wasn't guilty.

Striking a balance between my rising charun nature and the

morals Dad and the Canton PD instilled in me made me wish I could slice out the Conquest parts of myself and go back to the simple life of policing crimes committed by humans against humans. Too bad burying my head in the sand wasn't an option.

"Luce," Miller called from the living room. "You need to hear this."

I had been sitting in a rocker on the porch, staring down the driveway, wishing my past self would barrel up the road in her Bronco so I could wave my hands and yell at her to turn back, to go anywhere but here.

Shoving out of my seat, I let myself in and passed Thom curled up in Dad's shabby recliner, in his tomcat form, with Phoebe. I allowed myself a moment to soak up their cuteness before joining the others in the kitchen.

"How bad is it?" Super not great if his expression was any indication. "Do we have hard numbers yet?"

"Four clans are missing members." Miller sounded distracted, but he kept going. "The total number of confirmed dead is thirty-four. There are still twenty-odd people unaccounted for at this time."

"Cause of death?" I could guess, but I couldn't afford to speculate.

"Their throats were slit," he confirmed. "They appear to have all been killed by the same weapon."

"Does same weapon mean same person?"

"Slight deviations in the kill strokes *might* indicate multiple attackers of varying heights, but it could also be explained away depending on if the victim was sitting or standing, and if the injury was inflicted from behind or in front." He rubbed his eyes. "Without access to the bodies, we can't be certain. The bodies were collected, buried, or burned within hours. Whatever evidence they carried is gone."

"What do we do?" I leaned my hip against the counter. "We can't hand Kapoor over for a lynching, but we can't let these crimes go unpunished."

The fastest way for me to lose support would be allowing my people to get away with crimes I would hold anyone else accountable for, and murder was a biggie. I couldn't shrug off these numbers. The issue had to be resolved before our allies decided the cost of allegiance was too high.

Much of our forces expected Luce Boudreau to lead them. That was the campaign promise. If I wanted to hold up my end, I couldn't afford to act like a politician with a mouthful of lies. I had to act like . . . me.

"We can buy some time." Miller palmed my shoulder. "We'll think of something."

"Until we do, Kapoor has to stay conked out. That means Thom will have to stick to him like glue."

Word traveled fast with charun, and if news broke that scouting parties were being picked off by friendlies, I wouldn't have allies for long. Oncas might be willing to forgive in the name of Conquest, but other factions wouldn't be so quick to follow their lead.

"Do we have an ETA on Portia and Santiago?"

"Two more hours, and they ought to be finished passing along their condolences."

The pace of the last few days was making me twitchy. It had been quiet. Too quiet. Now this. The first sign of aggression, and it came from within. But if toppling a self-styled deity was easy, then someone would have knocked Ezra on his ass long ago.

I left Miller to monitor the situation remotely and stepped outside in time to watch Cole angle in for a landing. He started walking toward me, dragon one minute, man the next, and I folded myself against him.

"The resistance is falling apart." I shut my eyes, wished I could stay in the comfortable dark. "This is the first blow, and Ezra struck it without us knowing. Who's next? What's next? How do we get ahead of him?"

Cole wrapped his arms around me, a protective cage I would gladly inhabit for the rest of my life. "You've done all you can."

"I could hunt him." I tightened my fingers in the fabric of his shirt. "We could hunt him."

"Wu hasn't had any luck finding him," Cole reminded me. "None of our scouts have located him either."

After the meeting with Wu that resulted in Conquest being unleashed, Ezra vacated the usual places. Wu hadn't been able to pin him down yet, and wasn't that a kick in the teeth?

"I can't keep sitting on my hands." I growled low in my throat. "I need to do *something*."

The front door opened and then shut, drawing my attention to Miller.

"Two more squads are MIA." He crossed to me, handed me the tablet. "They should have checked in this morning, but they've been out of touch for three days."

"I don't understand." I read the strings of correspondence. "These are in addition to the previous total?"

"Maggie called these in," he explained. "Neither clan is proficient with technology. They hadn't recharged their tablets, so they had no means of communicating with us. Until Portia and Santiago arrived, they weren't overly concerned. Delays happen."

Too bad I wasn't standing near a brick wall to bang my head against. "The only way to be certain Kapoor is responsible for these attacks is to contact Haven and get an idea of how long he's been gone. He would have had to be on a killing spree from the time he left to the time he showed up here to hit this many groups, and how would he find them? He's been in Haven this whole time."

"Wu could have given him some intel," Cole said quietly. "Prior to this we had no reason not to share information with Kapoor."

"True." I drummed my fingers against the plastic case. "We can ask."

But the odds of exact coordinates of multiple groups coming up in casual conversation were nil. Wu might be walking on eggshells around Kapoor, but he would notice any marked interest in tactical information. It would shoot up a red flag not even he could ignore.

I found Wu where I saw him last, sitting vigil beside Kapoor with his face resting in his hands.

"Did you happen to mention the locations of any allied encampments to him?"

Sitting up straighter, he dropped his arms. "Why would I?"

"It's a yes or no question." I hated being a hard ass, but Wu was too slippery to handle with kid gloves. "Did you happen to mention the locations of any allied encampments?"

"No," he said on a sigh. "He hasn't been interested in talking. I called him daily at Haven, but I had to drag conversation out of him. Frankly, he didn't care enough to ask me any questions in return."

"Then we have a serious problem." I indicated he should join us downstairs and sent Miller up to keep an eye on Kapoor in the meantime. "How did he locate so many groups? These were scouts, trained in stealth ops, apart from the main group. So how did he find them? One or two, okay. Maybe someone got sloppy, but how —?"

"You don't understand what Kapoor is," he said earnestly. "He was the janitor for a reason. He could find anyone, anywhere. His record was spotless. He retired with a one hundred percent success rate." He pitched his voice lower. "He doesn't need a map or a hint. Once he's locked in, you can't escape him. I've never seen another charun like him. His mother refused to participate in any testing. They were unable to determine her powers and released her after sterilization. She's never been seen again."

"You're telling me his mojo works in reverse as well? He could have bolted, and we would never hear from him again?"

"Yes."

"He was cognizant enough to realize what happened to him, then." That was a spot of good news. "He came to us, to you, for help."

"Luce . . ."

"You're telling me he's an unparalleled tracker."

Wu must have picked up what I was putting down. "No."

"I get why you wouldn't have told me this sooner, seeing as how you were covering your ass for the day I found out about Ezra. You could hardly say 'My pal Kapoor could find him no problem' because you never wanted me to learn the truth."

"I've apologized for what I've done and explained my motives for doing it. What more do you want from me?"

A big red button to smack with my palm that reset everything. I wanted a do-over. Stat.

"I want you to glue Kapoor back together. I want you to sic him on Ezra. I'm tired of waiting for the other shoe to drop. I want to find the shoe first this time and beat Ezra to death with it."

"Kapoor won't stop until he finds Ezra. Be very sure you're ready before you unleash him."

"We're as ready as we'll ever be. You know it as well as I do. We've rallied an army, we've stocked our larders, we've hidden our loved ones. There's nothing left to do but fight. The longer we put it off, the more time we give him to think circles around us." I gripped his arm. "Kapoor was a Trojan horse. For all we know, Ezra gave him orders to slit our throats in our sleep. Since we weren't handy when he activated, he could have done the next best thing to get relief. This is our chance to turn Ezra's cunning against him. And it will help Kapoor atone."

"He will bear the guilt as he always has done."

"You know as well as I do that when the others find out he's responsible, they'll want blood."

Charun were big on the whole eye for an eye thing.

"Do you think this will earn him forgiveness?"

"No." I had to be honest about the odds. "I think there's a good chance we'll all die, and none of this will matter anymore."

Wu studied my face, his pale and tight. "I can't tell if you're joking."

That made two of us.

That night, after the coterie gathered together, we put the matter of Kapoor to a vote. Wu, to my surprise, threw his weight behind the plan. But he wore his true feelings on his face, and you only had to look at him to see he already mourned his friend. All I had done by suggesting this course of action was give him a villain to point at down the road when he needed someone to blame.

There was a difference in him declaring his friend unsalvageable and me setting Kapoor on the path to self-destruction.

I acknowledged my part in it. I accepted it. They wanted me to lead, well, follow or get the hell out of the way. The longer we sat around twiddling our thumbs, the more people — human and charun — would die. We didn't have the luxury of waiting out Ezra, who had won this game each time he played. We had to topple the pieces, toss the board, take a page out of a book he hadn't read so many times the words were emblazoned in his memory.

Ezra was used to being the aggressor. He was used to calling the shots. He was used to being one step ahead of us, of everyone.

If we wanted to shake his confidence, we had to be the aggressors this time. We had to hit him where he lived. We had to knock the legs out from under him.

With the vote unanimous, I searched the faces of everyone gathered for signs of doubt but found none.

Maybe I was more than the antidote we had to shove down Ezra's throat. Maybe I was the bitter pill Wu had to swallow if he wanted to outthink and outmaneuver the male who had raised him, made him who he was, turned him into this vengeance-driven machine.

"We start tomorrow," I announced in closing. "Pack what you need and keep it light."

The coterie dispersed, off to gather their things in preparation for what came next.

Wu kept his seat, and so did Cole. So did I. And I waited for one of them to speak.

"I'm going to sit with him tonight," Wu said to the floor.

"All right." I had no doubt Thom had gone straight to check on the patient. "We'll bring a cot for you."

"The chair is fine." He rose, angled toward the dining room. "You're doing the right thing." He still couldn't look at me. "I don't want you to be right, but you are, and I know that."

"You don't have to like it," I told him. "I don't."

"But you'll do it," he said, and I heard the accusation he tried to hide.

"I will."

"You're everything I hoped you would be, Luce."

He left before I could form a comeback that didn't throw my creation in his face.

"Let it go." Cole took my hand. "He's hurting, and he knows he only has himself to blame."

Hauling me to my feet, he took me outside for a moonlit stroll to cool my temper.

"I could tell by how he tried to make me sound like a monster there at the end. The compliment almost sold me, but the disdain dripping from every word is going to make one hell of a stain on the floor."

"He has to lash out at you. It's the only way he can avoid castigating himself."

"He's brittle around the edges, isn't he?"

"He's old, Luce. Very old. He's been holding onto his anger for a long time. It's what's been fueling him. Without it . . . he's got nothing."

"I couldn't see it at first." I kicked a piece of gravel into the dark. "But the more things go wrong, the realer it gets, the easier it is to see the cracks in his façade."

"It's one thing to think you're ready to kickstart a war you can't win. It's another to realize you've begun something that can't be stopped, that you can either run to catch up or wait until it circles back and crushes you before rolling on."

"You make it sound like it's up to us to begin the apocalypse. I'm not sure I want that on my tombstone."

Here lies Luce Boudreau. She started the end of the world. Oops.

"You can't take all the credit." Cole chuckled. "Wu and Kapoor have been working behind the scenes to bring this about for decades at least. On Wu's part, we might be talking centuries."

"You don't sound panicked," I noticed. "You're always so chill and calm. How do you do that?"

"This isn't my first war," he said simply. "I've been in many battles during my lifetime."

"But the fate of the —" I began and then stopped before I made a fool of myself.

"Conquest was true to her name. She conquered many terrenes between her home world and this one."

Including Convallaria, his home. She had wiped out the entire royal line, his family, smote them to ashes, and presented him with an urn as a keepsake.

"This feels so big to me."

"It is big." He pulled me to a stop and faced me. "For you, it's everything." His gaze went distant. "I remember the desperation, when it was my home and my people at stake. I remember fighting against the clock, making any deal I could to save those I loved. I remember, and that's why I want you to conquer, one last time."

"I really don't deserve you." I placed my palms on his chest, smoothed them over his shoulders. "You're too kind and too forgiving."

"I've had a long time to make my peace." He cradled my face in his palms. "I will never forget, and I will never forgive her. But you're not Conquest. You're Luce." He brushed his lips over the stubborn line of my mouth. "You're mine."

"Want to go someplace quiet and make out?"

His teeth scraped over my jaw. "Do you even have to ask?"

"I do try to be polite." I smiled into his kiss. "It's not easy, mind you."

He and I had made the tent in the woods Portia and Maggie arranged for us our own. It wasn't too far from the others, but it gave us the privacy any couple still exploring each other required without putting on a free show.

As I guided Cole into our home away from home and knelt on the mound of pillows that made up our mattress, I couldn't imagine how Conquest had known him, loved him in her way, and had the heart to break his. But that was another Cole, lifetimes ago, and he was no longer that person any more than I was her. We had both changed, and the breaking of us made the fit perfect when we came together in this life.

Unable to hide my grin, I let him strip me naked and look his fill. He traced the delicate lines of the *rukav* across my shoulders, allowing himself to get sidetracked by the curve of my breast. That was fine with me, I had my own exploring to do.

I shucked his polo over his head and spread my palms across his pecs, marveling at the sheer size of him. He was all muscle, probably thanks to the amount of time he spent in his other skin, and I couldn't touch enough of him.

When my fingers bumped across the ridge of his abdomen and hooked in the front of his pants, he growled approval that melted me into a puddle beneath him. I had to make a conscious effort to finish the job of working the button free and yanking down the zipper, and then I had him. I closed my fingers around his length, and he punched out a hard breath against the side of my throat.

Abandoning my breasts, he smoothed one of his wide palms down my torso until he cupped me between my legs. I didn't imagine his chuckle at my gasp as he speared first one finger and then another into my core.

"I love you," I panted. "I'll love you even more if you invite your thumb to the party."

One expert brush of his thumb, the pad calloused and textured, over the tiny bundle of nerves begging for more, and I exploded around him.

I was still catching my breath when he spread my legs and sheathed himself with a single thrust.

Drifting on pleasure, I stroked my hands down his back, relishing the feel of him. The flex of muscle, the beads of sweat, the catch of his breath. And as he coaxed me back up to that perilous ledge, he toppled over it, growling my name into my ear, dragging me after him.

"What do you think?" I murmured sometime later, after I found my voice again. "We could run away together, do this every day, and never look back."

"Depends." A thoughtful sound moved through his chest. "Does *every day* mean once a day or . . . ?"

Happier than I had any right to be, I chuckled as I snuggled up against him and let sleep take me.

CHAPTER SIX

———◦———

The starlit night birthed a gray day that suited everyone's mood down to the forked lightning that struck in the distance and the rolling boom of thunder that could have been a growl from any of our throats.

One look at Wu told me he hadn't slept last night, which made me feel guilty for the warm and loose-limbed way I greeted the day. The others looked rested enough, though. That had to count for something.

While the coterie waited outside, I joined Wu alone over Kapoor's bed. He held an injector of the serum that would bring Kapoor out of his induced coma like it might come alive and bite him.

Hands resting on my hips, I stared down at Kapoor. "How does this work?"

"He was trained to hunt on command." Wu pressed the needle to Kapoor's skin hard enough to dent but not deep enough to pierce the flesh. "I will tell him his target and give him the order."

NSB training for their charun division bordered on torture from what I could tell. "It's a compulsion?"

"Part of it is his nature, but yes. The NSB wanted to guarantee their control over him."

"Yeah, they wouldn't want to turn a trained killer loose and risk him getting any ideas."

"He served a purpose, and he performed his duty with more compassion than any of his predecessors."

"That's why he burned out on the job," I surmised. "His productivity declined."

"He was too well trained for that." Wu exhaled and depressed the plunger. "But he lost weight, lost his edge. The hope was he would rebound if given a different position. His stint in management was never meant to be permanent."

How depressing for Kapoor. "Did he know that?"

"I don't know."

"You never told him."

"No."

"He's your best friend."

"He's the closest anyone has ever come to claiming the title, yes."

"Do you not understand how that works?"

"I . . ." He watched as Kapoor's eyelids fluttered. "Farhan?"

Farhan, not Kapoor.

Wu was definitely slipping up more often.

"You're . . . loud." He wet his dry lips. "Water?"

Prepared for his cotton mouth by Thom, I passed over the bottle of cold water from the fridge.

Wu took it from me and held it to Kapoor's lips while he drank, somehow managing not to get a dribble on him.

Watching them, I could see Wu cared about Kapoor. And Kapoor had already shown how far his loyalty to Wu extended.

He had allowed Ezra to capture and torture him for Wu's sake, and for the enclave. I could also tell from the fumbling overtures that Wu hadn't realized Kapoor was more than a cog in his revenge machine. Along the way, they had become friends. Somehow. And Wu was struggling to cross the finish line. Too bad the race had already begun. He ought to know. He's the one who pulled the proverbial trigger.

"Could you give us a moment?" Wu placed the bottle on the bedside table. "I would prefer to do this in private."

"Sure."

I left them with the understanding that Wu had more than a vague inclination of Kapoor's capacities as a tracker. The guilt? It was multifaceted, as were most things where Wu was concerned. But I had no doubt, none, as Wu lured Kapoor into a trancelike state behind me, that he had trained Kapoor himself.

And maybe that was how he could speak to his father's skills with such certainty. Perhaps what he had done to Kapoor, to others under the auspices of the NSB, was learned at his father's knee. So when he told me Kapoor was broken, he meant it.

And I had to wonder, if the ability to program and reprogram at will was one of the gifts of his species, had he used them on me?

I credited my core beliefs to my father. Edward Boudreau had raised me a certain way, and his friends, who had become my family, further reinforced that moral code. But what if Wu had whispered in my ear the night he made me? What he wanted me to be, how he wanted me to behave, what he wanted me to value?

Alone in the kitchen, I stuck my head in the freezer to cool the summer heat off my nape and shock my senses.

I couldn't pick apart the threads that wove together to make me. Start with one loose string, pull on it, unravel it, and it would take another and another and another with it until no more Luce remained. Conquest would be all I had left, that immutable core hidden inside me like a dormant disease waiting to spread through my system with cancerous glee.

"You're doing it wrong," Rixton said from behind me. "You're supposed to put your head in the oven to commit suicide. Common mistake really. Freezer, oven. I can see how you'd get the two confused."

Giving up on finding absolution in conveniently frozen portion sizes, I shut the door. "When did you arrive?"

"About five minutes ago." He popped a potato stick into his mouth. "I caught up with Maggie then went looking for you." He crunched through another one. "There are easier ways to go if you're looking to cash in your chips."

"I'm not trying to kill myself."

"Um." A cough stopped him mid-crunch. "This isn't one of those hormonal things, is it? Where you have the hot flashes and night sweats? Commercials have led me to believe women don't go through that until they're older, but I usually flip the station to avoid hearing the side effects, so I could be wrong. I don't know that I've ever sat through an entire ad, so maybe I missed pertinent details."

"I'm not going through menopause either."

Comprehension dawned on his face. "You're out of ice cream."

"Yes," I said, deadpan. "I'm out of ice cream."

"No problemo." He tossed me a silver packet. "Hope you like Neapolitan."

"This is astronaut ice cream." The foil crinkled in my hand. "Why do you have astronaut ice cream?"

"Mags told me to pack the essentials. I can't very well bring a carton of the frozen stuff into the field, now can I?"

"Here." I tossed it back to him. "Something tells me you need this more than I do."

We joined the others out in the yard and waited on Wu to finish setting Kapoor on the scent.

Miller drifted to my side. "When do you plan on bringing in Death?"

"We need a location first." I rubbed the base of my neck. "I don't want to pull that trigger until I've taken aim."

Several of her coterie, who she viewed as her children, had died in our last confrontation, and her mate had been seriously wounded, as much as a reanimated corpse can be injured. I wasn't certain what the shelf life on Janardan was, but she had almost come unglued when he was hurt, so he must be killable. That or he was only as salvageable as his corpse.

"All right." He nodded. "I can see the logic in that."

Thom sidled up to me, brushing his shoulder against mine. "I haven't hunted like this in an age."

We had hunted Drosera together, other charun too, so he must mean targeting a power.

That must be old hat for Conquest, and therefore the coterie. Much like Cole and his levelheaded approach to defending this terrene, he was pulling on his vast knowledge of how to bring a world to its knees in order to keep this one standing.

Not ten minutes later, Wu emerged with his lips mashed into a bloodless line.

Kapoor followed on his heels, his eyes gleaming silver, and his body farther gone into his transformation than I had ever seen it.

"He's ready," Wu rasped. "Are you?"

"As I'll ever be."

Wu snapped out a command in a language that tickled my hindbrain, and Kapoor shot into the sky.

Wings burst from either side of Wu's spine, and he blasted off in pursuit.

Cole shifted while the coterie gathered around us, and I hopped on his back.

With an eager trill, Phoebe shot down the front of my shirt then stuck her head out the neck while threading her tail through the nearest loop on my jeans. It's not like we had to worry about her splatting if she fell, but we tried to keep her safe, even though she was determined to fight us every step of the way.

"Stay in contact," I shouted to the others. "Ears and eyes open."

Miller and Thom took one SUV and Portia, Rixton, and Santiago took the other.

They would be our backup on the ground, in charge of securing food and lodgings as needed until this hunt concluded, one way or another.

The quick dart of Phoebe's raspy tongue across my chin brought my attention down to her.

"Are you sure you don't want to stay with Granddaddy?"

Far away from the action, nice and safe in a mountain fortress, hidden away from it all.

She bared her teeth.

"I'm willing to supply you with cats to chase."

Her lips stopped quivering while she thought it over.

"I might even let you eat one or two."

Sorry, cats.

A decisive shake of her head sealed the deal.

"Stay close and do exactly what I tell you, understand?"

This time when she showed her teeth, it was with glee.

The thing I kept forgetting about her was she was charun, a person and not a pet. She might look like the cutest little dragon to ever be born — hatched? — but she was a child, and according to Cole children on Convallaria matured at a wicked fast rate until they hit puberty. I wasn't imagining that she was bigger in the *time flies when you have kids* way most parents viewed their offspring. She was putting on weight, gaining length. Her mind was sharpening, her reflexes quickening.

As she settled in to nap, I kept tabs on Wu and Kapoor.

With the sun beating down on us, it promised to be a long day.

Wu called Kapoor to heel at nightfall, and we met up with the others to eat and sneak our sweaty, sunburnt party into our hotel rooms. Wu and Kapoor shared a room, since Kapoor was fully under Wu's control as far as I could tell.

No wonder Wu hadn't shared Kapoor's ability with us. It meant exposing his own and acknowledging that no matter how much he despised his father, he was still very much his son.

The coterie, plus Rixton, had three rooms up for grabs. I expected Thom and Miller to share, then Portia and Maggie, who were, of course, a combo deal, to stay with Rixton, and for us to get stuck with Santiago.

I wasn't disappointed.

"We've got a problem," Santiago said as he shoved into our room and claimed one of the queen-size beds.

"How is that different than any other day?" I flopped on the other mattress, sore and achy and glad Phoebe had settled on the dresser in the nest of blankets Cole made for her. "There's always a problem. Multiple problems. If we didn't have problems, I would think the world was ending."

A bit too on the nose, but I was tired and hungry and hungry and tired.

"Mateo Vega is reporting five missing Cuprina scouts." He tapped the tablet screen he pulled from who knows where. "They're more tech savvy than most. They all wore smartwatches to keep in contact with their home base."

"That's good news, then." I frowned at his glum mood. "That means you can track them."

"I'm working on it." He manifested three more tablets and began to search in earnest.

Forcing my brain to do its job, I asked, "When did they go missing?"

"Today."

"Kapoor was with us the whole time." The news drew me upright. "Are you sure it happened today?"

Most scouting parties left on days or weeklong missions, only returning home to report and tag in the next group. Radio silence wasn't uncommon. Technology was easily tracked, so most left their phones and other gadgets at home.

"They left this morning, got a few hours out, and the signal disappeared. Mateo attempted contact an hour after, in case they had flown into a dead zone for coverage. No one answered his calls."

"We can't afford to divide our forces." I sounded very much like the general leading her troops, and I hated how naturally it came to me. "We have to stick together. It's the only way we've got a fighting chance against Ezra."

"We can't hang our allies out to dry," Santiago said, "or they're going to start thinking you're more like Conquest than the brochure says."

"I didn't say I wouldn't send help." I was practical, not heartless. "Contact our allies. See who's nearest them. Request a search party. Keep the details as vague as you can. We don't need to start a panic."

"Yeah," Santiago agreed dryly. "We wouldn't want our allies to know they're being hunted."

"They knew what they signed up for," Cole rumbled from behind me. "We need to keep a lid on the Kapoor situation for as long as possible."

"There." After a few keystrokes, Santiago powered off his tablet. "Help is on the way. Problem solved."

He turned to go, but I put myself between him and the door, blocking his easy exit.

"What is your problem?"

"Problem? What problem? I don't have a problem."

"Are you questioning orders?"

"There she is, ladies and gentlemen." He tucked the tablet under his arm so he could clap. "Conquest."

A warning rumble filled the space between us, but I couldn't blame Cole. It was all mine.

"I'll ask you one more time before I shift and swallow you whole. What is your problem?"

"That right there." He jabbed a finger in my face. "You're more like her every day."

"What do you want me to do? Bail on Wu and Kapoor — on you guys — instead?"

"Yes," he hissed. "Go prove you're willing to put your money where your mouth is."

"I set Kapoor on this path. It's a collision course with Ezra. I'm not going to search the bushes for what we all know they're going to find. I can't protect those people. I made that clear. They chose to follow me, to deify me, and I hate that I can't slap them sober, that we need willing sacrifices." I slapped his hand away. "Coterie is family. You guys and Dad are all I've got left."

"Ezra has held this terrene beyond memory, beyond time, beyond —"

A bucket of ice-cold comprehension dumped over my head. "You're scared."

Horror contorted his features. "I am not."

Now that I knew to look, I couldn't stop seeing it. "You are too."

"Am not."

"Are too."

The door swung open behind us, and Portia sashayed in without waiting for an invitation.

"I can't believe you picked a fight with Santiago and didn't invite me to join." She rubbed her hands together. "What are we making fun of? His face? His pea-sized brain?" Behind her hand, she said, "His pea-sized other brain?"

"Forget it." He shoved past her into the hall. "Forget I said anything."

As much as I wished I could, I had an inkling of what would make this better — and worse — and I owed it to him to suck up my distaste and do it.

"He left." Portia gawked after him. "I offered to insult his manhood, both north and south, and he left." She wheeled on me. "What did you do to him? He's broken."

"I have an idea how to fix this." I pushed out a sigh. "Stay put. It won't work if there are spectators."

When all eyes were on him, he couldn't help but live down to their expectations and pitch epic mantrums worthy of his reputation.

My first order of business was hitting the vending machines for his favorite soda and snacks. Only after I had that peace offering in hand did I track him down to the parking lot where he sat under a tree planted in the median between our hotel and the strip mall behind it.

"Catch." I tossed him a bag of those rock-hard corn things, ranch-flavored, that would chip my teeth if I tried to eat them. "I would toss your soda, but that would be cruel."

Eyes narrowed on me, he tore into his treat. "That's never stopped you before."

"Yes, well, normally I would shake it all the way from the vending machine to here and then given it to you for the joy of watching it explode in your face. I might have even recorded it for Portia."

"What's stopping you?" He accepted the can but eyed it with distrust. "You're not exactly known for your mercy."

Ignoring his sprawl that screamed *no girls allowed*, I kicked his ankle until he made room for me to sit beside him. Then, since he was being a scaredy cat, I took his drink and popped the top myself to prove it wasn't rigged. I handed it back, and he slurped loudly and suspiciously.

There was nothing to do but spit it out. "You're trying to protect me."

"No, I'm not."

"Yes, you —" I gritted my teeth against falling into the childish rhythm that was his comfort zone. "You're trying to provoke me into personally checking on the missing Cuprina. There's no tactical reason why you would do that, so it's got to be an emotional one."

"I have no emotions."

"Yes, you do."

"No, I don't." A smile tipped the corner of his mouth he must have thought I couldn't see. "Is there a point to this? I'm not against you hand-delivering me snacks, but I could make a list for next time. It would cut down on the number of trips you have to make."

"You're worried we're going to find Ezra," I pressed on. "You want to scare me off so I'm not there when you die in a blaze of glory."

"There's no glory in death," he scoffed. "I don't like you enough to spare you from the psychological scars witnessing my imminent demise would inflict on your wannabe human psyche."

"Of course you don't." Risking life and limb, I leaned my head against his shoulder, ignoring how he stiffened, and let that contact soothe him through the coterie bond. "I remember how guilty I felt after Thom . . . " I couldn't finish, but I didn't have to when

Santiago felt that burden as heavily as I did. "I wouldn't want anyone to feel that way if I got hurt. That they were responsible. I wouldn't want them to think it was their fault."

"We don't have to go looking for trouble," he said quietly. "He's going to find us. He probably already knows we're on the way."

"He's got all the advantages," I allowed, "but he's not going to see us coming. He's too used to being powerful, too certain we're going to cower before him. He doesn't expect to face his enemies head-on. He throws Malakhim at all his problems until they go away. He's not expecting a fight. He's expecting to wear us out and then hunt us down."

The tension beneath my cheek ebbed a bit, and I kept my own smile hidden.

"That still doesn't solve the problem of who is attacking our allies."

"That's true." I plucked a blade of grass and twirled it between my fingers. "There's always a chance that it's Malakhim."

"I don't see the point in picking off the outliers."

"Surveillance? Kill the lookouts then creep up on the main camp for recon?"

"Why stop there? Why not wipe out each encampment? They have the numbers."

"These attacks divide our focus," I pointed out. "I've cultivated a reputation among the cadre and their coteries for weakness. That same outlook will carry over into each cadre members' followers. They might hope that I'll peel off from the group to put out fires in person."

Santiago tensed again then rolled his shoulder to dislodge me. "Then they'll be disappointed."

Figuring that meant my work here was done, I stood and dusted off the seat of my pants. "Coming in?"

"I have to brood for another hour or two."

"Long enough for Portia to notice and come check on you?"

The cut of his scowl was betrayed by the tremble in his lips that begged to be a smile.

"What are you up to?" I looked to either side of him, but I didn't see anything obvious. "Spill."

Santiago didn't do happy without a reason. Usually one that sucked for the other person involved.

"A tin of itching powder might have come into my possession while we were in Virginia City. The general store had all kinds of awesome gift ideas."

"You could have bought her one of the gemstones. She might like that more."

"Sometimes, it's like you don't know her at all."

Raising my hands, I backed away. "Just make sure Maggie doesn't get stuck with the cleanup."

"I won't hurt Maggie." He snorted. "Miller would swallow me whole."

"Yeah, he would." The poor guy had it bad. "But that's nothing compared to what I would do to you."

With a wink, I left him to stew and plot, the two things he did best. No doubt an ugly surprise would drop into my lap thanks to the comment I had made about his pouting until Portia took notice. He preferred to strike first and apologize ... well ... actually never. He wasn't much for *sorries*.

Healing my relationship with Santiago might be a stretch, but I had slapped a solid bandage on it.

CHAPTER SEVEN

The next morning, Kapoor led us farther across the country, in a northwestern slant. I was going to laugh my butt off if it turned out Ezra lived in Hollywood, but that was the exhaustion and nerves talking. A high-density area would be the worst-case scenario. There was also the fact he viewed himself as above it all, so I doubt he would want to live among the common or uncommon, since we're talking Hollywood, rabble.

When we broke for lunch, I got served more bad news.

"Are you sure?" I sat across from Santiago on a picnic bench, devouring the fried chicken and biscuits he had selected for lunch. "How many were lost?"

"Two more clans are reporting scouts missing. The total between them is fourteen."

Overnight, I seemed to have come down with a case of humanity.

"Tell the other clans." So much for strategy. "Warn them it's started. Let them know they're being hunted. Bring in the scouts except for the perimeter patrols around the encampments. Make sure they're armed."

"Will do." Santiago set to work. "I'll send aid to the clans who require it."

"Thanks." Drumstick in hand, I rose and started pacing off my anxiety. Within minutes, Cole joined me. He wore Phoebe like a necklace, which was one of her favorite modes of transportation. "What's up?"

"You're doing the right thing."

"Am I?" I tossed Phoebe the rest of the meat, and she snapped her jaws closed over the bone, breaking it into pieces. "The fact they're being targeted can't exactly be breaking news." I repeated the phrase meant to ease my guilt. "They know what they signed up for."

"You'll save lives by putting them on alert."

"They should already be on alert."

"What's really bothering you?"

I got the feeling he was handling me now the way I handled Santiago last night, but it worked.

"Conquest knows what she's doing. She could handle the strategic points without so much emotion getting in the way." I rubbed my wind-chapped palms down my face. "People are dying. They're being picked off. I know it's not my fault. I know they wanted to join the fight. But they have this stupid idea of who I am that makes them think dying is worth it to support me."

"Luce, the pain you feel over every life lost in your name is what sets you apart."

"I hate this." I anchored my hands on my hips. "I feel like the baby King Solomon ordered cut in half."

"I'm not as familiar with Christianity as you, but that seems extreme."

"Two women were fighting over a child. Both claimed to be its mother. The king ordered the child cut in two so each woman could have a half. One said go ahead. Basically, if she couldn't have it, no one could. The other said she would rather give up the baby than have it killed. That's how he determined the real mother."

"It's been my experience that when the stakes are this high, if you feel torn, if you worry you're not doing it right, if you worry you're not doing enough, then you're on the right path."

"Conquest —"

"— wouldn't blink when her allies were murdered. She wouldn't take breaks to rest her coterie, either. She would demand Kapoor hunt until he produced Ezra, or she would kill him for wasting her time. You can't compare yourself to her. She's the same as every other Conquest before her, and you see how well their methods have worked up to this point."

"They haven't," I grumbled reluctant agreement. "I know it in my head." I pounded a fist over my chest. "It's my heart that's giving me fits."

"It's your heart that's going to win this."

"Or cost us everything."

"You've got to have faith."

"I'm still not on speaking terms with God. He let me down, and I haven't decided if he deserves a second chance yet."

"I meant faith in yourself."

"Oh."

"Is it really easier to place your trust in a being you have never seen than in the face in the mirror?"

"Yes. A thousand times yes. A hundred thousand times yes."

Fed up with being ignored, Phoebe leapt from Cole's shoulder onto mine.

"We can play fetch." I scratched under her chin. "With a stick, though. No more chicken bones."

"She can digest them, and they're more nutritious than sticks."

"Daddy is spoiling you rotten," I cooed at her. "He probably has a drumstick in his pocket."

"It's a thigh," he confirmed. "It's best if we travel with snacks."

"Mmm-hmm. I wouldn't want her to eat all the cats between here and wherever we're headed."

Wu, who refused to leave Kapoor's side while he remained lost to his tracking fugue, waved me over to join them.

"Looks like you guys will have to play fetch." I passed Phoebe back to Cole. "I'm being summoned."

Wu took his time updating me, as if the information cost him. "I have an idea of where we're going."

"That's good news. A location would cut down on our travel time."

"Kapoor can't deviate. He has to follow the trail to its end."

"Okay, that's less good."

"You and the others go ahead," he offered. "I'll stay with him."

Letting Wu out of my sight wasn't happening. I stood a greater chance of surviving his machinations with him around to buffer me.

"There might come a time when I have to take you up on that offer. For now, we stick together."

"All right."

The fight was draining out of Wu right before my eyes, and the fun hadn't even started yet. Maybe this close to confronting his father, to ending it, he regretted the cost of freedom being his mortality. Well, he could join the club. I didn't have much empathy left for him. He set us on this path, and he had no right to drag his feet if he expected me to jump into a suicide pact with both of mine.

"Have you eaten?" I tried for levity. "Or are you morally opposed to eating winged relatives of yours?"

The smile he attempted was a pitiful thing that ended before it began.

"Come on." I took him by the arm, and the warmth in my palm

told me our connection was strengthening, more confirmation the bangles were weakening. "You and Kapoor have to replenish the calories you burn during flight."

Kapoor trailed after Wu, his eyes blank and dark. His presence at my back caused the hairs on my nape to stand on end. It was easy to forget what Kapoor had been when most of the time he resembled every other harried agent scooped out of the field and dumped behind a desk for the sake of what the higher-ups called a promotion.

"There have been more attacks," I told him when he didn't appear interested in chitchat.

"It's to be expected."

"You know Malakhim strategy. Do you think they're responsible?"

"No." His eyes cleared as he thought it over. "They're apex predators, not ambush predators."

Ambush predator. I remembered thinking that about Death when she sneaked up on War and killed her. It made me recall who else had witnessed that end, had schemed to bring it about, and growled, "Sariah."

Wu held very still. "You think she's picking off your allies?"

"She wants to be the next War. This seems like a very War thing to do."

"Where's the gain?" He frowned. "Killing you won't earn her a title, and it won't help her situation. Why pick a fight with you?"

"Do you think she was telling the truth about taking orders from Ezra?"

"He would have killed her for the impertinence of engaging with him as if they were equals."

"This complicates things." These days, waking up in the morning complicated things. "Kapoor is convinced he committed the murders, and the evidence suggests he's guilty, but he also believed the victims were Malakhim. What else might he be confused about?"

"Do you think Sariah framed him?"

"Your guess is as good as mine."

"Kapoor might have been caught up in a delusion, stumbled across the Onca massacre, and his brain filled in the blanks once his thoughts cleared."

For all we knew, he had been hacking up corpses, convinced they were Malakhim invaders. Or he could have spotted them, swooped down to investigate, and gotten blood on his hands when he checked their pulses. With Kapoor so far gone, there was no way to know what was true.

A chill swept through me when I checked on Kapoor, who had sat and began eating mechanically. "I set him on this path."

A path he couldn't deviate from, according to Wu. Kapoor wouldn't stop until he found Ezra. Back when I thought he wore the blood of innocents on his hands, I deemed his life in trade for theirs fair. Now I had to wonder if I hadn't condemned him unjustly.

This was a prime example of why I missed being a cop. I enjoyed apprehending bad guys, and I enjoyed dumping them in jail, which made them someone else's problem, even more. I made life or death judgement calls in the field, true enough. But the rest of the time? Lawyers, judges, and juries fought it out to determine innocence or guilt.

"You made the best decision based on the information you had at the time."

"Did I?" I had to glance away from Kapoor. "Or was I engineering the solution I wanted?"

"You can't second-guess yourself." He gathered his wits, appearing more present in this moment than he had in days. "Trying to outthink yourself is the worst thing you can do."

"It's not me I'm worried about. It's her." I shook my wrists. "They're failing. How much longer until they can't hold her back? We're racing so many clocks, but this is the one I hear ticking loudest." Worry that I had manipulated Kapoor into this situation gnawed on me. "We need to find Ezra while I'm still myself. We need to end this before Conquest gets a say in the matter. She's not going to sacrifice herself for this world or anyone in it."

Wu slowed until we both came to a stop. "I'm sorry, Luce."

"You're a liar, Wu." I gave him the smile he deserved. Sharp, hard, pitiless. "You wanted revenge, and you'll get it. That's fine. You deserve it. But I'm getting what I want too, and that's for my people to be safe after I'm gone. For this world to be free once I'm no longer in it."

"You'll have it," he said quietly. "I swear it."

"Again," I reminded him. "You're a liar. I can't take your word at face value. All I can do is pray that if you loved your wife as much as you claim, if your descendants are as important to you as they seem, that you'll want to preserve this world for them too. If not for their sake, for hers."

"I deserve your anger."

"Yes, you do."

"I should never have let you reunite with your coterie."

I blinked at the change of topic. "What does that have to do with anything?"

Slowly, slowly, Wu cupped my cheek. "I could have made you fall in love with me."

The truth, that I had been halfway there since puberty, made denying the claim impossible. I had been fascinated with Ezra. He had been my savior. He was the one link to my otherness, and I cherished him. I would have done anything, gone anywhere, to meet him just once. I had wanted to believe so very much, and I thought I would fit with him if he gave me half a chance.

I never wanted to be Wild Child Boudreau. I wanted to be normal, if not by human standards then by someone's, but I was an anomaly in both worlds. Thanks to Wu.

Searching his face, I felt the dim echo of resonance between us. "Could you have loved me?"

Wu hesitated, and he dropped his hand. "Would it matter to you if I could? If I did?"

The truth hurt, but I had to tell him. "My heart belongs to Cole, from corner to corner. I might have fit you in there had you been honest with me sooner, but now? No. It doesn't matter. There's nothing you can say or do to change who I chose."

"Then all is as it should be."

He walked off, and I let him go. I stood there, staring after him, the imprint of his hand on my cheek still warm, and imagined how life might have been if he had revealed himself to me as Ezra before I received the call about Jane Doe.

All things considered, I ought to count my lucky stars Wu didn't see to it I was raised to believe my sole purpose in life was sacrifice. He let me have the most normal, the most human upbringing anyone in my position could receive.

Cole's hand landed on my shoulder. "Time to go."

"What?" I jerked back, got my head on straight. "Sorry, I was woolgathering."

"I could tell." He massaged the knots aching near my spine. "You've been staring off into the distance for the last ten minutes."

"I was reflecting on all the ways we might have ended up somewhere other than here."

"Wu has feelings for you," he stated matter-of-factly. "He's not sure what they are or what they mean."

"You think so?" I laughed. "I'm in no position to tell him."

He made a thoughtful sound but didn't elaborate.

"What does that mean?" I elbowed him and immediately regretted my life choices.

"You chose me." He smiled a little, the corners of his eyes crinkling. "I enjoy remembering that."

"Good grief." I walked off. "Boys."

Phoebe, who had been flitting here and there, spotted me and landed on my head. She stuck out her forked tongue at her father in a show of female solidarity that made me teary. Or maybe my watery eyes were the result of straining my neck to hold a dragon upright. Sheesh. This kid was growing fast and getting heavy. Cole must be feeding her rocks behind my back.

Energy prickled along my spine, and a much larger version of her prowled up beside us. I set Phoebe on his back then climbed up and stuffed her down my shirt where she curled against my collarbone and let the neck of my shirt act as a sling to hold up her head.

And then we were off again, trailing Kapoor and Wu while the coterie tracked us from below.

Belly full of chicken, I almost dozed off. I would have if juggling Phoebe at these speeds and at this height wasn't so dangerous. She might be a better flier than me, but she was still a baby, her wings so membranous and delicate the wind could shred them as fast as Cole flew.

With napping off the table, I kept watch on the horizon.

Night approached, and we ended another long day of flight. I was sunburned and sore, and Phoebe was showing her tail out of boredom. I was going to foist her off on her Uncle Santiago for the first leg of the journey tomorrow and see if that made a difference. I was imagining his horror at being asked to babysit, but they had an understanding. He put on cartoons, and she sat and behaved like an angel.

The trick only worked for him, which was unfair if you asked me.

An inquiring noise rumbled through Cole, and I searched for what had caught his eye.

Below us spread a hundred or so tents. From them poured a thousand charun sporting armor. They raised their axes overhead and roared loud enough for even my ears to catch their salute.

Speak of the devil, and he'll appear.

Aunt Nancy used to say that all the time.

Well, thinking of Santiago was enough to summon his handiwork apparently. These must be new recruits he wanted us to vet while we were in the area. I couldn't imagine any other reason for us to be crossing their path.

"Santiago has a way of ruining everything without even trying," I grumbled, tired and ready for a long soak. "What is that?" I squinted down at the field. "There's no way." I swallowed. "Uh, Cole. That's a catapult." The dragon made a noise of agreement. "I hate to be an alarmist, but they're loading it." I started kicking him in the sides. *"They're aiming at us."*

That caught the dragon's attention. Cole was used to gliding invisibly through the skies. It was a nifty trick, but not everyone here knew the same ones. Wu must have some way of concealing himself, but Kapoor? I had no idea. I was far from an expert at charun species, and I had never seen anyone like him.

A quick feint by Cole spared us a direct hit, but whatever they hurled at us exploded in a shower of colorful sparks overhead.

For an instant, one teeny second, I thought it might be fireworks to welcome us, and I was ready to laugh off my paranoia. But smoke from the display clogged my lungs and made my head feel weighted with marbles. I stuffed Phoebe down my shirt to spare her as best I could, but we had flown through the black cloud, and it clung to my skin, stinging worse than a jellyfish.

Worst of all, the dragon beneath me began to sway. At first,

I thought it was my vision going wobbly, but no. Cole was as affected as me, and we were going down.

Nothing I did would stop this from happening, but I had to try.

"Phoebe, stay with your dad no matter what." His odds of survival were about to be much higher than mine. "No funny business. This is serious."

Gritting my teeth, I leapt off Cole's back into open air and swallowed the scream rocketing up the back of my throat.

A chill skittered down my arms, Conquest's survival instincts kicking in, and I changed in a burst of energy that consumed me from the inside out, a transition unlike any I had experienced up until now.

Crimson flooded my vision, and my dragon heart pounded at the sight of my mate and offspring spiraling toward the earth. I let out a roar that challenged the skies and sped toward them, ignoring the ants scattering across the field below us with their wicked machines.

Thanks to playing tag with Phoebe, I was a stronger flyer than I had been, but Cole was a mature male dragon, and I had no illusions about how this would go. That didn't stop me. It didn't even slow me down.

Cole was managing a wicked fast glide rather than a plummet, but his wings trembled. Whatever they shot at us, it wasn't wearing off him the way I was burning through its drowsy suggestion. Whether that was because I was Conquest, half human, or seconds from a coronary, I didn't know.

A warning growl was all the heads-up I could give him before sliding under him the way he had once to correct my flight. Our bodies were long and sinuous, but our hindquarters were muscular. This wasn't going to be easy.

Pumping my wings as hard as I could, I took on Cole's weight and turned him out of his spiral into an even glide straight into the field below us. It made us sitting ducks, but that couldn't be helped. This was the only way I could keep him and Phoebe alive.

The razor-sharp sting down my left wing caught me by surprise. At first, I didn't understand. I thought I might have been struck by something launched at us from the ground. But then it got worse, red-hot pain searing through that side, stealing my breath. When I turned to examine the injury, I tasted bile rising up my very long throat.

I had torn my wing. There was a split ripping its way through the dead center, right where a reinforced ridge of cartilage helped it keep its shape. I didn't remember childbirth, but I had to imagine it couldn't be worse than this.

The ground rushed up at us, and I shut my eyes. It was all in God's hands now.

Impact broke something in me. Maybe several things. The trail I was blazing through the field on my stomach began working the scales loose. When that protection failed, I started losing skin, but I could hear Cole's indignant roar above me. Distantly, I made out Phoebe's frantic trills.

They were alive. They were going to make it. That was what mattered. It was all that mattered.

Trees loomed ahead, a forest encroaching on farmer's land, and I didn't have the strength to lift my head to blunt impact with those weathered trunks.

The next snap I heard . . . was my neck.

CHAPTER EIGHT

Chains bound me when I woke, and familiar laughter pierced the veil of unconsciousness.

"Hi, Auntie."

"Sariah," I hissed through bloody teeth. "Where . . ." I swallowed hard and tasted stale copper. "Cole?"

"Oh, he's fine. Just dandy. He's in the cage next to yours."

Primal instincts screamed at me to ask after Phoebe, but if Sariah wasn't rubbing her capture in my face, I was going to pretend that meant she was okay. The alternative, that she hadn't survived our crash landing, caused a more critical thing than my ribs to break.

"What do . . . you . . . want?"

"What I've always wanted."

At that point, I grasped that my eyes were open, but I couldn't see. I had a bad feeling the issue wasn't a blown lightbulb in my cell. And judging by the echo and the moldy smells, I was underground, probably surrounded by concrete.

"You might have . . . noticed . . . I'm not currently at my . . . best."

"See, in my mind, this is how it was going to play out. The Bushtas stun Cole with the nerve agent they've been developing for just such an occasion, he turns all heroic, demands to sacrifice himself for you, and you ride him to the ground like a surfboard." She snickered at the description, clearly enjoying herself. "I planned on using what was left of him to motivate you to cooperate. I expected him to be the mess of road rash, not you." She sighed. "He barely has a scratch on him, and you're ... hamburger."

Thank you, God.

"Sorry to ... disappoint."

"Now I have a matched set. I'm not too upset. You've still got the bangles on, which means you're only half the threat you could be. Honestly, I wouldn't have tried this without them, so thanks for going the noble sacrifice route." She clasped her hands together. "Here's the thing. I've gathered my allies, and you've gathered yours. We both want the same thing: control of this terrene. I propose we fight it out. Winner take all."

"Ezra," I panted, "will kill you."

"First, I don't plan on losing. Second, I intend to make him a peace offering he can't refuse."

Even with my brain rattling like a rock in a can, I could see where this was headed. "Me."

"You."

Motion blurred the darkness as my vision attempted to come online. "He'll kill you."

"No." She paced outside what I assumed was my cell. "He won't."

Yes, he will.

No, he won't.

A laugh escaped me on a wheeze as I imagined how it might play out if I kept engaging her.

Apparently Santiago wasn't the only one who could devolve into childish taunting.

The sudden quiet unsettled me more than my present circumstances. "What makes you so sure?"

"You're not the only fish we caught in our net."

Wu and Kapoor. Had to be. Damn it. Damn it. Damn it.

"I bet Daddy pays a pretty penny to get his boy back."

"You have no idea who you're dealing with."

"A xenophobic charun with a god complex."

"Okay." Fair point. "Maybe you do know who you're dealing with."

"I've done the research," she reminded me. "There's nowhere to go once I turn you over. Not back down, and certainly not up. For better or worse, this is home. It's not a bad place to live. Humans are soft and sweet on the inside, and they'll bargain anything away if it means getting what they want when they want it. They're incredibly shortsighted that way. They would rather have the latest phone in hand before their friends than a lifetime to experience future technological advancements."

Other coteries had hidden themselves away in the human population without drawing Ezra's immediate ire. She might survive if she kept her head down. She was good at that. Surviving. The flaw in her plan was in thinking she could confront him, make demands of him, and then walk away to enjoy that life.

He would bristle at her gall and kill her if she was dumb enough to bargain with him. He wanted me dead, and some days I wasn't sure he didn't wish the same on his only child. Still, it was a bold plan. It spoke to her ambition in claiming her mother's title. More than that, these Bushta must be War's allies.

Sariah couldn't have established a reputation for herself in time to raise her own followers. She must be dipping into War's known cohorts, no small feat considering most former coterie members shrugged off each ascension once their player was out of the game. Sariah must be pitching this as the battle to end all battles for them to be so eager to do her bidding.

We had no way of knowing how much information Sariah had at her fingertips after infiltrating the coterie's database. No one aside from Wu, Kapoor, and I were aware of the cost of sealing the terrenes. Of that I was certain. Otherwise, I would be bound in bubble wrap and taped to a chair in a basement somewhere.

Killing Ezra would be enough for my coterie, I was certain. As much as I wished I could be satisfied with that, I couldn't call it a win. Ezra had cost me my aunt and uncle, and my future with Cole. I wouldn't stop until he was dead, and his empire crumbled to ashes.

Unless we sealed the terrenes, future wars were inevitable. The Malakhim would keep falling, bringing those like Ezra and Wu with them. The cadre would keep climbing, until yet another set of harbingers emerged with battle lust and a taste for destruction.

Commotion down what sounded like a long hall silenced Sariah for a beat or two.

"There's a healer on the way," she informed me. "I got a cramp from holding your head in place while your cervical fracture fused. I'm guessing it was C2, maybe C3, but who knows? It's not like I carry a pocket x-ray machine." She hesitated. "Try not to die before he gets here."

The reminder made me flinch, and God that hurt. I had forgotten about my neck. It was one hurt lost among myriad others, a single note in a symphony of agony. It's not like I could move it or anything else, but relief slid through me, hot and greasy as it mingled with the knowledge I had worse things to worry about now.

"Why not?" I fought to untangle my thoughts. "What does it matter?"

"Ezra strikes me as the sort who enjoys playing with his toys before he breaks them. He won't be as motivated to bargain if I have to roll you in to the meeting in a wheelchair."

Faking exhaustion, which wasn't hard since I was halfway to dead, I slumped back and let her think I had passed out again.

"Sleep well." She made a happy sound, one of anticipation. "Our healers aren't as skilled as yours. When a Drosera patches you up, the healing often hurts worse than the injury."

When I made no comeback, she accepted I was unconscious and left me to my rest.

An hour passed, maybe longer, before I heard a familiar gruff whisper from next door.

"The guard they posted left."

"Ah." I kept my eyes shut since the view didn't change much when they opened. "I wondered what took you so long."

Thanks to the bangles failing, I had sensed him nearby through our mate bond. That frail connection had been the only thing chaining me to my sanity. It gave me the strength to wait for Cole to make contact.

"I was unconscious there at the start," he admitted. "Her evil chuckling woke me."

"I hate we lost our package," I said, unable to swallow my fear for Phoebe a moment longer. "It was small, but valuable."

"I'm glad you think so, but we didn't lose it."

"Oh." Moisture gathered on my eyelids. "That's good then."

Phoebe was alive and well. I didn't have to know where to be content. We couldn't risk getting more specific in case there were other security measures in place Cole hadn't noticed. Usually, I wouldn't doubt his senses, but he was still shaking off Sariah's cocktail. Until he was back at one hundred percent, we couldn't afford to take any risks.

"You should rest. You'll need your strength for the healing."

"It's as bad as she says?"

"Worse." He exhaled. "It's the difference in a battlefield medic and an acclaimed surgeon."

A butter knife and scalpel more like it, but I didn't want to dwell. Knowing would be as bad as not knowing, maybe worse.

"I'm spoiled to the second." Thom had all manner of healing properties that didn't require invasive or painful procedures, even if it did require ingesting his various bodily fluids. I promised myself right then I would never question where any of his medicine originated if I could only have some now. "The first doesn't sound like much fun if I'm being honest."

"Let me see what I can do to help until then." Chains clanked across the stone floor. "Can you reach?"

"I don't know." I hadn't fully grasped that I was on the floor too. That was good to know. "I can't see well."

"Extend your left arm." More shuffling on his side. "There."

His warm hand clasped mine, and the coterie bond poured in through my fingertips to sweep through my abused limbs. It didn't heal me, and it didn't numb the worst of the pain, but it was a comfort I felt down to my bones. The resonance I shared with Cole sang through me, connecting us, and I slept.

The Drosera medic Sariah brought me resembled the freckle-faced boy in those vintage Coke ads but taller. He didn't look old enough to be a doctor, but the skin suit he wore could be concealing any manner of monster. None of Sariah's coterie were her age, she killed anyone too clever before they became a risk, but the eyes on this one betrayed his years.

"This is Adder," Sariah said, letting him into my cell. By now I had regained my vision and could see what was happening. Then again, ignorance might be bliss. "He's the best we've got, which isn't saying much."

The male didn't twitch, didn't show any indication if her insult stung his pride.

An electric lantern swung from his fingertips, illuminating the space. No wonder Cole hadn't shifted and busted us out of here. This cell could hold two people, barely, but his? It was comically small. He sat with his back to the wall, and his feet brushed the bars in front of him. He couldn't shift in there, and I couldn't shift in here. He had no room, and I had no stamina. I was too injured to do more than lie there and let the healer cut away my clothing.

"Don't break her more than necessary to fix her," Sariah warned. "You like to play, and usually, I like to watch, but we're short on time."

The frenetic energy in her voice drew me upright. "Do you have a meeting set?"

"I do." She rubbed her hands together in an exaggerated fashion, living up to cartoon villain standards. "Exciting stuff, right? I'm doing all the things I was told I can't by my unsupportive family."

There was a difference between *can't* and *shouldn't* but she ought to be old enough to know it by now.

"I would like to begin," Adder rasped in a sibilant voice. "May I?"

"Yeah, yeah." She waved a negligent hand. "Piece her together so there are no scars. No matter how long it takes. I don't know what Ezra plans on doing with her, but I want her pristine."

"I take great pride in my work."

"That's what makes you the best." Her lips pulled to one side. "And the worst. It's all a matter of perspective."

The healer waited until Sariah left before putting his hands on me. The first touch almost made me scream. I had unlinked my hand from Cole's while I slept, so there was no relief there. The entirety of my body was one exposed nerve.

"It hurts, doesn't it?" Adder ran his hands down my torso,

over the worst of the damage. "That's a rib, dear. That's why. They aren't meant to be worn on the outside." He wheezed in laughter at his own joke. "I'll put it back where it goes, don't you worry, but first we must begin regenerating your skin. It's the longest part of the process, and I regret there are no shortcuts." He smiled, and he was close enough I distinguished the glint of braces on his teeth. "As I said to the pretender, I take great pride in my work."

At last he'd said something that piqued my interest. "The pretender?"

"Just so." He massaged a salve onto my feet and up my legs. Cold pervaded my skin, but it didn't hurt any more than you would expect when someone was touching a raw wound. "She is not War. She was forged by her mother, I'll give her that, but she is not cadre."

"You're following her."

"With her gives me a better chance of survival than against her," he said pragmatically. "I'm old. Not as old as some, not as old as her, and I have taken great care to make myself useful."

As far as strategies go, it wasn't a bad one considering the depths of depravity War allowed in her coterie.

"You want to survive." Breath whistled through my clenched teeth. "Have you considered you're on the wrong side?"

"It did cross my mind when our mistress was slain." He hesitated, thoughtful. "I expected you to kill us. I would have killed us. Anyone else would have, I believe, in your position."

"I should have," I agreed upon reflection. "Starting with Sariah."

"Perhaps you'll get another chance."

"Perhaps."

Amused, he asked, "Do you sing?"

"No."

"You will."

A flint struck, and light filled his palms. Or so I thought until its flickering betrayed its true nature.

"This will burn." He chuckled again, clearly a huge fan of his own jokes. "Best grit your teeth."

I opened my mouth, but whatever it was I meant to say dissolved into a pathetic whimper.

Determined not to give him the satisfaction, I buttoned my lips to hold in my screams.

Uncle Harold used to pick on me when I filled in on the choir. He claimed I couldn't carry a tune in a bucket. If he could only hear me now. Adder was right. In the end, I sang like a freaking canary.

"I'm going ... to kill ... you," I swore to Adder the next time I saw him.

"You're weak as a kitten." He clucked his tongue. "You might scratch me, but that's it."

The first thing I did was check on Conquest. She was no longer sleeping, but she wasn't poised for a takeover. She seemed content to sit back and let me bear the brunt of the punishment. Sadly, that counted as the good news.

"How does this feel?" He pressed on the fractured ribs, paying special attention to the one he had shoved back inside me at some point. "Tender?"

I didn't have enough air to scream, which encouraged him to deepen his examination.

My eyes rolled back in my head.

"Luce."

Wrapping my arms around my middle, I curled on my side. "Ow."

"Thank the old gods and the new," Cole breathed. "Adder has come back twice. You didn't wake either time."

"Small mercy." I ran my palms over my abdomen, relieved to find the flesh smooth. "How do I look?"

"Beautiful."

Relieved to find my neck worked again, I cranked my head toward him and did what I could to put him at ease. "Are you saying that because I'm naked?"

One small mercy was Adder got off on the pain he inflicted, not my body. Clothes or skin, I don't think it made a difference to him.

A faint thread of amusement surfaced, barely there and then gone again. "No."

"I'm better." I didn't use the *I'm okay* line. We were in cells in God knows where and at Sariah's mercy, or the lack thereof. "I'm not going to run a marathon anytime soon, but I could probably crawl to the bars to receive a bowl of gruel, assuming my chain stretches that far."

His exasperated sigh was music to my ears.

I had been warned against pulling the dragon's tail, but it was too much fun to stop now, and I could do with the distraction. "Any word on Wu or Kapoor?"

"No."

"That sounds final."

"This facility is similar to the one where we ..." He frowned, a gathering of darkness near his mouth. "The only way they could have known about this facility was if Kimora told them its location. Assuming it was built using the same blueprints, there's only one level of cells."

"Wu and Kapoor are being kept separate from us."

"Or," he said thoughtfully, "they might not have been captured."

"Cole." I sucked in a sharp breath. "Are you suggesting that darling Sariah might lie to dishearten us?"

"As much as the notion offends your delicate sensibilities, I'm afraid not everyone is as open or honest as you."

Strange as it may seem, bantering with Cole was what convinced me we would be okay.

As slim as the hope was, I had to believe he was right, that it was at least possible Wu and Kapoor were still out there. Even if they weren't, we didn't have to hang our hopes on them. The rest of the coterie was free, and they wouldn't rest until they found us.

Light footsteps started our way, and I braced for the worst, unsure if they meant Adder or Sariah.

"You're feeling chatty," Adder accused. "You must be recovering at a faster rate than anticipated. That's good. The pretender will be pleased."

"She lets you get away with calling her that?"

"I am careful with my tongue." His freckled, youthful cheeks creased. "Much more than some."

"Yeah, well." Easy for him to say, what with him being free and all. "Some of us don't have as much to lose as others."

"There's always more to lose," he chided. "I would have thought you, as a mate, as a mother, would realize that."

Icy sweat trickled between my shoulder blades. Conquest wasn't at fault. This was sheer terror.

"What's left that hurts?" He advanced on me, knelt beside me on the floor, and began a clinical examination. "Your skin is ninety percent regenerated. One more session ought to do it. The ribs will still be tender, but you'll look whole. That's all the pretender cares about, the presentation, so that's as far as I'll take you. Further would be a waste of my time if she's going to hand you off to this Ezra."

"I'm good." I waved him off me. "You patched me up, and I'll definitely live, so thank you."

"Alas, you're no healer or clansman of mine. Your opinions

matter less to me than the number of bones in the fish I ate for dinner."

Again, he coated his hands in ointment and applied it methodically over my abdomen and my chest.

Again, he struck a flint and cradled fire between his palms until they roared with heat.

And again, he put his hands on me, and I let the dark swallow me whole.

CHAPTER NINE

Adam woke in a field with Kapoor crouched over him, a guard dog ready to tear into anything or anyone who came too near. The gauntness of his features told him Kapoor hadn't left his side, even to hunt.

Groggy, he pushed himself into a seated position, his body throbbing like a bruise. "What happened?"

"Ambush." Kapoor's black eyes locked on him. "Bushta shot a neurotoxin into the sky to incapacitate Conquest and Cole."

"I was affected?"

"No." The old Kapoor would have smiled, maybe even laughed. "You got hit."

That explained the ache in his left ribs and hip. "I don't remember."

"The toxin affected me. I began falling." He gave the report without a hint of emotion. "You took a direct hit to spare me. You caught me and flew us a safe distance from the encampment. You were unconscious when I woke. This is the first time you've come around since then."

Hunger roared in his gut, and cotton lined his mouth. "How long was I out?"

"Two days."

He whipped his head toward Kapoor, and his eyes swam. "Luce has been a prisoner for two days?"

"Yes."

Already certain of the answer, he couldn't stop from asking, "Have you performed any recon?"

"No."

"What about the coterie?" He examined their surroundings, but trees were trees in this part of the country. No identifying markers gave away their location. "Have they made contact?"

"Your phone rang."

"You didn't answer?"

"I wasn't ordered to, so no."

That spark of defiance gave Adam hope Kapoor might yet survive intact. "I'll try Santiago."

The phone in his pocket hadn't sustained any damage, for which he was thankful, but the stream of texts and calls didn't give him much hope the coterie had had any success in liberating Luce while he recovered from his injuries. The last text contained one line: *Since you're not answering, you better be dead.*

As much as it hurt to bring the phone to his ear, he almost wished that was the case. "Santiago."

"Ah, so you're not dead."

"Not quite."

"Pity."

"Have you located Luce?"

"It's been forty-eight hours," he scoffed. "What do you think?"

Annoyance snapped in his tone "Could you be less hostile?"

"Nope," he seethed at him. "Could you be less of an ass nugget? Seriously. You let Luce and Cole get taken. You were right there.

Right there. What the hell good are you if you can't prevent two freaking dragons from getting shot out of the sky?"

"*I* got shot out of the sky."

"Whatever." Santiago covered the receiver, and a muffled argument broke out. "Kiss his ass if you want, Miller. I'm done puckering."

"Wu," Miller said, having taken over the call.

"Yes?"

"I want to be very clear that there's only one reason why you're still alive."

Since Adam doubted Luce had told them about the sacrifice required of them, he assumed Miller meant the next best thing. "I'm the only person who can destroy the upper seal."

"No." A faint hiss escaped him. "You're not within striking range."

Adam wasn't afraid Miller would unleash himself. To do so would mean destroying the world and all its inhabitants ... including Maggie. She was an unexpected weak spot for the ouroboros, and Adam filed it away with all the other rainy-day measures he might one day be required to take.

"You haven't mentioned the child," Adam said, redirecting Miller. "Did she survive?"

A tense moment elapsed while Miller decided if he wanted to share. "She's with us."

"Good."

"Don't pretend you care, asswipe," Santiago yelled in the background. "Do you even know her name?"

Names made things too personal, and Adam was out of time to get attached. Distance was best, for all of them. "She led you to her parents."

"Yeah," Miller admitted at last. "She cloaked herself, went in, verified their location, and came in search of us."

"*The child* is a badass," Santiago hollered then ended with an *oomph*.

"Shut up," Portia growled. "Let them talk."

"What's our next move?" Adam asked, willing to let them take the lead if it eased their hostility.

"We've intercepted two runners." Miller shut a door behind him, and the bickering on the other end went mercifully silent. "Both were carrying messages to post within charun communities."

Adam didn't have to ask, but he might as well hear the details. "What did they say?"

"Sariah is offering up Conquest in exchange for amnesty from Ezra."

Bitter laughter closed his throat. "My father will kill her."

"Yeah, and that would solve one of our problems. The issue is, she won't fork Luce over to anyone but him, and if he puts in an appearance, he'll kill Luce and Cole too."

"Then we'll have to make sure he doesn't receive her summons."

"We're working on that. Santiago killed their cellular service, so they can't text, call, or email. We're picking off the ones chosen for hand deliveries." Miller exhaled. "We're keeping them as contained as possible, but Sariah is quick, and she knows how we operate. She'll figure out we're to blame when she doesn't get an RSVP. We have to come up with a plan, and we have to move fast."

Adam massaged his nape. "Where is she being held?"

"Underground." Miller hesitated. "Possibly in one of the enclave bunkers."

A twinge in his chest stole his breath. Kimora must have told Sariah, before or after she became host to a Drosera. Adam didn't keep track of each bunker location. They were scattered across the country, their coordinates entered into a database to ensure they got routine maintenance, but he didn't keep tabs on that program now that it had been in effect for so many years. The enclave handled it on their own.

"I can get us in." He could call up Knox and get the proper code. "We'll have to —"

"It's too dangerous."

"It might be our only shot at getting them out of there before Father catches wind of this."

"Luce protected Cole when they went down. She's injured. Badly. We inspected the crash site. There are scales everywhere. Blood and tissue too. Sariah knows Luce is worthless to Ezra dead. She'll bring in a healer, but she's not dumb enough to restore Luce to full strength. She's too afraid Conquest will get out. That means we must be prepared for triage. We can't count on her being able to fight her way out, or even walk on her own."

"I have an idea." He got to his feet, tested his balance. "Give me another day. Be ready to move in twenty-four hours."

Adam hung up before Miller could protest.

Kapoor stared at him, waiting, but asked no questions. He couldn't care less what happened to Luce and Cole at this point. His entire being was focused on Ezra, a tuning fork vibrating with the need for harmony.

Aside from tracking, Kapoor was all but worthless to him in this state. "I need your help."

Wings twitching, he wet his lips. "We hunt?"

"First, we hunt Drosera." Adam noted the droop of Kapoor's wings. "Then we hunt Ezra."

Eyes gleaming, Kapoor flexed the claws on his fingertips. "What do you need?"

CHAPTER TEN

I jerked awake gasping and soaked to the bone. For a humiliating instant, I thought I had wet myself.

"There now." A stooped female holding a bucket peered through the bars at me. "That ought to do."

"What ought to do?" I scrambled back, relieved when my limbs obeyed me. "Why did you do that?"

"Mistress wants you clean." She shrugged. "But not too clean."

"Don't worry." Grime caked me from the sticky ointment and now the water formed bloody muck underneath me. "There's no danger of that."

Humming under her breath, she walked off, leaving me in a rank puddle. Guess a change of clothes wasn't on the menu.

"Have they fed you?" The menu thing got me thinking about Cole. "Given you water?"

"No."

Weird that it hadn't occurred to me until now, when I was soaked, that I ought to be thirsty or hungry.

Scooching to a corner to dry, I asked him, "How long do you think we've been here?"

"Two or three days," he estimated. "I'm hungry enough to eat the next jailer who comes to my door."

For him to admit that, things must be dire. He wasn't normally so obvious with his carnivorousness.

"I'll get you food." I had no idea how, but there must be a way to bargain. "And water."

"We can't trust anything they give us not to be dosed with whatever they shot at us. We need to save our strength for when it will do us the most good."

A door opened and shut in the distance; our jailer come to gloat no doubt.

"You can't keep going on air."

"Oh, why not?" Sariah strolled down the hall. "He's a dragon. He's got wings. Air is practically sustenance for his kind."

"I could say the same was true of betrayal and yours, but I seem to recall you have a healthy appetite."

"Ouch." She chuckled gaily. "Your aim is getting better, Luce. Good for you."

"Can I help you?" I faked boredom. "I was in the middle of a conversation."

A fraction of her amusement dimmed, but she rallied before I glimpsed the depths of her annoyance.

"I just wanted to let you know I've made contact with Ezra. He's willing to negotiate." She leaned in, looking me up and down. "You've looked better, but that can't be helped. I'll send down some clothes in a few. He strikes me as the kind who doesn't appreciate seeing a woman's pink parts. Or any other parts, honestly. Pretty sure there's a reason the Malakhim are all male."

How fun would it be to end Ezra's reign by flashing him my

boobs? I would do it in a heartbeat. Sure, it would be degrading, but could you imagine the bragging rights? I could be like Agnès Sorel, *Dame de beauté*, the chief mistress and love muffin of King Charles VII of France. As the first officially recognized royal mistress, she ensured her place in history. Her taste for risqué gowns, baring her breasts in public, and the portrait of her as *The Virgin and Child Surrounded by Angels*, didn't hurt.

Either I was loopy from the healing, the hunger, or the thirst, or I had lost my damn mind from watching a mixed bag of Discovery Channel specials with Dad over the years.

All things considered I felt good about what I asked next. "Kapoor didn't kill those scouts, did he?"

"Please." She snorted. "We had to dose him with the toxin to implant the suggestion. I learned from the time I spent with Kimora that Malakhim are very pliant, and Kapoor had undergone similar training."

"The suggestion," I clarified. "You're saying he didn't kill the Oncas either?"

"We drugged him, hacked up a few charun with his sword, then told him to find you." She shrugged. "I hoped to get more mileage out of him as a distraction, but leave it to you to see the best in everyone."

Guilt pressed on my shoulders, the weight of my decision to use Kapoor a stone around my neck. "Why kill the scouts?"

"All this prep work has left the coterie with quite the appetite. I figured why not let them have a little fun? Best case, you blame the deaths on Kapoor. Worst case, you lose more time walking around in a circle while scratching your head."

And that's exactly what we had done. Point to Sariah.

"Gotta go, Auntie." She checked her phone for a missed call or text. It must have been on silent. "I have to finalize a couple of things before our guest of honor arrives."

She all but skipped down the tunnel, reminding me of the young girl's skin she wore the first time I met her.

"That doesn't sound good," I said once we were alone. "I can't believe Ezra would entertain her."

Cole rubbed where the shackles reddened his skin over the rose gold silver bands encircling his wrists. He didn't get a chance to reply. Yet another Drosera, I assumed, trundled down the hall wearing a middle-aged woman and straight to me. Her eyes were fever-bright and drool formed at the corner of her mouth.

"Mistress says put these on." She shoved them through the bars. "Mistress says hurry up about it."

Happy to have clothes, I didn't put up much of a fight on that front.

"Mistress says not to eat the aunt," she murmured to herself. "The aunt is not food."

This must be one of the younger siblings. The skin she wore covered any physical deformities she might have in her natural form, but there was no hiding the twitch and jerk of her limbs as her coordination struggled and failed. I didn't feel great about her talking to herself either.

"Mistress will fetch you soon." She bared her teeth, hissed, then erupted into giggles. "Soon."

I wrestled on the leggings then disappeared within the over-sized shirt provided for me. There were panties but no bra, socks but no shoes. The garments all had tags, which comforted me. Except I spotted bloodstains on a few items that made me wonder if the Drosera hadn't broken into a store to procure them.

"This should be fun." I stood and began stretching to limber up from my healing and captivity. "I'm not sure if you'll be allowed to watch the show, but I'll take excellent notes to pass on later."

If there is a later . . .

"Come here." He reached through the bars, and I went to him. "Do whatever it takes to survive."

"Are you telling me to run?"

"Yes."

Lacing our fingers, I sighed. "You ought to know me better than that by now."

"I do, but I can still hope." He pressed his forehead against a gap in the bars. "There is the package to consider."

Returning the favor, I stared at him, wishing the bars were thinner so that I could steal a kiss goodbye. "The package will be kept safe by the coterie and my dad, with or without us."

He searched my face. "I love you, Luce."

"I love you too." I relished the texture of his fingers, coarse against my skin. "I'm going to get you out of here. The package likes you better anyway."

A smile tickled the edge of his mouth, but he couldn't hold on to the expression, and it slipped away.

We stayed like that, breathing each other's air, hands linked past the point of pain, and waited.

Sariah didn't keep us long.

"Ugh." She ignored us while fiddling with the lock. "I never understood the fascination. It's like a mental illness with you."

Having my hunger for Cole compared to Conquest's always left me cold. No doubt that was the point.

"Ezra is here?" I stood, putting a wobble in my balance, and limped over to her. The puny act wasn't a total lie. I didn't have much *oomph* left. But that moment Cole had warned we should save our strength for? I could see it coming around the bend. "He came?"

"He's waiting topside." She got the door open and studied me. "You look like you just rolled out of your lover's bed with that shirt and that hair." She noticed the dirt on my socks, the wet spots that had turned slushy. "Or rolled in the mud." She shrugged. "Not everyone could pull it off, but you do it well, Auntie."

"Are you going to unchain me for this walk of shame, or do you expect me to bring the whole cellblock with me?"

"I'm getting to that part." She snapped her fingers, and a dozen Drosera appeared holding weapons that varied from a pocket knife to a crossbow to an assault rifle. "These gentlemen will be keeping Cole company while I make introductions. No harm will come to him if you're on your best behavior for our guest. I'll even let him go after, if you leave willingly with Ezra. But . . . " she gestured to the men, their eyes dark and wild, " . . . misbehave, and I'm sure your imagination can supply how things will go."

Long before I was attached to Cole beyond a surface attraction, she had known he would be my weak spot. He and I were so inter-twined, our fates knotted, there was no separating us. So I didn't kick myself for letting her see how much he meant to me when she would have done the same if Conquest were in my position.

"Don't hurt him." I put a growl in my voice, offset nicely by the knee I let buckle once. "I'll cooperate."

She frowned at my performance, and inwardly I cursed my dramatic streak. I had overplayed my hand. I was supposed to be healed. Stiffness and soreness were acceptable, but I shouldn't be a total invalid. The closer I came to her, the more I shed the act until it appeared I was walking off stiffness. That appeased her, if her smile was anything to go on, and I made small adjustments as we went to prove I was sound enough for the auction block but too weak to cause much trouble.

"He's agreed to allow you to coexist?" I made my voice faint but getting stronger. "You think you can trust him?"

"Nah." She waved a hand. "I'm not a total idiot. He's going to do whatever he has to do to get his hands on you, and then he's going to attempt to wipe me off the face of the planet with his Malakhim flyboys. The coterie is watching them, but his forces are keeping a respectful distance to give the impression this is an honest transaction."

"If you don't trust him to hold up his end of the bargain, why risk antagonizing him?"

"I'm going to kill him." She ran her tongue along the edge of her upper teeth. "You might have noticed I've been busy recruiting too. We're going to make an end run at Ezra, bump him off, and then — sorry about this — we're going to kill you and your coterie. That will make me the next best thing to the only cadre left on this terrene."

"As much as I admire your ambitious plan, and I do, I've got to point out that it takes more than motivational speeches and a can-do attitude to become cadre. We're born, not made. War is dead. There is no War 2.0 this ascension. All you'll ever be is exiled coterie, the same as everyone else." I shrugged. "Assuming he doesn't smite you. I've heard he's got a thing for smiting."

Temper infused a tremor in her voice. "I should kill you for that, but I need you alive."

"Too bad you don't have a handy phonebook to beat me with. I hear those don't leave marks but hurt like a mother. I can't remember if the urban legend is to smack the victim with the book or hold it in place on your victim while you punch the book, though."

A thoughtful expression stole across her features. "What is a phonebook?"

"They don't make them anymore. Well, I guess they do. They just don't circulate them. It's pretty random. I would go two, three, five years without getting one and then bam! There it was, wrapped in a bag and tossed on the doorstep."

The randomness of my thoughts made me question a possible head injury. Surely the healer would have patched up my brain.

What fun was murdering your enemy if they didn't know it was happening?

That left me with the possibility it was sheer terror responsible for my guts turning to water, and how ridiculous was that? I set Kapoor on the path to find Ezra. What did I expect but that he would, you know, find him? That then, I would have to, you know, confront him. That he might then, you know, kill me.

Oh, God.

I was rambling.

Yep. Definitely terror. Worse than any I could remember. Not to give Ezra too much credit. Without Conquest, I didn't have the cold place to retreat when I needed my reality buffered. This was the first time in my life I was dealing with raw fear the way a human did, with nothing but their wits to aid them. Except for my inner dragon. Humans didn't have those. So I guess I wasn't having a one hundred percent authentic experience —

Damn it, Luce. Get your head in the game.

Slow inhales and exhales kept me company on the walk down the long hall to where all the action happened. It was a cement tube that ended with a metal ladder leading up through a hatch they had left open.

"Age before beauty," Sariah said. "Just take it easy. Wouldn't want you to trip on your chains and break your neck. Again."

Grateful my hands were free at least, I used them to pull myself up the ladder. I gripped the sides, pulled my bound feet up the next rung. Gripped the sides, pulled up my feet. Gripped, pulled. Gripped, pulled.

A hulking Drosera with a rifle slung over his shoulder waited for me at the top. He reached in, hooked me under the arms like I was a child, and lifted me out. He set me beside him, and I wish I could say I kicked or fought for my freedom, something more dramatic and befitting Conquest, but I had been down in the dark for a long time. In the sudden light, I couldn't see. Not a damn thing. And my legs were wobbling for real from the exertion after so much confinement.

"Keep an eye on her, Teddy." Sariah hopped out next and dusted off her hands. "I'll go receive our guest. He must be eager to see what he's buying with his cooperation."

The way she prattled on, like the deal with Ezra was legit, like she hadn't admitted she planned on killing him, made me wonder how much her coterie knew about her intentions. She couldn't expect to win a battle without priming her soldiers first. That was madness.

Either they were all in on the plan, or Sariah figured she had enough non-coterie support at this point that she could afford to sacrifice them. She might prefer it that way, building her own coterie instead of inheriting her mother's mixed bag of offspring, who were already pushing back against her.

Squinting at my surroundings, I tried to get my bearings. I had a general direction we had been traveling, but I was clueless when it came to our actual location. We had been following Kapoor, not coordinates.

Had we gotten close enough to Ezra for this to be a daytrip for him? And if Kapoor and Wu weren't captives, where the hell where they? While I didn't entertain any fantasies of Wu charging to my rescue for altruistic or romantic reasons, the fact remained he needed me to die at a predetermined spot and time. This would seriously put a kink in his plans. That alone comforted me that help from that quadrant was incoming.

The coterie was a given. They would have been lying in wait for this exact moment — when I appeared aboveground, making me easier to rescue than fighting their way down into the reinforced bunker. The problem would be, after they sprung me, how would we retrieve Cole?

My dragon could crunch through the metal given enough time, but we had none to spare if Ezra and his forces were really here. It's not like they would let me call for a timeout while I helped my mate escape.

A blinding light that might as well have been a miniature sun come to earth stabbed me in the eye before I could formulate any kind of plan. I raised my hands to shield my face, but the delicate skin on my palms felt sunburned from the brief exposure.

No one told me Ezra harnessed solar energy to barbecue his enemies like a kid with a magnifying glass going whole hog on an anthill.

Beside me, the guard wasn't faring any better. He grunted and ducked his head, but not before clamping a beefy hand on my upper arm to keep me from getting any ideas about making a run for it before his eyes adjusted.

Damn it.

That was an excellent idea. Too bad I hadn't thought it up thirty seconds ago. Not that it would have helped much since I would have been staggering around blind just like everyone else. I stood as much chance of stumbling off and falling back in the hole as I did clearing the gathered Drosera. That didn't count the allies Sariah had gathered who camped farther away from the action.

The other clans might grumble that the Drosera got to have all the fun, but they'd shut up once Ezra retaliated. Sacrificing her coterie to protect her new buddies would win her brownie points if nothing else.

"I have come," a rich voice boomed, deeper than thunder, harder than marble. "Bring Conquest to me."

Gradually, vision returned to me. He must have flipped the switch on his dimmer dial. I was still fielding spots when a smaller hand grasped my elbow and hauled me toward the honored guest.

"Cadre scum," he growled. "Your reign ends here and now."

"Not quite yet," Sariah interrupted. "We have a deal."

However much of her intel was pure bluffing, she had known enough to pop on a pair of shades. Considering Ezra burned like staring into the flaming heart of our solar system, I envied her forethought. Though, now that I thought about it, Wu had never mentioned his father was a supernova. Anyone who based their assumptions about him on scripture might expect him to appear one way or another, but Wu had already debunked him for me.

Ezra might think he was a god, but he wasn't God.

"Your immunity is granted," Ezra thundered. "Give her to me."

"That's it?" Sariah kept her tone light. "We don't need to shake on it or . . . ?"

"You will not touch me." The brightest point centered on his face, and I couldn't look at him, but I could imagine him curling his lip. "Deliver Conquest to me, or you will suffer my wrath."

"Don't get your wings in a bunch." She gave me a shove into the light. "There you go."

The push slammed me into Ezra, and my breath caught. Up close, he was even more electric, more vibrant, more . . . resonant.

Tipping my head back, I tried peering through the gilded haze, but I couldn't divine his features.

Thanks to the mate bond, I didn't have to in order to know this, however improbable, wasn't Ezra.

It was Wu.

The fact he hadn't smited me for clinging to him should have been Sariah's first clue too.

"You must come with me to face justice," he intoned. "You have my thanks, demon spawn."

"I don't suppose you could arrange a front row seat for the justice you're about to serve?" she said, still polite. "I would sleep better at night knowing she was dead."

"I am not held accountable to you." His power flared. "I owe you no comfort or assurances."

"Can't blame a girl for trying." She shrugged and turned. "See you in the funny papers."

"Our bargain included her mate. Where is the coterie filth?"

"I decided to keep him. I've always wanted a pet, and I hear lizards are easy to care for."

A dangerous stillness swept through Wu, and I sensed his hesitation. Fight or flight. Push for Cole's release or escape with me. Risk me punching in his teeth to get back to Cole 'cause leaving him behind wasn't happening. Sadly, Sariah, being a predator, did too.

"I'm fond of wings as well." She turned back. "The creatures wearing them taste just like chicken to me."

Sensing the gig was up, Wu killed the light show and stood before the gathered Drosera with the haughty air of a king among kings.

"Release the dragon," he commanded. "Or you will suffer the consequences of your actions."

"I'm not much for suffering," Sariah admitted. "I prefer inflicting pain over experiencing it."

"Mistress?" The hulking brute behind her narrowed his gaze on Wu. "What are your orders?"

"Kill them." Sariah pivoted on her heel and walked into the throng of charun, but she yelled back, "I'm rooting for you, Auntie. Really, I am."

And this, right here, was how she kept surviving. She not only threw her people under the bus the second odds tipped out of her favor, but she also threw the driver, the passengers, and the whole damn bus too.

The order sent a ripple through the gathering, and they converged on us.

"This was your plan?" I snapped at Wu. "What were you thinking?"

"Sariah almost caught Father's attention. This was the only way to beat him to the punch."

"Kapoor?"

"He's here."

"The coterie?"

"They're here too."

Eyes dry and tender from his entrance, I couldn't focus much beyond the second row of charun eager to murder us. Sheesh. Didn't anyone settle their differences with a spirited game of paper, rock, scissors anymore?

Battle cries erupted, blasting chills down my spine. No, those weren't challenges, those were screams.

The coterie must be closing in from the rear. Energized by their arrival, I gave myself over to my dragon and was grateful Cole's advice had gotten me to this point.

Color bled from the world into a crimson wash that tinted my view as my head rose higher and higher.

With a metallic whine, the shackles binding my ankles snapped as I outgrew them.

I lashed out with my tail, knocking down the first row as they advanced, giving Wu room to draw his sword and dive into the chaos. A dark blot landed in a crouch a few yards away. Kapoor didn't carry a sword. He didn't have to when his fingernails had lengthened until they rivaled butchers' knives.

Janitor was far too sanitary a name for a man with skills of his caliber.

Without a word, he flung himself into the fight. Soon he dripped with blood, and he smiled as he tasted it. Working his way to Wu, he covered his friend's back. He was a beautiful fighter and terrible to behold. No wonder Wu had recruited him, befriended him. Kapoor was a lethal weapon. Eyes black and hard, he was blind to sentiment.

A gap appeared where Wu and Kapoor had broken through the Drosera's line. Craning my neck toward the entrance to the bunker, I rumbled my intent to anyone listening. Swiping my tail through the stragglers, I bought myself time to shift and go for Cole.

"I got this." Santiago sprinted past me. "Keep the exit clear."

Happy to oblige, I stood guard while Santiago skipped the ladder and leapt straight to the bottom.

Intent on standing my ground, I didn't notice the screams were tapering off until the lightning fast strike when Miller swallowed an advancing Drosera whole drew my eye. For dessert, he ate three Bushta who thought hiding behind their catapults would save them. Lucky for us, they couldn't risk firing into the crowd without dosing themselves with their toxin.

About to risk sticking my head in the hole for a status update, I blinked against the churning of loose dirt and debris, kicked up by a sudden wind. Looking up, I spotted the Malakhim force Sariah had mentioned. Before panic set in, I recognized the nearest one: Able.

These were our allies, and they threw themselves into the fray with single-minded purpose. With their gleaming swords and ornate bows, they rained death upon our enemies.

"Move over." Santiago shoved my claw. "You're in the way."

I snapped my teeth at him, but he didn't jump. He snapped back.

Inching to one side, I made room for him to climb out then searched for Cole behind him.

"He's coming." Santiago stepped up beside me. "Give him room."

Grumbling, I made them more space. Seconds later, Cole emerged. No sooner had his foot touched the earth than his dragon claimed his skin. His throaty warning explained what he had done, and I half galloped, half fluttered the heck out of Dodge.

An explosion engulfed the bunker, and the blast knocked me and everyone else in its path on our backs.

Once I got my feet under me again, I cut a path straight for him. He bared his teeth in a feral smile, and I did the same. In the distance, Portia and Santiago stood back to back, swords whirling, reminding me of a killer food processor. Until I took notice of how well they worked together, it hadn't occurred to me that Santiago never shifted in battle. Ever. I got the feeling I understood why he took his chances as a man now. He was Portia's backup, and he didn't make her feel less for not having another, more dangerous form.

Their friendship disturbed me on many levels, more than I could count, but I couldn't deny they loved one another in the way siblings love each other. No challenger could hurt or say a bad thing about one except for the other. It made me glad they had found each other. Conquest had done that much right at least.

A gleam in the distance caught my eye, and I risked glancing in that direction. Thom sat on a high limb in a tree. He carried a mean-looking pistol he must have taken from an enemy and had just taken a shot at a Drosera who attempted to scale the trunk to reach him. As if that wasn't enough to give me heart palpitations, I spotted a certain tiny dragon egging Thom on from her perch on his shoulders.

I trumpeted a call to Cole then sliced through the ground forces to make my way to them.

He grunted acknowledgment then snapped a Bushta in half with his massive jaws before impaling another on his horns. The balletic dance of his dragon in battle stole my breath, and I wished I could climb a tree and watch him cut down the army while I munched on popcorn, but I couldn't leave Thom. I was starting to think Phoebe didn't need my help, considering how she had survived the crash landing plus found her way to the coterie. The kid had serious survival instincts. I was in awe. Too bad we didn't have time for her to teach me half of what she hatched knowing.

I wasn't the only one who had noticed the vulnerables in the tree. Several fighters were hanging back, breaking off their part of the confrontation in an effort to seize the prize for their own.

Great.

Just great.

Perfect even.

I didn't stand a chance against charun used to how their bodies moved, who were able to use their heightened senses to their full advantage.

As I thought it, I tasted frost. The bangles vibrated where they rested against my skin, growing colder, and dread scooped out my middle. I couldn't lose control of Conquest, but the smell of carnage was waking her. Or maybe it was buried maternal instincts. Thom wasn't the only one stuck in that tree. She might not have loved Phoebe in a way I recognized, but through her memories I witnessed her twisted version of the pride she felt for her daughter.

"Forget it, lady," I thought at her. "You're not invited to this party."

The tug of war in my gut ceased, but the bangles didn't warm. She was still fighting to get out, and I couldn't afford to split my attention between her and the enemies swarming around me.

A squeaky trill announced Phoebe had spotted me. She bounced on Thom's shoulders, wings fluttering, then flattened her ears against her skull to growl at the Drosera. Pretty sure the kid was talking smack. Or cracking *yo momma* jokes.

Blasting an exhale through my muzzle, I forced my brain back on its task. I couldn't afford to splinter now. I had to keep a level head, or I risked Conquest picking up where I left off.

Teeth bared in an eager grin, I threw myself into the turmoil.

I used my tail to sweep Bushta off their feet, kicked a few Drosera into nearby trees, all the while biting and snapping at anyone dumb enough to get close.

"Behind you," Thom shouted. *"Luce."*

The goon who had been assigned to me must have tracked me this far. He was a freaking tank, and that was before — yep. His skin suit burst down the middle, and a massive alligator erupted. He didn't even lose speed. The transformation barely cost him a hitch in his stride.

With a quick snap of my tail, I took out one of his eyes. He screamed bloody murder, but he didn't slow.

Impact with him jarred my teeth as my shoulder rammed his, and I cried out when he slung his blocky head into my side then bit down above my freshly healed ribs. I lashed my tail at him, clawed at his armored sides, but I got nowhere. I was bleeding, and cold puffs clouded before me.

Flailing against the Drosera, I scrabbled for soft tissue until he roared. A lucky shot on my part relieved him of his other eye. He was fighting blind. He spun aside, and I lurched free, thankful to have escaped however I managed it. Thankful until I heard a faint squeak of indignation when the Drosera snapped its jaws closed over thin air.

Phoebe.

That stupid, stupid, brave kid had come to my rescue.

The pain in my side vanished, gone, forgotten. I leapt onto the Drosera's back, sinking in my claws to anchor me, and I wound my tail around his throat as many times as it fit before I began to squeeze.

It struggled against me, unwilling to go down without a fight. Phoebe kept buzzing him, distracting him, and she caused my blood to ice in my veins, a feat I couldn't blame on Conquest this time.

This kid was nursing a serious hero complex, and heroes didn't always win in the real world.

Tighter and tighter, I cinched my tail. Oxygen deprivation finally gave me a hand, and the creature slowed. Once he quit thrashing, I started chewing on his nape, gnawing through the hard plating an inch or so lower than my tail. Rich blood filled my mouth when I hit tendon and then bone, and I kept chewing for all I was worth, desperate to put him down so I could strangle Phoebe.

The Drosera finally stopped twitching, and I plucked Phoebe out of the air with my tail, interrupting her victory dance, and dropped her into my front claws. Her eyes shone up at me with admiration that both warmed my heart and exasperated me. She chittered away while I clutched her against my chest, and I wished again that whatever barrier prevented me from grasping Convallarian could be erased without giving Conquest a firmer toehold. I understood the tone and intent from Cole much better than from her, but he had warned me most of her jabbering was just that — childish noises of enthusiasm.

Tucking her close, I used one front claw and both back ones to climb the tree to Thom and deposit Phoebe in his arms.

"I won't let her escape again," he promised. "I didn't expect her to go after you."

I rumbled a sound that couldn't decide if it wanted to be a growl or a sigh.

"She is her father's daughter." Thom rubbed his cheek against the top of her head. "She's got a lot of you in her too, more by the day. She idolizes you."

This time there was no debating. It was a sigh. A kid idolizing me was dangerous on every level, especially if my reckless behavior encouraged her to emulate me.

A roar from farther afield drew my attention, and I scrabbled down the tree to rejoin the crush. I passed Adder's remains and chalked him up to one of Cole's kills based on the bite radius of his injuries.

Miller, whose coils resembled a sock full of bubblegum balls, shot in front of me, plucking a harried female Bushta out of my path and swallowing her whole. I grunted thanks and kept running straight up to where Cole was lashing anyone who advanced too close to Portia, and therefore Maggie.

Love for him spilled through me, and if I hadn't already given him every inch of my heart, I would have at that moment. Portia wasn't a weak link. She was experienced, savvy, and strong. But Mags was in there too, and she wasn't prepared for the realities of the battlefield. Not that I had any room to talk. This was all horrifying and new to me too.

Together we struck down the remaining Drosera and Bushta. Santiago sprinted toward the catapults and began disabling them while Portia checked the bunker for survivors. Downfield, Wu and Kapoor stood together, weapons clutched in their hands, and began the trek to join us. Above, the Malakhim lite picked off any stragglers. Once that was done to Able's satisfaction, he landed on the back of a dead Drosera in its natural form, seeming fascinated with it.

"Any sign of Sariah?" I panted. "She left before the fun started."

"Two of my best are following her. They'll capture her and return her to you."

Personal experience with Sariah taught me it was doubtful she would be captured but hope never hurt anyone. Malakhim were experts at rooting out charun. Maybe they would succeed where I had failed. Or, dare to dream, she might resist arrest and get killed in the process. One less problem for us to solve.

Ugh.

What a very Conquest thing to think of, let alone hope for.

When had wishing someone dead become okay? Granted, she had killed her fair share of innocents. More than. She was the engineer of Uncle Harold's bargain with Famine that resulted in his death. I had plenty of reasons to hate her before she captured Cole and me then threw us into an underground bunker, but mostly I was just tired of her scheming. I had enough on my plate without adding more, and her specialty was noticing when I almost had it clear before dumping extra helpings on top.

"We appreciate the assist." I stuck out my arm, and we shook hands. "You and your men are impressive in battle."

"We've trained hard for the moment when it might make a difference." He swept the field with a critical eye. "I believe this is a start."

Wu came to thank Able as well, going as far as to clap him on the back, and the young man beamed. I let them wrap up before summoning Wu to ask him a few questions.

"What's with the glow bug routine?" I had witnessed flares here and there, but his performance for Sariah was next level impressive. "You could always do that?"

"It serves no purpose." He rolled a shoulder, the fabric of his shirt red from the blood of his kills. "On our home terrene, the nights are long. The flares are meant to blind our nocturnal enemies to give us the upper hand. Here? It's a parlor trick. One Father relishes."

"I was impressed." Not gonna lie. "You had me fooled for the first minute or two."

"The bangles dampen our bond." He flicked a glance at them. "I regret the necessity. I didn't have a choice, and we had no way to get a warning to you."

"It's okay." I laughed. "More than okay. You sprung us. We're not picky about how."

"Kapoor needs to rest." Wu watched Kapoor check the fallen

and ensure they didn't rise. "He's growing more restless the longer the hunt takes. He's stopped eating or drinking. He's too focused on his end goal."

"I didn't expect Sariah to rally her forces so soon, or to use them to detain me. She's hung up on the idea of Ezra. She wants in his good graces. Makes me wonder if it's a manifestation of her mommy syndrome. She committed heinous acts to impress War and Thanases. Without them, who is she performing for? She's achieved the peak. In her mind, she is the new War. What's left but to reach higher?"

"Father will kill her eventually." Wu didn't sound worried about her, but I had made that mistake one too many times. I wouldn't again. "She can't have but a handful of Drosera left unless she was breeding them on the sly too. There's no telling how many clans she's allied with, but we put a dent in her numbers today."

"Let's hope she doesn't buff it out and come at us harder next time."

"Three more clans were camped out about five miles from here. They rushed in when they heard the calls go up but turned and ran when they spotted you slaying Bushta to reach Phoebe."

"Did you see that kid? She almost gave me a heart attack." I unerringly found Cole and prayed he had been too busy staying alive to notice me almost getting Phoebe killed. "Talk about little but fierce."

Wu attempted a smile, but it was too heavy, and it sagged on his face.

"How long do you propose we let Kapoor rest?" I rotated my shoulder, unhappy to find it tender again. "Are we talking overnight or . . . ?"

"He'll require a solid twelve hours at least. Twenty-four would be ideal. Either way, Thom will have to sedate him. He's too wired to sleep on his own."

"That works." As much as I hated to cede ground, I knew the drill. "Miller and Cole will be crashing soon." Miller, in particular, required sleep in order to digest. He didn't get a choice. He filled his belly, and his brain flipped the switch for him. The same was true of Cole to a lesser extent. "We might as well make it forty-eight. I would rather lose time than people." I exhaled. "I'll touch base with Santiago, see where he suggests we hole up to recover."

Once we came up against the real Ezra, there would be no handy rest breaks after each scuffle. We might as well make use of this one. Plus, I could get in some healing time with Thom. He could make sure Adder put everything back where it belonged, maybe take the edge off the new aches and pains I earned today.

I left Wu to keep watch over Kapoor while I checked in with the coterie. Portia and Santiago were drenched in blood, grinning from ear to ear. She was trying to get him to high-five her when I arrived, but he palmed her forehead to keep her at arm's length, smirking at her struggle to swat him.

"I assume you've mapped out our next pit stop," I said, interrupting their jostling.

"Fifty miles to the east is a city big enough for us to get lost in for a few days. I've booked us rooms on various floors in various sizes under various names."

"How various clever of you," Portia sniped. "Get it? Various?"

"I got it." He leveled a flat stare on her. "I didn't laugh because it wasn't funny."

Her harrumph made him glow with satisfaction. Yeah. Never going to understand those two.

"I'm going to check in with the others. We need to move fast. Miller was hitting it hard out there. He's not going to last long."

As luck would have it, Miller was the next person I stumbled across, and I rushed to wedge my shoulder under his arm. His eyes drooped, and a yawn cracked his jaw. He leaned on me, wilting on the spot.

"You ate too much." I poked his flat stomach with my finger, and he groaned. "Where does it all go?"

"It —"

Clamping a hand over his mouth, I shook my head. "I don't actually want to know."

Nightmares about hands climbing up the back of my throat to freedom were bad enough. I didn't want to learn the truth about where all the charun bits I ate ended up before they were digested. Then again, I never saw them protrude out of my stomach, so who's to say they ever passed?

And just like that, I gave myself fresh nightmare fodder.

What if the bodies never passed? What if they floated around in there — wherever *there* was — forever?

I helped Miller to a level spot clear of debris and bodily fluids and eased him down. Maggie was there before his butt touched dirt, searching him for wounds and generally fussing over him, which made him smile through his exhaustion.

When it became obvious she had things under control, I went in search of Cole. I found him crouching beside a Bushta, examining the boarlike tusks protruding from its mouth.

"I haven't seen one of these in a long time." He rose to join me. "They taste as good as I remembered."

Working hard to conceal my unease when I had no room to talk, I asked, "Like bacon?"

"More like ..." He humored me with a quick grin. "You don't want to know, do you?"

"Not really." I stared down at the corpse. "It's just too people-y for me to enjoy a debate about the subtle hints of flavor."

A copper aftertaste kept me wishing for a toothbrush and toothpaste, but that would have to wait until we reached our hotel.

"Able arranged transportation." He indicated a plume of dust kicking up behind what appeared to be two Humvees. "Everyone ready to go?"

"We have to collect Thom and She-Ra, but yeah."

"She-Ra?"

"Princess of Power?"

A thoughtful expression settled over his features. "It has a nice ring to it."

"Your child is a menace." I punctured his bubble of paternal pride. "However, she probably saved my life."

"I'll have a talk with her," he promised, setting out for the tree.

"Wipe that proud papa smile off your face before you do, or she's not going to take anything you say seriously."

"This was her first battle." Nostalgia tinted his voice. "She put her life in jeopardy to protect someone she loves, and she came out victorious."

"She could have been killed." I hated to be a Debbie Downer, but it needed saying. "She's still a kid."

"She's Convallarian." He slung his arm around my waist, tugging me against his side. "This is natural for her. She's a predator, and she's learning protective instincts from watching you with the coterie, who she views as extended family."

"I would never have forgiven myself if she got hurt. I figured you would think the same."

"I would be destroyed if she were lost to me again, forever this time. Do I want to put her in a bubble? Yes. Will I? No. I can't clip her wings."

Clip her wings.

That was the worst possible outcome for any flight-capable charun, even worse than death, and it hammered home how seriously Cole took her ability to make decisions for herself and act on them. I was all for her growing up to be a strong, independent

woman. But the human in me, who recalled my upbringing, felt
we ought to keep a steadying hand on her. In case she stumbled,
we could catch her.

"I can't help but imagine her as the child I saw . . ." The little
girl in the vision Conquest shared with me. "I picture her as this
chubby-cheeked toddler racing around corners and jumping out
to scare people. It's not fair to her, and I understand that. I'll try
to readjust my viewpoint, but Cole — she's still a kid. I can't make
any promises."

"Her first molt is coming up fast." The lines fanning from the
corners of his eyes deepened. "That will give you perspective."

Molt.

All too easily, I pictured a snake shedding its skin. I didn't need
the Discovery Channel for the image. I found them in the yard
as a kid. One of the hazards of living in the country. She would
most likely lose her skin in patches rather than in a single piece,
but still. I couldn't wrap my head around what that meant for the
child within her.

Dad might have had his hands full with me, but I matured at
a natural pace. He had time to grow into his role along with me.
For me, motherhood was a crash course with notes scribbled front
and back on an index card. Her childhood was zipping by on fast
forward, and I couldn't get the pause button to work. That, at
least, was a universal sentiment shared by parents the world over.
Maybe I wasn't so hopeless at this after all.

CHAPTER ELEVEN

—◆—

Our accommodations in the city were exactly what I expected from Santiago down to the single rooms he assigned Cole and me while he took a suite. Under normal circumstances, I would have fought him over it. That's clearly what he expected me to do and had primed himself to pitch an epic fit over my audacity, but I had other plans.

I had given Death enough time to mourn. However hard it might be, it was time she rejoined us.

Sariah was on the loose, and now we had to worry about her targeting us in addition to the Malakhim. I couldn't force Death to cooperate. She could kill me with a touch, so dragging her off to battle wasn't going to happen. She might choose to stand down, declare her losses too great to continue. As much as I wanted to begrudge her that, considering her coterie had been dead from the start, I would have been lost without mine. I couldn't very well slap her in the face with a double standard if I wanted to stay in her good graces.

"Where are you going?"

I turned from the window in the room with a single queen bed to find Cole watching me, his head denting the pillow, eyes already closed. "Who says I'm going anywhere?"

"You're not in bed with me," he pointed out, "and Wu is outside the door. I can smell him."

"Okay, fine. I'm going to pester Death." I joined him on the mattress. "We need her. I was going to wait until we had an idea of where to find Ezra, but our mini vacation drove home that the unexpected happens. We could be attacked and recaptured, and where would that leave us if the entire coterie got caught next time?" I couldn't bear to think of it, so I pushed it aside as I did all the things I didn't want to dwell on. "Death could have gripped those bars and turned them to dust or at least corroded them enough for us to snap them. That's assuming they weren't smart enough to stay out of touching distance."

"How long will you be gone?" He traced the designs embedded in my skin up to my shoulder.

"Two days tops. That will give you, Miller, and Kapoor the maximum amount of time to recover." I could use a nap too, but I hadn't earned my rest yet. I had farther to go before I slept. "We might not get another chance to recharge before we find Ezra. We'd be stupid not to take this opportunity."

"Thom is watching Phoebe?"

"He's sharing a room with Mags so they can take turns babysitting. Miller and Rixton are in the room next door in case they need backup."

"Kapoor?"

"He's locked in a closet in Santiago's suite." I shrugged. "Wu mentioned something about the dark helping him to relax. This way Santiago can keep an eye on him, so I'm not complaining."

"Be careful." He drew me down for a chaste kiss. "Come back to me."

"I will." I stroked his cheek, tracing his jawline, until he fell asleep. "I love you."

Backing out of the room, I slung a bag with clothes and supplies over my shoulder and made sure to lock Cole in tight.

"Ready?" Wu straightened from where he had been leaning against the wall.

"One day I'm going to get the hang of invisibility." I led him to the elevator, and we rode it to the topmost floor. "Then I won't have to keep bumming rides. I'll be able to zip off wherever I want whenever I want."

"Have you considered asking Phoebe for pointers?"

"You're a funny guy, Wu."

Until I got the hang of cloaking myself, I would be forced to keep depending on others for transportation when it mattered. With us taking refuge in the heart of a city, I had no hope of slipping away unnoticed. I had to rely on Wu to get me to Death's hideaway.

The flight, thanks to Wu's extra sets of wings, wouldn't take all that long. Maybe six hours. That gave me a whole day and change to get what I needed and then return before the others woke. I hadn't seen Death since she left Canton, and I wasn't certain of my reception. I didn't think she would kill me on sight, but I knew my appearance would remind her of her loss.

Once on the top floor, we walked to the end of the hall and shoved through the fire escape. We took the steps onto the roof and assumed the position. I had learned from experience that the best way for Wu to carry me was if I wrapped my legs around his waist and my arms around his neck. The position was intimate, and I didn't enjoy sharing that closeness with him, all things considered.

With his grip on me secure, he walked off the edge, snapping out his wings and soaring between skyscrapers until we reached a body of water. We followed its path, neither of us speaking, and I let my thoughts drift while we made the journey to petition my final sister for aid.

The sky was darkening when we arrived at a beachside home tottering on stilts. The ocean crashed and roared, so close you could almost touch it, it seemed. The breeze whipped hair in my face and made my skin sticky.

A sour taste flooded my mouth. "I have a favor to ask."

Startled, Wu said, "Name it."

Hoping I could trust him with this, I did, and he promised to make it happen.

Ghostly crabs scuttled over my feet when Wu sat me down, and I kicked off my shoes before setting out for a pair of loungers sharing a large red umbrella. A familiar couple rested there, gazing out at the surf, and when I followed their sightline, I spotted their remaining children frolicking in the water.

Janardan was Iniid, and so Death, as his mate, was biologically Iniid as well. Their children, in their natural form, resembled freshwater dolphins. They sported tentacles instead of flukes and smiled with seven rows of serrated teeth, like sharks.

"Dad took me to the beach a few times on family vacations," I said when I got close enough for the roar not to steal my words. "We usually went with my aunt and uncle since they had kids. That, and it gave Dad an excuse to dump me in Aunt Nancy's lap while he went deep sea fishing with Uncle Harold."

"It is a good place to bring young," Death murmured. "The sand is enjoyable, and the water . . . It's beautiful. So clear and blue. I've never seen anything like it."

"Your mate let you out of his sight?" Janardan, her mate, smiled warmly at me. "How unlike him."

Cole and Janardan had struck up an unlikely friendship during the early days of the cadre, and every time I met with Janardan, I marveled at how normal he seemed. I was thankful Cole had had one sane point of contact outside the coterie, and not just because Janardan had helped Death protect Phoebe.

"I might have slipped out while he was gorged on the flesh of our enemies and unable to physically stop me without falling asleep."

"Now that I believe." His laughter rang out, and Death joined him. "You've come for us at last then?"

"I've come for an answer." I sat in the warm sand in front of them. "You've got a good thing going here."

"How long would it last?" Death shook her head. "What is that ostrich saying?" She checked with Janardan. "Oh, yes. We can't bury our heads in the sand." He nodded that she had gotten it right, and he smiled. "It's only a matter of time before Ezra comes for me."

Janardan pushed upright from his reclined position, as if speaking his name might summon him. "Why don't you come inside and tell us what we've missed?"

"You should rest." Death searched my face, hers lined with concern. "You look exhausted."

Yes, well, imprisonment tended to wipe a girl out, but I didn't want to get into those particulars out here where the wind could snatch my secrets. And damn it. I hadn't thought to ask Thom for a healing session prior to zipping off to visit Death. I had gotten too tangled up in my head and forgotten, but the flight had reminded me.

"I have enough time for a nap." I sat downwind from them, and even Death wrinkled her nose at my smell. "A shower isn't a bad idea either."

My hosts rose to escort me into their home, and I stood, dusting off even though living on the beach came with the expectation sand would get everywhere.

Death called out, "One hour more."

An unholy racket erupted from near the shore, the sound a dolphin made when stuck between the jaws of a great white who was choking to death on a seal, and I whipped my head around in time to spot a writhing mass of oily black tentacles waving back above the foam.

I figured Death could only animate so many members of her coterie before it put a drain on her. I hadn't stopped to consider that the deaths of some of her children made room for her to birth more. *Birth* might not be the right word, but it was the least complicated. Clearly she and Janardan had been busy.

The longer I stared, the more clearly I saw what might have been a cross between a blue whale and an angler fish mixed in with a little crab. Swimming with it were a matched set of creatures who resembled nurse sharks who had glued bear traps down their spines and topped those off with a club tail that smashed the water at regular intervals.

I watched a few minutes longer, disturbed and awed in equal measure. All the specials I had watched on oceans made no bones about it being the last frontier. So little of it had been explored, comparatively, and new species were discovered all the time. Humans would crap their pants if they stumbled across anything like these creatures. Then again, who would have imagined the squidworm, the flamingo tongue snail, or the fathead? How many of those peculiarities were charun who had been discovered and forced to play scientific specimen until they could engineer their escape?

"Children." She clucked her tongue. "They only ever want to play."

"I can sympathize." I turned back toward the house and noticed Janardan had begun the trek alone. He was giving us a chance to walk together, and I marveled again at her mate's empathetic nature. "You'll never guess what Phoebe got it in her head to do."

As I relayed her antics, Death chuckled, indulgent. Much like Cole, she exuded pride in what our little terror had achieved. At the steps, she gave me a pointed look, and I spotted Wu lingering near the dunes.

"Give me a minute, and I'll shoo him off." I trotted out to him. "Any word on Sariah from the Malakhim lite?"

"They were unable to capture her."

Since that's about what I figured, I wasn't too upset over the news. It sucked, but it could have sucked worse. That was apparently my new barometer. Degrees of suckitude.

"Pick me up around lunch, and we'll head home. I ought to have an answer from them by then."

"I'll get a room in town," he decided. "I could use the break too."

The Southern girl in me wanted to feel like dirt for not checking on him, not playing the role of hostess since he was staying with the coterie. I kept reminding myself he had made his bed, and now he had to lie in it. It wasn't my job to tuck him in or make sure he had a glass of water, a teddy bear, or anything else. But I was my father's daughter, and I wanted to make my aunt proud. Even though I'm pretty sure she would have used Wu for target practice — angel wings or no — for all he had done to me.

"Make sure you get some food in you." I searched his face. "Sleep too. Don't sit at the foot of your bed and brood. Actually slide between the covers, shut your eyes, and dream."

"I'm not a fan of dreams," he said softly and shot into the sky.

I rejoined Death, who watched him go. "What?"

"You trust him further than I expected." She guided me into her living room. "Or you value us less than I had presumed."

"I trust him to say and do whatever is most beneficial to him." However, my perception had changed. I used to assume he wanted to step into his father's shoes. Now I grasped the scope of sacrifice required to unseat Ezra in the first place. "This was his grand design. I don't see him deviating from it just when all his scheming is coming to fruition."

The sentiment appeared to resonate with Death, who didn't question me further. That, or she trusted my judgement. How terrifying was that? All our lives were at stake, and I was doing my very best to keep us all breathing, but she was lightyears ahead of me with centuries more experience.

Who in the hell decided *I* got to call the shots? Had these people met me before balancing the world on top of my head? Had I lost a bet as Conquest I no longer recalled? There must be some reason other than I got here first, right? *Right?*

The possibility these people trusted me with their fates was too stark. It gave me chills. I didn't want this responsibility. I didn't want any of this. Too bad no one seemed to care.

Maybe they were happy dumping on me because it felt better to put your future into someone else's hands, even if they were coated in blood, than to hold onto it yourself. Who wanted to be responsible for their own actions? No one, that's who. And yet they had left me with no choice but to be accountable for the decisions I made that affected an outcome so much greater than my own existence.

"Have you eaten?" Death led me straight to the bathroom in a not-so-subtle hint she would like me to clean up first. "I have many television dinners I can prepare for you in the microwave."

Uncertain what she and her coterie deemed edible, I played it safe. "Do you have any pizza?"

"Many varieties." She brightened. "The combination, the pepperoni, and the supreme."

"I'll take the pepperoni."

"There are bathing supplies and towels." She flicked a glance at my bag. "Do you require clothes? I have decided I do not like the underwear. It's too constricting. I have shirts and pants you can borrow."

"Thanks, but I came prepared." I patted the side of the duffle. "I'll be out in fifteen."

Janardan began preheating the oven while Death rooted through the freezer to locate my dinner of choice. The scene was oddly domestic, and it warmed my heart to see them enjoying a normal moment together almost as much as it twisted my gut to know my arrival meant the last of these quiet evenings.

Ah well. As they say, all good things must come to an end.

I ate dinner on the porch overlooking the ocean. The pizza was burnt on the edges and frozen in the middle. It was the best meal I'd had in months. It reminded me of how Dad made them when I was a kid.

I wished I could visit him, but I had said my goodbyes a dozen times at least. With Phoebe's escape attempts bringing unwanted attention to Haven, I couldn't risk another visit even if I could justify one.

"I have chips," Death said when she joined me. "The barbecue, the salt and the vinegar, and the sour cream and the cheddar."

"This is fine, thanks."

"We should talk strategy." She shut her eyes, let the wind tease her hair. She still wore the Hollywood starlet look, and she fit here in a way she hadn't at the bunkhouse. "We must choose our battlefield."

"I was hunting Ezra when I was captured." I wiped my hands clean. "I thought a sneak attack would give us a chance to save lives, but that plan blew up in my face."

Expression solemn, she angled her head toward me. "Do you think it's wise to hunt a lion in its den?"

That was the question. Offense or defense? Which gave us

a better chance of survival? Which was the right choice? Was there even a right choice? Or were there simply less degrees of wrong ones?

"It's better than waiting on the lion to decide you look like dinner and ambushing you one night when it gets hungry."

Death crossed her slender legs and began rocking in her chair. "Have you heard of Hart Island?"

The name struck me as familiar, but I had to sort through a lifetime of documentaries to find an answer.

"It's an island east of the Bronx, in Pelham Bay," I recalled. "It's a mass grave. The famed Potter's Field. A million people, or close to it, have been buried there. Coffins run three deep in trenches. It's owned by the Department of Corrections, and inmates from Rikers dig the graves." I thought it over. "It's one of the largest mass graves in the United States. I want to say it's the biggest tax-funded cemetery in the US, maybe the largest of its kind in the world."

Embarrassed to recall so much, I had to admit I had definitely watched one too many insider reports in my life. Dad hadn't gone the *no TV is best* route. He had decided TV was perfectly fine as long as we watched educational programming. Together. As a cop, with an interest in criminal justice — a no brainer — we had sat through a ton of reality shows about life in super-max prisons and their satellites, such as inmates pulling grave duty on Hart Island.

"It is closed to the public. Visitation is rare. It would be an ideal spot."

Accepting Death's invitation to play in a mass grave sent faint hope of her having a greater plan skimming across the surface of my thoughts, but I couldn't afford to indulge in wishful thinking at this stage. Our planning had to be rooted in cold, hard absolutes.

"I'll mention it to Cole." It was only a few hundred miles away as a dragon flies. "Your coterie could swim. Mine could take the aerial route. It's not a bad idea."

The Malakhim, and Ezra himself, would have no trouble finding us either. The isolated location meant we could face him without endangering the lives of whatever innocents had the bad fortune to live wherever we were when Ezra made his move.

There was one component left. "How would we go about getting his attention?"

"You wouldn't have to waste your time baiting him. Word would carry that you and your coterie had holed up on the island. He would send scouts, and if you appeared well and truly isolated, cut off from your allies, he would attack."

"The whole point of raising an army was to put them to use." I set my plate aside. "The coterie and I can't take on Ezra and his Malakhim alone."

"You won't be alone." She covered my hand with hers. "Trust me."

Much to my surprise, I found that I did. With my life, apparently. "Okay."

Happiness brightened her face, and she smiled at me. "I'm so glad I met you, Luce."

"Me too." I patted her chilly fingers, even though contact with her gave me flashbacks of Malakhim falling after a simple touch from her. "I always wanted a sister."

CHAPTER TWELVE

Light tapping noises roused me, fingernails on glass, and I kicked aside my cover. Squinting against the morning sun, I padded to the window to find Wu hovering there and flung it open wide.

The dark circles under his eyes were less pronounced, which was a good start. He had showered and changed into fresh clothes he must have bought in town. They were expensive, but not tailored. I bet he felt like a hobo.

A deep crease bisected his brow. "Have you checked in with the coterie?"

"Not yet." I refrained from pointing out he had woken me from a dead sleep. "You?"

"I attempted to contact Thom this morning, but he didn't respond."

"He might have taken the nightshift. Did you try Maggie or Portia?"

Fingers tight on the windowsill, he swung himself in. "Neither answered."

Cole, Miller, and Kapoor were out cold. That left one person. "Santiago?"

He shook his head.

After scooping my cell off the nightstand, I tried all of their numbers, including the White Horse app, but no one answered. I almost called Dad, but he was attached to Phoebe, and I didn't want to worry him.

"We're leaving. Now." I yanked on clothes, threw on my pack, and burst into the living room to find Death and Janardan playing Monopoly. Piles of shells and sea glass appeared to be their preferred currency. "The coterie is incommunicado. Wu and I are heading back to make sure nothing has gone wrong."

"I have the tablet." Janardan removed it from a fold in his robes. "Please, let us know everyone is well."

"I'll do that." I smiled at him, panic worming through my gut. "We need to iron out the wrinkles in our plan anyway."

"Let us know what you decide." Death inclined her head. "We can meet you inland or on Hart Island."

That brought Wu up short. "Hart Island?"

"I'll fill you in on the way," I assured him before turning back to Death. "The island is more secure."

"All right." She stood, and everyone in the room rose with her. "We will begin our journey."

"Do you have a place to stay? What about supplies? It will take us at least one day, maybe two to gather what we need before joining you."

"We can catch our meals and sleep in the ocean. No one will see us, and the children will enjoy it more."

"That works." I didn't mention her newest additions, and she didn't elaborate. "I'll contact you with an update soon." On the porch, I jumped into Wu's arms, startling him. "Giddyap."

A lopsided smile touched his lips. "As you wish."

He carried me down to the second step then thrust out his wings and reached for the sky.

Anxiety got the better of me, and I caught myself muttering, "Come on, come on, come on" under my breath. There was no good reason for the entire coterie to be unreachable. Half of them might still be sleeping, but the other half ought to be wide awake and monitoring their devices in the event I reached out to them.

Wu's feet barely touched the roof before I twisted out of his grasp and jogged to the emergency stairs. The door was locked, but I didn't let that stop me. I shifted into a dragon, rammed it with my shoulder, and smashed the hell out of it, uncaring if it meant the security feeds would require wiping before we left. Shifting back in seconds, I hit the stairwell at a run, not checking to see if Wu followed.

I reached our floor and shoved through the door into the hall. Nothing appeared out of the ordinary. Everything was as I had left it. That didn't prevent me from making a beeline to check on Cole.

The second I touched the handle, I knew it would be bad. The door I had locked so carefully stood ajar.

"Cole." I reached for my service weapon before remembering I no longer carried one. These days, I was the weapon. "Cole."

A quick check of the bathroom confirmed it. Abandoning his room, I ran to where Thom and Maggie had bedded down. There was no sign of them or Phoebe. Miller and Rixton were absent too. Santiago's room was last. I searched every inch, but I found nothing to indicate where they had gone or why they had left without touching base with me.

"They're not here." Wu braced his hands on my shoulders. "Luce, stop. Listen to me. They aren't here."

"Who did this?" Heart pounding in my ears, I missed his answer. "Who took them?"

About the time I was ready to break every one of Wu's fingers for daring to comfort me, I heard a melodic beep that reminded me of a text chime but not. I didn't have to look far to uncover a tablet he had slipped beneath his pillow.

"Santiago left us breadcrumbs to follow." I picked it up and checked the home screen. Messages kept coming through, hard and fast, the newest crowding the screen before I could read the oldest, but the last was the one that turned my blood to ice. "It says *run*."

Heavy footsteps announced the arrival of four Malakhim kitted out in gleaming golden armor.

"Your reign of terror has ended," the first one intoned. "This is your last day on Earth."

Unlike when Wu cosplayed Ezra, these guys meant the rhetoric.

"As much as I enjoy the melodrama of dealing with your kind," I said dryly, "I'm going to cut to the part where I kill you."

Santiago's self-indulgence paid off when the dragon claimed my skin without asking permission. I wouldn't have fit in any of the other rooms, I barely managed to occupy this one without bumping my shoulders on the ceiling.

In the back of my mind, I sensed Conquest's rage. Cole and Phoebe mattered to her, and they were missing. Until she set eyes on them, she wouldn't rest. Neither would I. On this one matter, we agreed. For once, our goals aligned, and it was liberating to stop fighting with myself even for a few minutes.

With my mobility limited, I cut them down with my tail, a signature move I was coming to love. For the ones who got too close, I snapped my jaws shut over their forearms, forcing them to drop their swords in their severed hands. While I finished them off, Wu fought in an elegant dance with a blade he had taken from its master. Within minutes, we had killed them all. Thanks to Conquest, I could taste the cold place, a crisp tang on my tongue, and I had no pity for the dead at my feet.

Movement in the corner of my eye spooked me into a strike, and Wu narrowly missed me having wings for dinner.

"*Luce*," he snapped. "You've got to focus."

I didn't like focus. It was hard, and I was hungry. The man with feathers looked tasty, and I preferred live prey. I ran my tongue along the edge of my upper teeth.

"Bloodlust is getting the better of you." He put up his hands like that would stop me. "You need to get out, to fresh air."

A rumble built in my chest, and ice plumed on my exhales.

"We have to find your coterie."

I hesitated, shook my head to clear it, and advanced on him.

"Where is Cole? Where is Phoebe? Where is Thom? Where is Maggie?"

He hurled the names at me, rapid fire pings against my mind I couldn't comprehend but couldn't shake.

"Your mate, Luce. Your child. Your best friend. Your coterie."

I crunched through the ice in my mouth, and reason blasted through me. Before I lost the thread of my personality again, I tugged on the string and unraveled to my human form. I ended up in a heap on the floor with the mother of all headaches. The bangles burned against my skin, frigid as chips of ice.

"I'm back." I waved him off when he tried to come closer. "Just give me a second."

Focused on my breathing, I settled into my skin and tamped down Conquest. For now.

"I checked the tablet." He chucked it across the room. "It's smoking. Totally fried."

"Lovely." I shook out my arms, the left one still tender. "That means there's no way to tell if the coterie were the ones warning us." A thumping noise overhead shot tension into my spine, and I shot to my feet. "What is that?"

We followed the racket into the bedroom as a crash happened in the bathroom.

"Announce yourself," I shouted. "Or I *will* eat you."

"How did you know I was charun?" Santiago called back. "I could have been a poor human maintenance worker who had the bad luck to fall through the ceiling during a routine exam only to find myself threatened by a guest who wants to get her cannibalism on." He emerged covered in white dust and spiderwebs. "That's not very human of you. Tsk. Tsk. You've been hanging around with charun too long if your first impulse is to skip the questions and whip out the teeth."

I flung myself at him, which he wrongly interpreted as violent intent, and flipped me over his shoulder. I hit the floor on my back, the air knocked out of my lungs and stars winking in and out of my vision.

"She was going to hug you," Wu explained.

"Oh, I know." Santiago dusted off his shirt. "I'm not a hugger."

"Good to know," I wheezed, accepting the hand he held down to me. "Where are the others?"

"Not here." He held a finger to his lips. "Let's get moving. I promised I would have you home in time for dinner."

"Lead the way." I fell in step behind him, cocking an eyebrow when he hit the stairs. "Wu, you with us?"

Silent as a wraith, he drifted in my wake. "Yes."

We descended two flights then stepped into a hall identical to the one leading to our previous accommodations. Santiago walked four or five doors down, knocked, then let himself in using a keycard.

"Hey, Bou-Bou." Rixton stood and stretched his arms over his head. "I was starting to think you'd stood us up." Maggie was sitting on the bed. Until I arrived, she had been flipping through a photo album I saw from the doorway was chockful of pictures of his daughter Nettie. "Did you bring us good news?"

"I don't understand." I whirled on Santiago. "What the hell is all this?"

Rixton shot me a concerned look, but Maggie just stared at Santiago in expectation.

"I moved everyone two floors down after you left. I got a ping off a sensor on the roof. A group of Malakhim scouts found us, and I had to act fast. I scanned the area, and it came up clean. I don't know — yet — if that means they got lucky, or if they knew where to find us."

"Sariah?"

She had stuck her fingers in his technological pie. He hadn't noticed when it happened, and I wished anyone other than me had thought to ask. Coming from me, he would take it as an insult, as me throwing his past mistakes in his face. Santiago was big on looking for reasons to be offended, and it was never hard to find one.

"I burned my infrastructure to the ground." Amazingly enough, he didn't bristle. "I started over from scratch after Sariah outed herself. No one has an in to the system I've been operating out of for the past week. She couldn't have found us through me, or any tech she might have pocketed while staying with us."

"Good work," I praised him, earning a scowl that accused me of patronizing him.

I could not win with him. Could not. I don't know why I bothered trying.

"Whose idea was it for you to play ninja and drop from the ceiling *after* we killed the Malakhim?"

Now that I thought about it, this scenario explained his crack about having multiple rooms on multiple floors under multiple names.

"Say what now?" Rixton cocked his head. "What is she talking about, Santiago?"

"Cole told me to stay behind and relay our new coordinates," he said innocently. "That's what I did."

"He climbed up in the ceiling —" giving me hospital flashbacks to the time a journalistic vulture did the same to snap pictures of me while I slept, "— and watched the scene unfold. Four Malakhim were waiting for us in the bedroom of his suite, and we killed them. Only then did he grace us with his presence."

Failing spectacularly at innocence, he dusted his hair. "I honored the letter of the agreement, if not the spirit."

"I'm going to check on Cole." I rocked back on my heels. "What room is he in?"

"He's down the hall, third door on your right." Rixton reclaimed his seat beside Maggie. "I dropped off breakfast about thirty minutes ago. His eyes might have been closed, but he answered the door."

"Good deal." I regretted rushing through my own breakfast. "One last question for Santiago. Why didn't you call me? Make that two questions. Why shut down the lines of communication at all?"

"I was testing your reflexes," he said blithely. "Now I know how you react to crisis situations in which the coterie is endangered."

Waiting to hear the results, I cocked an eyebrow.

"You kill and/or maim anyone in your path."

"You really had to field test that?" Maggie exhaled through her teeth as she slid into Portia. "Why are you such an asshat? Seriously? Why?"

"You can thank me later," Santiago intoned, "when we've all survived because of these emergency preparedness drills."

All too happy to turn my back on them, I crossed the hall and knocked on Cole's door. He answered wearing boxers and smelling like coffee and waffles. My mouth watered. I invited myself in, slid my arms around his waist, and dipped my fingers into the elastic of his waistband near his spine.

A throat cleared behind him, and I froze. "Thom?"

"Yes." He chuckled. "Phoebe too."

Of course Cole would have moved her in with him, taking her favorite babysitter with her, after the Malakhim breached. Guilt clogged my throat that I hadn't asked Santiago for her location. I had been too wrapped up in finding Cole, in quieting the tension strung between us when we were apart for too long.

"I didn't get the memo." I popped Cole's waistband. "Yep. The elastic works. Just checking."

I dropped my arms, face on fire, and found myself the recipient of a lingering — if chaste — kiss.

"Later," he murmured against my lips, and my face flushed for an altogether different reason.

"I have an update on Death." I forced my knees to firm up and support my weight. "We should gather the coterie so I only have to give it once."

Granted, I had been willing to give Cole a private update, but now that naked charades had been cancelled, I might as well give the appearance of being a team player.

"Let me get dressed." He backed away, clearing the path for a tiny missile to launch. "Phoebe —"

The force of a miniature dragon smashing into my chest sent me staggering out the door, into the hall. I regained my balance with the help of the wall we crashed into, and I had no sooner wrapped my arms around the writhing bundle than the elevator pinged at the end of the hall.

"You are a menace." I nuzzled her quickly then sprinted for the safety of Cole's room and locked us in. She might be capable of invisibility, but I would still draw notice for juggling air. "Dad used to tease me, but I'm for real. You're always up for trouble, aren't you, short stuff?"

While Cole dressed, and I pretended very hard not to watch, I cozied up to Thom. "Did she behave?"

"Once she understood you would return shortly, yes." He scratched under her chin. "She wants to be wherever you are, but her father was a worthy substitute it seems."

Cole grunted what sounded like *ungrateful child*, but the curve of his mouth betrayed him.

That was when I lost all pretense of not ogling him. I found it nearly impossible to glance away when he let himself be happy. I might have ignited the spark, but Phoebe had fanned the flames. I cut myself a break since I was no longer sizing him up like a hunk of beef I wanted to sink my teeth into, more like I wanted to give him a good nibble.

Oh, wait. That was kind of the same thing.

Never mind.

"She enjoys getting in trouble almost as much as I did when I was a kid." I took a moment to be thankful she had no antlers on which to impale her enemies. Or, you know, stray cats. "While the gang puts on pants, I'll check in with Dad."

Moving to the window, I dialed him up and tried not to imagine what I might be interrupting between him and his mermaidlike girlfriend. *Girlfriend* sounded wrong, too young and weird when you took their ages into account. Womanfriend? Ladyfriend? Charunfriend?

"Hey, baby girl." He yawned. "Are you calling to ask for an update or to give one?"

"Just wanted to hear your voice." I cradled the phone, felt myself relaxing to hear him safe and sound . . . and alone. "Phoebe has made me regret ten times over all the grief I put you through when I was a kid."

"She's cute as a button." Pride sang through his voice. "I ordered a cat toy for her."

"Um." I rubbed my forehead. "The coterie is highly susceptible to stimulants for cats."

Famine's use of valerian had me ready to hump Cole's leg while the whole department watched.

Not one of my finest moments for sure.

"I don't mean for a cat. It's a plush cat. You put batteries in it, and it meows and rolls around on wheels hidden in its paws."

Stunned for a full second, I asked, "Are you telling me Amazon delivers to Haven?"

"All kids think their parents are idiots, but I do have a brain." He sighed, and I recognized the tone as one I had used only five minutes ago. "They make deliveries to lockers these days. I'm not saying you should put saving the world on hold while you fetch a toy for my granddaughter, but I am saying if you happen to be in the area and pick it up that I expect pictures of her playing with it."

Who was this man and what had he done with my father? I was supposed to be his baby. But here he was, shopping online, spoiling his granddragon from afar. As much as I wanted to blame Miranda for it, I suspected he was ga-ga over her the same as me. Guess that meant I would have to suck up my demotion and deal, as parents had before me, and accept there was a new baby in town.

Dad launched into a recitation of the address and strict instructions on what pictures he expected while I scribbled notes. I got off the phone quickly after that, before he added to his requests.

"How is your father?" Cole crossed to me. "Did he mention how Sherry and Nettie are doing?"

"He more or less asked if I would mind postponing the apocalypse long enough to hit an Amazon locker, pick up a toy he bought Phoebe, and then send him pictures and video of her playing with it."

Emotion brightened his eyes, and I couldn't stop myself from cupping his cheek.

"He loves her," Cole marveled. "He's only seen her in her true form, and it doesn't matter to him."

"Dad is like that," I said dryly. "He's got a soft spot for mischievous girls of mysterious provenance."

When my phone pinged, I panicked it might be Dad again, but no. I was rewarded with a text from Santiago, who had miraculously repaired the lines of communication now that the coterie wasn't in immediate danger.

One day I was going to pat him down and lock him in a cell with only a candle for company. I might even let Portia set up a card table facing him, so he could watch her play computer games but not see the screen. I bet he broke down in five minutes or less. In ten, he would be weeping. Twenty? He would be comatose.

Buoyed by that mental picture, I shooed the occupants of Cole's room into Santiago's much larger and nicer accommodations. Rixton, Miller, and Portia were already there, and their expectant looks put me on the spot before the door shut behind me.

"I had a sleepover with my littlest sister," I informed them, though I was sure the ones who had slept through it had already heard the news. "It appears we have a new game plan."

Hitting bullet points, I ran down Death's idea to use Hart Island for our showdown, and the others absorbed the suggestion with reluctant nods. The nods became smiles when I told them what she had spent her time away creating.

The aquatic charun would have limited utility, but they could make a difference before the fighting broke out, and every little bit helped. They would be our first line of defense, and our last, as they picked off any deserters or Malakhim attempting to return for reinforcements. Or, if our bait strategy failed, return to bring Ezra after we were good and wiped from the battle. He could finish us off in minutes if he let us exhaust ourselves with limited access to our allies.

God, it was a gamble. Every step, every detail. It all went counter to my instincts, which screamed to hunt Ezra down and end this before it got started. But Death had a good idea too, one less likely to kill or injure innocents in the process. She had done what the others were reluctant to do and advised me, put the weight of her experience at my disposal, and maybe that's how it was always meant to be. The cadre counseling one another. Who understood the full burden we bore better than our own?

And just like that, I grasped the insidious whisper in the back of my head coaxing me to lean on my sister, solely because she was cadre, and to discount the counsel of others who were not.

Closing my eyes, I inhaled through my nose then exhaled through my mouth. The move let me pause, reflect, and fill the cracks gaping wider as Conquest threw herself into fracturing me.

A dull horror throbbed at the base of my spine when it hit me how easily she had swayed my viewpoint seconds before I grasped the line of thought wasn't mine. All this time I thought she was contained, she was biding her time, chipping away at me, and only when she managed to dislodge a noticeable chunk of my morals had I sensed her before I crumbled.

When I opened my eyes, the entire room stared at me, and the coterie wore identical grim expressions.

"We scented her." Thom wore his heart on his sleeve. "She's gone now, but she was there."

"The bangles are failing," I confirmed. "I'm not sure how much longer I have before Conquest punches through the barriers separating us." Given how easily she had manipulated me moments earlier, I had to admit, "Whatever Ezra did to me shifted the balance. She's stronger now than she's ever been, closer to the surface." I toyed with the cool metal on my wrists. "I'm not sure there will be anything left of me once she succeeds."

Silence choked the room. Even Phoebe had gone silent as faint tremors shivered through her delicate wings. If I didn't know better, I would think she was afraid. Of what happened to me or of the whiff she caught of Conquest, I wasn't sure, and it's not like she could tell me if I asked.

"We'll find a way," Cole promised me then shared a long look with Wu, who nodded he would help.

The promise meant nothing to me. Wu was a con artist. He would say what Cole wanted to hear, a thing Cole himself never did, in order to keep his head on his shoulders. But if Cole took comfort from the lie, or thought I did, I wouldn't disabuse him of the notion.

"You can fight this." Maggie clutched her hands in her lap, her fingers cramped and bloodless. "You've got this, Luce."

"I want you to knock me out if it looks like she's surfacing," I told Thom, hating to burden him with the task. "It's the only chance you'll get to contain me before there are any casualties."

"And then what?" Santiago challenged. "Are you going to sleep through the siege on Hart Island?"

"I don't know what else I can do." I made fists at my sides, my knuckles itching to crash into his clenched jaw. We couldn't count on Conquest to fight on our side, and he knew that. She was as likely to smite the coterie in a fit of pique over them allowing me to keep her bottled as she was to pitch in. "I'm doing the best I can."

"Then your best sucks." He sneered at me then shoved out of the room. Slamming the door behind him, he yelled through the wood, "And cutting out our allies is stupid."

"I don't care if hate is how he shows his love," I snarled, "if he doesn't pull his head out of his ass soon, I'm going to lace his brownies with Ex-Lax. Then he'll be a bone fide shithead."

Portia, who had claimed Maggie and was halfway to rising, no doubt planning to hunt down Santiago, snorted a laugh that rippled through the others in the room. Just like that, the worst of the tension evaporated, and we all took a collective breath.

"Where do you think you're going?" I cocked a hip and planted a fist there. In all the commotion, Phoebe had slipped away from Thom and made her move. "Get your scaly . . . buns . . . over here."

I wasn't going to curse at a child, even if I had let my potty mouth get away from me seconds earlier. All I could do was be thankful Dad wasn't here. He would have shoved a bar of soap in my mouth so far bubbles shot out of my toes.

Ducking her head, Phoebe made halting steps over to me, and a horrible realization seized me.

"You're afraid." I staggered back, tripping over a footstool. "Of me."

"You're projecting." Maggie had worked with kids for years, so I trusted her judgement in matters three feet and under. "She's slinking in because she was about to do something bad and got caught. It's worse because she admires you and doesn't want to let you down. She doesn't want to get punished either."

But Phoebe had smelled Conquest on me for the first time. That was enough to spook any kid.

"Thom, can you take her back to Cole's room?" I strode to the window, ignoring my troubled reflection. "Mags, you and Rixton can take one of the White Horse credit cards to go stock up on supplies. We're going to need it all. Tents, blankets, food, water. There's nothing on Hart Island, and we don't have time to circle back to Canton."

A nudge at my calf prompted me to glance down where Phoebe

was busy curling her tail around the same ankle her father preferred, her shorter length only making the full loop once.

"You should go with Thom." I bent down to rub her silky mane.
"He'll take good care of you."

Once my hand got within grabbing distance, that's what she
did. She hooked her tiny kitten claws into the long sleeve of my
shirt and hauled herself up my arm and over my shoulder until
she could wind her tail around her preferred anchor — my throat.
Using that hold to stand on my chest an inch from my nose,
she stroked my cheeks, claws sheathed, with her small paws and
butted her head against me while purring her tiny purr.

I cradled her in my hands, holding her lightly so I didn't hurt
her, and gave her what passed for a hug when your kid was a
squirmy dragon with better things to do.

Without a backward glance, she sped across my torso, down my
legs, and leapt onto the carpet. She trotted after Thom, swishing
her rump, clearly pleased with herself even though I wasn't sure
what she had accomplished aside from convincing me she loved
me, warts and all.

"Cole?" I didn't seek him out, afraid of what I might find in his
expression. "Care to do some light recon with me?"

He came up behind me, set his hands on my shoulders. "Do
you have to ask?"

CHAPTER THIRTEEN

Hart Island was as desolate as a quick internet search promised. The entire island was a mile long and maybe a third that wide. I expected it to be barren, and it was in its way, but there were several ruins and wooded areas as well. Those would provide an ideal place to set up camp away from prying eyes.

Once I had looked my fill and checked with Cole that we had all the intel we required to make our next move, I pointed him toward the hotel. As much as anyone can point a dragon any-where. And that is why it shouldn't have surprised me to find he didn't go where I expected him to but where he wanted.

He landed on the muddy edge of an unfamiliar riverbank and shed his dragon skin almost quicker than I could dismount.

"I give up." From this vantage, I couldn't tell this city from any other. There were no postcard-worthy feats of architecture in sight. "Where are we?"

"The where doesn't matter." He walked to the edge and peered into the murky water. "This is the closest point of contact for the Diorte."

Thanks to the influx of new allies, I had to think back to identify the species in question.

Joining him, I studied the rippling surface below us. "Was this meeting your idea or Santiago's?"

They had discovered Jean Ashford, one of the humans Janardan had infected when he was trying to make first contact with me. The only other thing I could recall was their size meant they had to cull their own in order to survive undetected in the rivers and lakes where they lived.

Reproduction was illegal, according to the NSB, but Wu let some species willing to police their numbers off the hook. Yet another reason getting a bead on him was difficult. For as many of his bad attributes I could name, I could list two or more acts of kindness he had shown species his father would have wiped off the face of the earth without losing sleep.

Really, when I framed it that way, it cast Wu in the light of savior and me in the role of sacrificial lamb. Everyone not chosen for team death-by-pointy-object loved the guy, and I'll be honest, it pissed me off they didn't see the conflicting sides of him I did.

No one was wholly good or wholly evil. I wasn't arguing that point. He was a mostly good guy. There. I admitted it.

What burned my biscuits about Wu was how quick he was to make life or death decisions for the rest of us when half the time we would have volunteered to follow his cockamamie schemes for the greater good, but we never got the chance to choose. He was too busy railroading us at every opportunity to ensure his grand vision for the end unfurled as planned and on schedule.

That was what tempted me to ask Thom to knock Wu out so I could pluck him like a chicken while he was unconscious.

Cole's lips pulled to one side. "What do you think?"

"Ugh." I leaned my shoulder against his. "He's adjusting his recruitment strategy."

We had named Hart Island ground zero, and now he was refining our options to suit the conditions.

Santiago might be an ass, but he was smart, and I was glad to have him on my team.

Except when forced to interact with him. I was definitely gladder to have him on my team when he wasn't also in the same room as me.

"Here they come." Cole squared his shoulders, and I took the hint to do the same. "Their leader is Castro."

Charun come in every size, shape, and color imaginable, so I didn't waste energy attempting to picture them. It was easier all around to wait and let them reveal themselves to me. Good thing I had adopted that mentality. What parted the waters was nothing I would have imagined on my own. I wasn't that creative.

The closest match to a known, if extinct, animal my brain supplied was a plesiosaur. Its conical head, however, was bloated in comparison, far too large for its slender neck. Its sleek hide was black except for its face, and red and white flesh streaked its cheeks, shifting to darker colors as I watched, telling me they could shove their heads out of the water to breathe and scout, and as long as no one got too close or paid too much attention, they could pass for buoys.

Really, really terrifying buoys. The bone structure in their jaws that allowed for sinuous muscle to rope over their broad foreheads mystified me. The Discovery Channel had definitely not prepared me for this. I bet every paleontologist in the world would give their eye teeth for a look at her, let alone an opportunity to observe her in the wild.

"Child of man," a gentle whisper glided over the water. "Well met."

Child of man. That was a new one. I liked it better than other names I had been called: scourge, plague on humanity, etc.

"Well met." I knelt at the soft edge to put our heads at a similar level, given the steep embankment. "I hope you and your kin are well."

A pleased trill rippled through the water, proof she approved of my good manners. "We are, and for that we give thanks to the Mother of the Deep."

Cole stepped in to save me before things got awkward, what with me having no clue what we were doing here aside from likely recruiting a new clan. For that I was grateful. I routinely made an ass out of myself by heading into these things without any talking points. Probably because I avoided recruitment missions like the plague.

"Your elders contacted our coterie." Cole joined me on his knees, a little behind and to the side of me. "The message indicated you wish to cooperate with us."

"It is the time of the culling," she murmured. "Our numbers have blossomed, and our young have outstripped the resources we have available. For the good of the pod, we must abide with tradition." The colors fluctuated along her nasal passages. "However, we wish to prolong our deaths if our lives might yet be paid in service to you."

A knot formed in my throat as I recalled what precious little else I knew about their kind. They thinned their population in accordance with the number of children they birthed, the adults willing to sacrifice their lives in order to welcome new ones into this world.

"I would be honored," I said, and I meant it. "It is my greatest wish to preserve this world for all our children."

The curve of Cole's lips told me he hadn't missed the slip. The circumstances of Phoebe's conception and birth might exist beyond me, but I loved the kid. I was one hundred percent my father's daughter in that regard. All it took was looking at that adorable face, and I was lost. She was my daughter as much as she was Cole's because I already loved her with a depth I hadn't known I was capable of, let alone in so short a time. But Dad told me once he knew from the moment he saw me that I was his. It must run in the family.

"We too wish for this world to survive." Her head tilted, and only then did I notice the black bead of her nearest eye as she took a gander at me. "It will take a few days for us to reach the Sound."

"You prefer lakes and rivers. Can you survive in saltwater?"

"Long Island Sound is a caldron swirling with freshwater from tributaries and saltwater from the ocean. It is enough for us to acclimate and survive for a short period of time. Long term exposure to saltwater will kill us." Amusement shone in the one eye I could see. "But we are already dead."

I bit my lip to keep from saying what I might regret later. I had the wrong perspective to question their commitment. I should be grateful, not sad. I should applaud them, not mourn them. They were making this choice. For that alone, I ought to be glad. No one had forced them to this point. They had reached it on their own.

"We heard you were different." A slender filament extended from the tip of her nose to caress my cheek, capturing a tear I hadn't noticed falling. "We are pleased to see the rumors, for once, were true."

"I'm not sure different is better," I admitted. "Different has cost a lot of good people their lives."

The alternative, allowing Conquest to rise uninhibited, would have cost more. I tried remembering that, but it was hard when the reason grief clouded my judgement was because I was different, because I was Luce, I had been the catalyst for more death and destruction than I could sometimes bear.

"Change requires sacrifice, child." A warm glow emitted from the filament. "We are pleased to offer what we can to help you further your goals, as they are ours as well. You are unique, and that which is unique must be sheltered and allowed to thrive for the good of all."

"I didn't mean to lessen your offer by questioning it." I kept my joints locked in a stiff pose, uncertain what protocol demanded when a charun caressed you with its shiny nose hair tentacle. "I respect your decision and appreciate your help."

"The longer charun live, the less empathy we possess. It is a kind of mercy for our kind that we choose to shorten our existence in order to preserve that brightness of spirit. The future belongs to the young." Her touch retreated. "Despite the weight of your soul, you are young. Your future . . . is what you make it."

A fraction of the weight pressing on my chest lifted as her meaning sank in. Without knowing the entirety of my circumstances, she had given me a way of spinning what Wu had done to me. He might have orchestrated this, but he couldn't carry it out on his own. He required my help. I had to be willing to take my own life in exchange for saving everyone else's. In that sense, it was my choice. I wasn't helpless. I could decide to spend what time I had left with my family and tell the rest of the world *screw you*. It was a small consolation, but it gave me some of my own back, and I needed all the spunk I could muster to get through the next few days.

"We should return to the others," Cole said, perhaps sensing my distraction. "They'll be expecting us."

"Go on." Castro patted my cheek and then withdrew. "We will meet again soon enough."

I rose, Cole standing in tandem with me, and we backed away as she glided deeper into the water.

After he embraced his dragon, I climbed onto his back and, thinking of Castro's choice, buried my face in his mane.

*

Santiago waited on us in the hall below the roof access door at the hotel, tablet in hand. I was starting to wonder why he didn't just amputate one and fuse the device to his wrist. He didn't acknowledge us at first, which wasn't unusual for him, but he didn't let us pass either.

Emotionally drained after the meeting with Castro, I sighed. "I'm guessing you've got something on your mind."

"You need to lock the kid down before we leave." He glanced up, shot Cole a pointed glance, then settled his ire, as usual, on me. "She's got a fighting spirit, but what you propose to do on that island ... It's no place for a kid. She's small, fast, and she's got invisibility on her side, but the Malakhim aren't going to leave any survivors. No matter how cute they are."

I hated to agree with him, but he might as well have been plucking my thoughts straight out of my head. "Are you that certain we'll lose?"

"I'm that certain we'll win, at great cost." His focus slid past us, down the hall. "You don't want her death on your conscience. She's a good kid, and she's been through enough. You're going to have to figure out a way to keep her butt at Haven or something. I don't know."

Short of supergluing her paws to the floor, I didn't see that happening. She was too crafty.

"She'll only come after us." Cole softened his voice the way he did when explaining the facts of charun life to me. "She's a predator, and her bond to us is ironclad. Convallarian young are rare and treasured. It's part of their genetic memory to stay close to their parents to better their chances of survival."

"I figured you'd say that."

Santiago resumed his typing. "I had to try."

"I didn't know you cared," I joked, mostly.

"Portia is torn up about it." He kept busy, tapping and reading.

"I promised I would mention it. She didn't want to come off as questioning your parenting skills."

The hit landed, right on target, and I debated kicking him in the junk to make myself feel better.

Portia's father had sold her into marriage. Her husband beat her, shared her with his men, and generally made her life a living hell. Those things, she gritted her teeth and endured. But when he crushed her eggs as she laid them, because he couldn't be certain who fathered her offspring, that's when she snapped. She struck her bargain with Conquest, they killed him and all his men, and Portia joined the coterie.

Kicking up an eyebrow at him, I kept my tone even. "Clearly you don't have that problem."

"Nope."

"I wanted her to stay with Dad, at Haven, where they would both be safe." I sought out Cole's hand, classic united front body language. "It's not like we're thrilled about the prospect of her joining in, but we can't stop her. She's too clever and too capable. At least if we allow her to participate, we get to set the ground rules instead of her sneaking off to do what she wants how she wants behind our backs."

Trust flowed both ways. I had tied myself into knots as a kid to earn Dad's approval, and it still meant the world to me when he gave it. We had to hope Phoebe shared similar values and craved parental approval enough to obey orders.

We rejoined the others in Santiago's spacious suite, and they all made a point of not looking at us.

In my experience, that was never a good sign.

"Fess up." I stopped in the middle of the room. "What happened after we left?" I noticed who was missing, and my heart flung itself against my ribs. Pretty sure a few got cracked in the process. "Is Thom . . . ?"

"He's fine." Mags rushed to comfort me. "Phoebe just kind of . . . well . . . exploded."

"*Exploded?*" The strength sapped out of my knees, and they wobbled. "Where is she?"

"Phoebe hit a growth spurt," Miller clarified before I had a full-on heart attack. "She's fine, she was just disoriented. Thom took her back to Cole's room to lie down."

"Okay." I sank onto the couch until my legs quit wobbling like Jell-O. "Cole?"

"I did warn you Convallarian children experience rapid growth spurts."

The tone was calm, but the look on his face? In his mind, he had already rushed across the hall and scooped her up in his arms to do a thorough examination. Meanwhile, I was still trying to recover from the exploded comment and the mental picture it supplied.

"Will she be okay?" The conversation we had with Santiago on the roof still applied, but a bigger Phoebe would be even more difficult to contain. "Miller mentioned disorientation."

"Children adapt to their new size within a few hours. Their minds make similar jumps." He reached out to me, rested his hand on my forearm. "She won't be the same as when we left her."

Swallowing hard, I nodded and stood, unable to put off checking on her myself.

From across the hall, Thom's voice carried. That was a comfort. Or it would have been had a softer voice not answered him too quietly for my ears to pick out the individual words. Cooing or babbling, okay. But this was a conversation. They were chatting. With words. Actual sentences.

Years of development had sped past while we were on coterie business, and there was no turning back the hands of time. This must be how parents felt when they picked their bundle of joy up from daycare and found out they'd missed its first steps. Drop off a baby, pick up a toddler.

Fumbling for Cole, I leaned against him, and he wrapped a steadying arm around me. "She shifted."

"She's older, stronger." He kissed my temple. "She's integrated into the coterie and trusts us to protect her. Enough she's willing to assume a more vulnerable form."

"This will be like meeting her all over again." I folded my hands together, wary like the knob was a snake ready to strike. "I'm not sure I can —"

The door swung open, and I was out of time to waffle. The baby dragon was gone. In her place stood . . .

"Hi, Mom."

The hotel mattress was comfy, but I couldn't figure out when or why I had climbed into bed alone.

"Cole?" I sat upright, puzzled to find I still wore my clothes and shoes. "Thom?"

After I swung my legs over the side of the bed, I experienced a dizzying moment of vertigo as the reason for my nap crystalized into being before me.

"Are you going to faint again?"

Seated in a chair across from me, Phoebe had definitely experienced a growth spurt.

She had also chosen her human form, and it shocked me to my core to sit there looking at a mirror image of myself from ten years ago. She resembled fifteen-year-old me so perfectly I had no doubt she had memorized one of my pictures from a photo album Dad must have shown her and copied me down to the mole in my right eyebrow.

For a person who had spent her life avoiding mirrors, photos, and reflections, I had trouble holding her gaze. My eyes kept wanting to slide away, find somewhere else to focus. I had to force them back to her or risk hurting her feelings. What she had done ... it was a huge honor. Dad would have a cow. Hell, he would have a *herd*.

"Maybe." I swallowed to wet my throat. "I didn't expect ..."

"You're my mom." A snort escaped her, evidence of her dry humor. "How did you think I would look?"

"The last time I ..." I gestured to her. "You were a toddler. I—" I had to give myself a break, to study her clothes like I cared what she wore other than, you know, *my face*, or else the thoughts drained right out of my head. "I expected you to snap back into a little kid. This is not ..."

Phoebe crossed to me slowly and hit her knees on the carpet in front of me. She rubbed my arms until I awarded her my full attention, her eyes — which I hadn't noticed were the same meltwater blue as Cole's — held understanding beyond her years.

"It's okay," she soothed. "I'm still your little girl."

"Come here, you." Tears sprung to my eyes. "Of course you're still my little girl." I gathered her against me in a hug that drove home how much she had changed in so short a time. "I just didn't realize how *big* my *little* girl had gotten."

"I used to dream about you." Her slender arms wound around my waist, and she burrowed against my chest. "When I was in the pod."

She meant during her time with Death, when my sister had kept her in stasis to protect her from the cadre. Phoebe had slept away the centuries, safe from her other aunts ... and her mother.

"You mean Conquest," I said, shocked at how much it stung.

"No." Withdrawing, she sank onto the floor into a lotus position with her hands folded in her lap. "I don't remember much about her. I was only a few weeks old when Death placed me in the pod."

A human child would remember nothing from such a young age, but she was a charun on steroids. The toddler I recalled so vividly ... was *weeks* old? She had been a freaking infant by human standards.

"I wasn't awake, exactly. I wasn't asleep, either." She chewed on her bottom lip. "I made up stories in my head about my mom. I pretended she was a superhero and that a supervillain had kidnapped me." She laughed softly. "I didn't know those words until Uncle Rixton got me hooked on cartoons, but it fits." She flicked her gaze up to me. "All I thought about was the day my mom would come to save me."

"I can see how you might mistake Death for a supervillain." I rubbed her shoulder. "But she took care of you when we couldn't, and for that we owe her a lot."

All that time, she and Janardan had risked their lives for a potential payoff. There were no guarantees our cadre would reach Earth, let alone that I would be in a position to honor the bargain Cole had struck. I might be a wild card this ascension, but Death possessed more empathy than all the others combined. As much as I wanted to pin all the credit — fine, the *blame* — on Wu, I wondered if Death wasn't more than a caricature too. And then there was Sariah, so eager to claim her mother's title.

For a repetitive loop, nothing about this cycle struck me as normal. Wu could hardly pat himself on the back for all of it.

"Oh, I know." She covered my hand with hers. "Just like I knew the day you came for me at Haven that you were the mother I had been picturing in my head."

"Does this mean you'll listen if I tell you to go stay with your grandfather? He would love to meet you."

"He already has," she pointed out, quick to use her newfound voice and logic against me. "And no, I'm not leaving you." A smile hooked up one side of her mouth, warmer and more natural than any I had managed at her age. "I would rather stand beside you and Dad on the battlefield than cower in the dark until Ezra finds me."

"Are all charun kids this brave?" I couldn't stop the tears. I was a regular leaky faucet lately. "Or did we get lucky?"

Proving she had also mastered the art of sucking up, she grinned. "I had great role models."

The reminder had me searching the room a second time. "Where is your dad?"

"Waiting in the hall." She jumped up and yanked tissues from the complimentary box and passed them to me. "We could tell you were coming around, so I asked if I could talk to you alone first."

"Do you mind if we bring him in?" I dabbed my cheeks and blew my nose. "I want him to be here for this conversation."

Allowing Phoebe to join us on Hart Island when she was a slip of a dragon with a child's comprehension was one thing. She was a teen now, or resembled one. She sounded older. The knowledge in her eyes put me in mind of a contemporary. Maybe she had chosen to appear younger to give me time to process her sudden physical maturation.

"Sure thing." She dashed over to let him in, and he couldn't take his eyes off her. "She's asking for you."

With his hearing being what it was, he would have already overheard. I was, however, pleasantly surprised to find how well-mannered she had turned out. I would definitely be patting myself on the back right now if I wasn't doing my best to keep my brains from leaking out of my ears.

Human minds weren't meant for this. They weren't elastic enough. Mine, apparently, was more human than any of us anticipated, thanks to Wu turning me into his personal science experiment. I heard things, saw them, and I understood. I told myself I accepted them. But all the while, that nagging scream

that began the night I learned my true identity kept droning on
and on and on.

How long before it finally shut the hell up? I didn't have time
to cope. My brain knew this. Why couldn't it put a cap on the
wailing already? It wasn't like I needed the reminder my world was
shot straight to hell. I was the one loading the bullets, itching to
take aim and claim the first kill.

I wanted this over, for life to return to some semblance of
normal, and . . . oh.

Yeah.

Hmm.

Maybe that's why that most human part of me hadn't shut her
yap. People tended to not want to die, and I was no exception.
The only way I was getting through this was to pretend this ended
with a *happily ever after*. There was no fooling myself, though. No
wonder it kept right on wailing.

Lying to my loved ones hurt. Looking ahead to their future
without me in it hurt. Listening to them make plans, me faking
my contributions, hurt worst of all.

But they'll be alive.

That was what mattered.

That was the only thing that mattered.

"Before you guys start in on the reasons why I shouldn't be
allowed to go with you," Phoebe began in a rehearsed tone,
"there's something I ought to show you."

"Okay." Fists clenched in the sheets, I braced myself.
"Let's see it."

"We'll need to go up to the roof." She bounded through the
door and down the hall ahead of us. "Catch up, slowpokes."

Typical teen, she didn't wait on her lame parents but
rode up alone.

"Can you honestly tell me this doesn't freak you the hell out?

Come on, at least a little?" I checked with Cole. "She was cooing and trilling this morning. Now she's formulating arguments against us sending her to my dad. She's articulating all the reasons why she belongs with us on Hart Island."

"I'll admit, it's jarring." He took my hand, interlaced his fingers with mine, and led me to the elevator. "Even knowing this is the order of things, it's been a long time since I witnessed it firsthand." He cut me a glance. "And never with my own child."

"I keep thinking Kapoor had it right."

"What do you mean?"

"He saw a therapist regularly."

"I'll schedule you an appointment myself, as soon as this is all over."

When this ended, I wouldn't need to see a shrink. I would be at peace, one way or another.

CHAPTER FOURTEEN

———◆———

I had a vague idea of what Phoebe wanted to show us, but I wasn't prepared for the reality of it. One minute a teenage mini-me stood there, and the next an adolescent dragon more than half the size of mine had taken her place.

"Man up," I grumbled at my wobbly knees. "What good are you?"

An inquisitive noise rumbled up the back of her elegant throat.

"You've broken my knees," I explained. "I might have to have replacement surgery before Hart Island."

Now she laughed, a sound that left her father grinning. Seriously, the man was so proud he could pop.

"I get that you're trying to show me you're bigger and stronger," I said gently, "and therefore a greater asset, but at the end of the day, you're still our kid."

Cole crossed to Phoebe and stroked her muscular shoulder, admiring her frilly mane and scratching behind her wings. He didn't say he was on her side. He wasn't going to call me out in front of her, remind me my human ideals had no place here, and I liked that. Having been raised by a single father, it was pretty cool to see this co-parenting thing at work. But he had physically taken her side, whether he realized it or not, and I was well aware it was a losing battle.

Be true to yourself was the advice everyone kept parroting at me. Their belief that my unique outlook was the key to our success meant accepting I wasn't the Conquest they had come to know and loathe, but my own person. I was myself, and that was what I brought to the table. Fresh perspective, heart, and the determination to protect at any cost. Given my current situation was a testament to the power of the individual contribution, I didn't have a leg to stand on.

Phoebe wasn't human. I couldn't shove her into that box and expect her to stay there. She had already proven time and time again she would burst out of it the second my back turned. Putting a lid on her wasn't slowing her down. It was forcing me to run out of lids. Or, in this case, excuses.

"I won't lie and say I'm happy about this," I told them both then singled her out for the rest. "I'm human enough to want to hide you away to keep you safe, but I'm charun enough to accept your instincts run counter to mine." Her tab ears perked. "If you want in, and it's okay with your dad, you're in."

Barreling past Cole, she ran at me, trading shape seconds before I experienced how it felt when a runaway train smacked into you head-on. The impact of a teen girl was more survivable, but still enough to leave bruises when she wrapped me in a hug that toppled us both onto the roof tiles.

"This seems oddly familiar." I tickled her until she rolled off me. "What is it with you tackling people?"

At least this time she didn't pee on me. There really was a silver lining to every situation, no matter how painful.

"Not people." She scooched closer and rested her head on my shoulder. "Just you."

I wasn't lying when I said, "Lucky me."

*

Now that I had survived my psychologically traumatic reintroduction to Phoebe, it was time to gather the coterie and figure out our next steps. I'll admit, I snickered at the expression wreathing Maggie's face when she saw Phoebe and me side by side for the first time. It's a good thing she was sitting. Otherwise, she might have fallen down.

"It's uncanny," she said to Phoebe on a laugh. "You look exactly how I remember Luce at that age."

"You could have chosen anyone to mimic?" Rixton slumped forward on the couch, dejected. "I always wanted a twin. Can you imagine the fun we could have had? Talk about your missed opportunities. I'm *much* more attractive than Luce and at least five times as awesome. Seriously, I have references. How could you choose her over me?"

"She's a girl," I pointed out then covered Phoebe's ears. "Do you really want her to be an exact copy of you?"

Eyes widening, he formed an *oh* with his lips. There I was, thinking I had brought the point home, but no.

"Are you saying I could have made requests?" He stared at his crotch. "I have ideas. Big ones."

"Ugh." I curled my lip. "Men are so predictable."

"Can you imagine?" Wonder shone in his eyes when he raised them to mine. "I could be a modern-day Mercury with wings on my ankles. How cool would that be? Do you think it would work? How much of a dragon's wingspan is responsible for keeping it afloat versus magic? Would I have cute little wings like on the cartoons, or would I trip over them because they were so long?"

Leave it to Rixton to break the curve with a unique wish. He had been staring at his feet, not his . . . um.

Just saying wings weren't what I had expected him to be worried about tripping over.

"Sorry, Uncle Rixton." Phoebe bumped shoulders with me. "I'm a momma's girl."

"Uncle Rixton," he repeated, choking up as he soaked it in. "I'm an uncle. I have a niece."

Grateful for the distraction, I didn't further disillusion him by implying Mercury had worn winged sandals, not had actual wings attached to his ankles.

"I didn't blubber this much when you named me your kid's godmother," I grumbled. "Dry your face, Rixton."

"No," he countered, dropping the pretense. "You acted like you had been sentenced to life without parole." He snorted. "The first time you held Nettie, you might as well have been walking the last mile on death row. You had that whole *bound for the gallows* thing happening. It was pretty hilarious, actually."

"I had never held a baby," I argued. "I didn't know what to do with her."

Honestly, I still didn't know how to handle an infant. Nettie was getting bigger, but she was still tiny. I would rather wait until she was walking to attempt holding her again. Or maybe until she started college. Somewhere in there.

Stepping in to break us up before Rixton got carried away — even more carried away — Maggie grinned at us. "That makes me Auntie Maggie, right?"

"That was the plan." Phoebe returned her smile. "You're a two for one."

The shock of being included melted Maggie into Portia, who clearly hadn't expected the honor.

"You're a good kid, Pheebs." Portia sniffled. Unlike Rixton, her emotion was genuine. "It's nice having young blood in the coterie, not to mention another girl. There's been way too much testosterone for way too long, if you ask me."

"No one did." Santiago grimaced. "Enough with the tears and

snot." He stepped back like emotion was contagious. "This is a tactical meeting, not a baby shower."

As much as I hated to agree with him, we were getting sidetracked. "Where are we on supplies?"

"I've placed the orders." Rixton lifted a handful of receipts from the cushion next to him. "I arranged for the delivery of nonperishable items to be made to a locker near the subway. The food will require a truck, but we can ditch it at the pier and let the dragons fly it over."

Ugh. I was a dragon. Still, no apocalypse got started without a team effort.

"I bought a boat. A pontoon." Santiago's fingers twitched with the childlike eagerness he only ever showed when about to play with a new toy for the first time. "We can rip out the seats we don't need to clear deck. We all pitch in, load it up, and I'll drive it over." He pointed to a stack of papers on the desk. "Boating licenses, etc., etc., in case we attract attention from local LEOs."

Law enforcement officers would be thin on the ground in that area, but it never hurt to be prepared.

"We'll have some shelter as long as we set up camp in the buildings." The tents would protect us from the elements, so that wasn't a huge concern. "Portions of the roofs are intact, so we'll have partial concealment from aerial scouts."

"Any gaps in the walls and ceilings will give us easy ways out," Miller reasoned, "but they'll also make it simple for the Malakhim to get in. We need to walk through the buildings and familiarize ourselves with their layouts. Otherwise, we risk getting trapped."

The rest of the details didn't take long to hash out. The real strategizing would occur once we arrived on the island, explored it at ground level, and got a feel for the terrain. With the broad strokes decided, we broke apart to gather our things and make last-minute preparations.

Rixton walked off talking to Sherry on his phone. Portia and Santiago settled into a bickering contest. Miller looked on, amused. Thom was herding Phoebe back to Cole's room. Soon only Cole and I were left, and we parted ways as if by unspoken agreement. I went to call Dad, and he went to spend time with Phoebe and relieve Thom of his babysitting duty in case he had other matters to attend.

No one was saying goodbye, but the heaviness of reluctant farewell hung in the air all the same.

CHAPTER FIFTEEN

An unnatural fever ravaged Farhan, turning his skin hot and spinning madness into his thoughts. He had forgotten the all-consuming insanity in the long years since his last hunt. His body remained on the bed, muscles locked, strain giving him the appearance of shivers, but his mind whirred with eagerness to pick up where he left off.

The hunt, the hunt, the hunt.

Tension bowed his back as his instincts fought against Adam's orders.

Ezra, Ezra, Ezra.

With his eyes closed, the backs of his lids made a perfect movie screen, and he kept reliving the time he spent at Ezra's mercy. He hadn't realized until Luce gave the command to sic him on the wannabe god how deep his hatred for him had gone, the bottom of his loathing an endless tunnel that loomed dark and foreboding beneath him. Every move he made shifted his weight, pitching him closer to the edge, nearer to the drop.

Ezra had to die. He had to. Had to.

It was the only way to make it stop, the oily twist in his gut, the frantic thumping of his heart.

Hunt, hunt, hunt.

Ezra, Ezra, Ezra.

The door opened on a sigh, and Adam entered the room, his scent too familiar to mistake.

"We have a problem." He took the bed opposite his, the springs in the mattress groaning a complaint. "You won't stop until you find Ezra, but Luce has decided we're no longer searching for him."

"*No,*" Farhan raged in his mind, unable to speak, unable to roar his intent. "*He's mine.*"

"She's luring him to Hart Island." Adam exhaled. "You'll have your shot at him there."

A fraction of the mania animating Farhan's thoughts eased, but the insult of having his prey presented to him on a silver platter stung. He was a hunter. He was one of the best. Perhaps even *the* best. The only reason he landed a supervisory role was management's fear the stress he was under would cause him to snap. They worried their favorite assassin might turn against them if that happened, and they were right to worry. He had no control over his mind, his body, his thoughts. When the hunting fugue gained control of him, he regressed to a creature more animal than man.

"We're going to keep you sedated until then." Adam hesitated until the door opened again. "Thom is going to bite you. Just hold still. When the sedative wears off this time, you'll be ready for Ezra."

The promise soothed as much as the bite stung.

Hunt, hunt . . .

Ezra.

CHAPTER SIXTEEN

———◆———

I'm not sure if it's the same for all girls raised by single fathers, or if they have to also be outdoorsmen like mine, but I spent a lot of time in the woods. We camped, we hiked, we fished, we hunted. I got ticks, I got chiggers, I got stung by mosquitos, bees, wasps, and yellow jackets. I also learned the value of packing my own toilet paper because guys have different priorities than girls in survival situations.

I had never been more thankful to Dad for my rough and tumble upbringing than when Cole and I claimed our weed-ridden corner in the barely standing former mess hall we had chosen for our camp. The black tents had been erected and leveled, the supplies tucked out of sight, and the exits located in case we had to make quick use of them. All that remained were the finishing touches.

"Are you sure we should split up?" I finished unrolling our sleeping bags. "Scattering the coterie across the island makes me antsy."

"It was your idea," he reminded me. "Having second thoughts?"

Leave it to Cole to spin it around until I had to face the consequences of my own decisions. I was hoping one day I would trick him into giving me advice, but it hadn't happened yet. He had just a tiny bit more experience in evading probing questions than I did in asking them.

"It seemed like a good idea at the time." I chewed on my bottom lip. "Smarter to spread out the targets than cluster them together." I bit through and tasted blood. "God, we're not *targets*. That sounds so clinical. I hate how my brain slides into facts and logic so easily."

The terms gave me distance, yes. They made strategizing neater, yes. They helped me think clearer, yes. But I was playing with people on the ground, not pieces on a board. No matter how much of a game the rest of the cadre considered their ascensions, I didn't want to play. There was no choice. *No choice.*

Maybe if I kept telling myself that, one day I would believe it was true.

"Have you considered it's not all Conquest?" He caught a zigzag, a type of spider I found cute because of the noticeable zigzag pattern in its web and walked it to the nearest window. Then he went back to sorting equipment we had yet to mount. "You were a cop for several years, and you were raised by one. You have an analytical mind. There's nothing wrong with that. Conquest might slip into your subconscious now and again, but you're more than the sum of your parts. Your perspective has been forged by your life, your job, your commitment to your community."

"You always know the right thing to say." I kissed him on the chin. "I like that about you."

The thing with Cole was he didn't believe in sugarcoating anything. Ever. So when he did give advice or his opinion, it was always worth hearing — no, worth *listening* to — and it was always one hundred percent from the heart.

"You'll feel better once we start patrolling. I volunteered us for the first shift."

"Aww." I placed a hand on my chest. "Be still my heart."

Proof positive the man was perfect. Setting eyes on the coterie was about the only thing that would settle my nerves.

"You guys aren't going to do any mushy stuff, are you?" Phoebe tromped in, dirt streaking her face, her hair wild, looking more like me every minute. "I heard kissy noises from outside and came in to remind you to keep it PG."

"We'll try not to disgust you too much." Unable to resist, I flung myself at Cole's back and shimmied up his body. "Oh, no. Phoebe, look away. I'm climbing your father like a tree."

"Gross." She backed up, slapping her hands over her eyes, until she hit the wall. "Make it stop."

"You'll have to endure the horror for like two more minutes." I kept climbing until I settled on his shoulders. "I need to hang a lantern and wedge an antenna in a crack somewhere up there." I snapped my fingers. "Pass me the goods, kid."

"Maybe I should have postponed my growth spurt," she grumbled, peeking between her fingers before lowering her hands. "This isn't how I imagined aiding the resistance."

"Right? Hollywood makes out like the end of the world is all human sacrifices and explosions, but it's pretty much like every other day until it's not." I snapped my fingers again. "Gimme."

Phoebe passed me the equipment as I requested it, and I finished rigging our station. She had chosen to bunk with us instead of Thom, which meant Cole and I couldn't get up to any questionable behavior. Not that we would, since that whole impending doom thing was happening. When the apocalypse happened, I did *not* want to be caught with my pants down. How embarrassing would that be? Definitely not what you want to go down in history about you.

"Phoebe, you get to guard the camp." I slid down Cole's back, and if I squeezed his butt where no one could see it, then sue me. I planned to enjoy him with all the time I had left. "Cole, you're with me."

He strapped on his sword and passed me mine. I had used it enough now that it felt less like I was marooned in a medieval cosplay fantasy and more like a natural extension of my body. I only wished I wasn't getting better the more I used it. It's not like I had been practicing, and it's not like I had taken any lessons. The more accomplished I became with a blade, the more I had to admit to myself that Conquest was seeping through the cracks she worked to widen in me every day.

The length of the island meant it would be a quick lap, but it would give us a chance to check in with each camp before we returned to our own. With stations at key points on the island, and the waters full of our aquatic allies, we were guaranteed a warning before the Malakhim converged on us. Even a few precious seconds could make all the difference.

The glow of screens announced we had found Santiago and Portia. They each held a tablet while several others fanned out around him. She was watching Netflix. He was ... I'm not sure. But it made me think he was busy rigging the island with cameras and motion detectors, anything to give us a slight advantage. And to keep his mind and hands occupied while the clock ticked in the backs of all our minds.

"Are you guys set?" I tried to come off as official-sounding, but the worry bled through. "Need anything?"

"All good." Portia stuffed a handful of buttered popcorn in her mouth then swore at the screen. "Don't choose him. He's a player. He just wants in your pants. Take that rose and stab him through the neck with it."

"You heard her." Santiago flicked his fingers at me. "Run along."

Annoyance zinging through me, I set off with Cole. "How did Conquest not eat him?"

"She must have assumed he would give her indigestion."

"He's the kind of person who would swallow a block of C4, shower in barbecue sauce, then allow himself to get swallowed with the detonator in his hand."

Cole burst out laughing, the sound bold enough to startle the scant birds in residence from the trees.

It wasn't often I tickled an actual laugh out of him, let alone one on this scale, and I felt downright proud of myself. Maybe Santiago was useful for something after all. He played the role of ass to the fullest, so he couldn't very well complain if that also made him the butt of a few jokes.

"I was hunting that pigeon," Thom grumbled, dropping in front of us from a scraggly tree limb over our heads. "It was fat and smelled like buttered popcorn."

That must be Portia's doing, though I had no idea where she got popcorn from unless Santiago packed it for her. Kernels hadn't been among the other supplies, neither had butter, or I might have been tempted to steal a cup to pop over the fire with Phoebe the way Dad had with me.

"I'm sorry." I placed a hand on my chest. "It's my fault."

Cole's shoulder still bounced with amusement, and I couldn't find it in me to nudge him to silence.

"I saw gulls near the water." Thom scanned behind us. "They're not as fat, but they do smell like fish."

"Well, there you go." I examined the sagging brick structure behind him. "Where's Miller?"

"Mixing explosives." He twitched his nose. "He's in the far corner, beneath the largest hole in the ceiling. Make noise if you go in, let him know you're coming."

"I don't want to startle him into blowing off any appendages."

I took a healthy step back so as not to disturb him. "We're just checking in. There's no need to distract him." I didn't spot the third wheel to their party. "What about Rixton?"

"He's helping."

"Then I'm definitely not going in there." I rocked back on my heels. "I want plausible deniability if Rixton blasts himself into next week."

"We drew the next patrol." Thom's attention kept sliding past me to where I heard the call of seabirds. "We'll be around to you in an hour. You can check on them then."

"Sounds good." Cole and I left Thom to hunt his dinner. "Did Wu tell you where to find him?"

"No."

"You're going to love this." Not long after, we came across a chapel. Its stained-glass windows had been broken long ago, but the frame hinted at the design, and it had once been beautiful. "Irony, am I right?"

This time I didn't earn so much as a grin from him, and I was starting to wish I had kept my mouth shut when I spotted the reason for his quiet.

Kapoor perched on the roof, his body black as a crow, his eyes dark as the oncoming night.

"Wu isn't here," he murmured absently, staring across the Sound. "He'll be back soon."

Alarm zinged down my spine. "Where did he go?"

"He didn't say." He reached down to scratch his ankle where a black cord wound around it and knotted to a nearby dormer. "Do you think we'll go hunting soon?"

Forget a crow. The tether and the question put me in mind of a falcon's jesses. From here, he resembled a bird of prey eager for his master to unleash him on a target. The regression into a more primal version of himself worried me almost as much as the way he kept wetting his lips, like his prey was so close he could taste it.

"Soon," I promised him and backed away without pressing him for details.

God only knew where Wu had flitted off to or when he would return. *If* he would return. He wasn't known for keeping us in the loop, so I shouldn't be surprised to learn he had waited until the eleventh hour to run his own errands without telling us first. It's not like he was the one who kickstarted the apocalypse.

Oh, wait.

Yeah.

He was.

"We should go take care of dinner." I started back in the direction of our camp. "We need to eat before it gets too late."

"There's no rush. The solar panels have stored enough energy to heat our meals."

MREs were not my favorite thing, but I had eaten boatloads of them. Lot of folks left the military to join the police force, and tons of them brought those as novelties to inflict on their friends and family.

A text from Santiago informed us he had the island under surveillance. Foot patrols were now optional.

Just how many solar panels had he smuggled over? There were phone chargers, lights, a stove for each camp and a tangle of cords in the bottom of the bag we hadn't gotten to yet.

As much as I liked to kid that Santiago was living his prepper dreams, I was starting to think the joke had been on me. None of his equipment required charging. He had it ready to go the second the need arose. Not only had he already owned it, but he had assembled it and topped off the batteries.

"The next time we make our rounds," I said, "we should check in with our allies. See who's arrived."

Since we had decided each camp would take turns walking the perimeter, we had three hours until our next rotation. Regardless of what Santiago said, I wanted us active. How else could we gain Ezra's attention? With Wu MIA and Kapoor in his peculiar state, I wasn't trusting either of them to pull their weight. I would much rather Kapoor keep right on roosting. Pretty sure the cord around his ankle was just that. A string. I bet Wu had leashed him with an order then left him bound as a tangible reminder in his absence. Meaning Kapoor could blast off in pursuit of Ezra if his instincts overwhelmed him.

"Death and Janardan will seek us out when they arrive." Cole kept pace with me. "The Diorte have a longer trip ahead of them. Any allies they recruit will be along the way. Odds are good we're the first ones here."

"You're probably right." Shaking out my arms, I exhaled through my mouth. "I'm getting antsy."

Cole parted his lips, about to reply, when a plume of dirt exploded beside us. He dove for me, knocking me to the ground, and covered me with his body. His heart pounded against my chest, and I struggled to shove him off. There was no way I was letting him play shield for me. Not this time.

"Sorry, I didn't see you there."

With my ears ringing, I couldn't identify the voice, but people who intended to blast you to kingdom come usually didn't apologize for it afterward. That implied this was friendly fire.

The mountain on top of me rolled aside, stood, and helped me to my feet.

Miller rushed over with a jar of white powder, a teaspoon, and a pocketful of plastic Easter eggs.

"Thom said you circled back. I thought you would have reached your camp by now." He blinked several times, his eyes red and watering. "I didn't expect you to be out here."

"Can you see?" I started toward him. "At all?" I caught a whiff of what he held and stumbled back. "What is that?"

"It's a recipe I brought from home, modified for this terrene." He held up an egg. "I miscalculated on the first batch. This one is better."

This close, I could see he was missing one eyebrow and his eyelashes were matted snarls. His eyes were demon-red with inflammation, and his complexion would make lobsters envious. His tee was charred, with a hole eaten through the center, the skin beneath crispy.

"I'll have to take your word for it." This was the kind of reckless behavior I expected out of Santiago, not Miller. Usually, he was far too cautious to make such a careless mistake. "Should I take you to Thom?"

"He's already patched me up." He shifted the materials in his hands. "He said I'll be fully recovered within the hour."

"And you thought — Hey, I'm half blind. Now is a great time to randomly lob homemade grenades on an island only populated by my coterie?"

"We need more practical weapons," he countered. "Fast." He lifted one of the eggs. "There are humans here."

Ah. Now we got to the ooey-gooey heart of the matter.

"Technically, there's only one human here. Maggie is a charun host, and that makes her sturdier than the average mortal."

"She has no battle form, no fangs, no scales, no venom, no claws. All Maggie has is soft, pink skin, and Portia is only as durable as the body she inhabits."

None of this explained why he felt his time was better spent mixing homemade explosives. Santiago must have packed one of every weapon known to man. For this exact reason. He wanted Portia armed so she could protect herself. That meant Maggie was also covered. Literally. Santiago had altered the suit of flexible armor he made for her. They were wearing it now. There must be more to this, but I couldn't see the angle.

"Miller." As much as I hated playing devil's advocate, someone had to do it. "What if she had been the one out here walking instead of us?" His stricken expression caused my heart to physically ache. "I know you want to protect her, but you have to take care of yourself too. What would she say if she saw you right now? You look like you stuck your spoon in a light socket, and the light socket won."

Glancing away, he mumbled, "She would be mad."

"Santiago made her suit up before we came to the island," I reminded him. "You saw Rixton wear the suit in battle. You know how durable it is. It can save human lives. It could save their life if it comes down to it."

Thankfully, Santiago had an earlier prototype far enough along he was able to modify that one for Rixton. Since it didn't have any sequins, Rixton didn't complain much. Even if it had saggy flaps across his chest meant to accommodate the larger boobs of the host Portia had been inhabiting at the time.

"Go clean yourself up." To make sure he did as he was told, I hit below the belt. "I'm going to tell Maggie you got hurt mixing chemicals. I'm sure she'll be around to lecture you more thoroughly within the next hour or so."

Miller whipped his head toward me. "Luce —"

"Nope." I turned to go. "That's your punishment. Suck it up and deal."

Once we reached our camp, I wrestled with an uncharitable thought that popped into my head.

"You don't think he did it on purpose?" I scanned the area behind us, but it's not like I could see him. It was full dark now, and he had retreated back to his camp. "That would be ... diabolical."

He had given himself a boo-boo in an uncharacteristically reckless manner, drawn our attention to it by compounding his mistake. He almost blew us sky high, ensuring I would use Maggie as a threat and likely tattle on him even if he did as he was told. Talk about a perfect excuse for Maggie to take the reins and ditch Santiago in the middle of Portia's movie night.

"Coterie dynamics give me a headache." I massaged my forehead. "Did we pack any aspirin?"

Digital alarms screamed into the night, and I dropped my arm, muscles clenching in anticipation.

Cold sweat beaded on my spine, and I tasted frost when a second plume of dirt shot high in the air.

Always the first to scent Conquest on me, Cole angled his face away before I read his expression.

Phoebe leapt the rubble to join us. "The Malakhim are here."

We had seconds to spare, a formation to determine, but I wasted them gathering Cole and Phoebe to me in a hug that lasted the length of a heartbeat.

When I turned them loose, they traded their human skins for their dragons. Since one of us had to be able to communicate with our allies, most of which had mastered English, that left me on two legs until the absolute last possible second.

"Here we go," I said under my breath and leapt onto Cole's back. "Move to defend the right side of the island." That's where our most vulnerable were stationed, not that I would ever say that to Rixton's face. "We need to give Miller and the others a chance to make a dent in their lines."

From high above the island, I had a bird's eye view of the Malakhim host, three times the size of the last one, an almost incomprehensible number, converging on us. Heart in my throat, I twined my fingers in Cole's mane and swallowed the impulse to tell him I loved him. He knew, and I knew he knew.

I couldn't distract him with sentiment. I had to focus, to let him focus too.

Sweat turned my palms clammy as I waited for our first line of defense to strike, and when it came, I sucked in a shocked breath as a robust Diorte leapt from the water and swallowed two Malakhim whole. The kill bloodied the waters, so to speak, and I sat back and gaped as a chain reaction sent more of the massive beasts rocketing out of the water where they devoured our enemies in twos and threes before slashing down, soaking others and causing them to lose altitude.

Now, I had watched enough Discovery Channel in my day to know great white sharks achieved insane air when they breached off the coast of Seal Island near Cape Town, South Africa. But I hadn't been ready to witness similar feats in person. Neither had the Malakhim.

Cries rang out, and their neat lines scattered as more and bigger creatures began preying on them. Their slow advance toward the island became a race to avoid becoming fish food.

As soon as the Malakhim crossed over dry land, plumes of dirt blasted them, blinding them, giving Rixton a chance to hurl more of Miller's bombs at them to blast through what remained of their front lines.

There was no question of when Death joined the fray. The smell would have clued me in even if the shock of watching corpses in various stages of decay claw their way free of the earth hadn't explained why she had chosen this place. That earlier kernel of hope, barely a wish, blossomed as she worked her magic on a scale I had been too afraid to dream. Her forces came in all sizes, some nothing but bone, others fresh enough to make my eyes water, more caught between the extremes.

Our numbers doubled, then tripled, then quadrupled as she summoned the slumbering dead to our aid.

They swarmed the fallen Malakhim brought down by the coterie and tore them to pieces with their brittle hands and cracked teeth then moved on to the next victim and the next, leaving a trail of wings, blood, and feathers in their wake.

Death wavered on her feet, the strain on her obvious, but she kept her arms upraised while Janardan and her coterie guarded her from attack.

The tide was far from turning, but we had a better chance now than when we started. I'd take it.

The best thing about Death's risen army was they were already dead. They had nothing to lose, and that's how they fought. Frenzied. Maddened. Frantic. They cut through Malakhim like winning meant they could claw their way back to life.

I watched a second longer then jerked my attention away from Death, who clearly had things under control, to pinpoint Phoebe, a master of invisibility if ever there was one.

I had pictured myself as a general yelling orders to her troops, but my troops had it under control. Or maybe it was just that at this point, all the hard calls had already been made. There was no time left. This was happening.

Now.

Right now.

Finally.

Sliding off Cole's back, I embraced my inner dragon, shifting in midair, trusting that form to save me.

A feminine roar blasted over my shoulder as Phoebe flanked me, covering me while I gained my bearings. As soon as my wings quit wobbling, she was gone. Vanished. But I tracked her steady progress via Malakhim dropping from the sky without a scratch on them.

Since it was a favorite move of mine, I didn't have to see her to know she was snapping their necks with hard cracks from her muscular tail.

The hitch in my chest winded me, but there was no time to mourn her loss of innocence. I had to do my part. And, as much as I hated it, so did she.

Gunshots rang out below where Rixton clipped a Malakhim, wounding him enough for Portia to …

A harpoon gun? How did …? Who authorized that?

Sure enough, Portia gut shot a Malakhim with the massive rod, its hooked end punching through the wannabe angel's back, then she and Rixton pulled him down using the attached cord. As soon as their victim got within range, she lopped off his head, he tossed the body, and they began the cycle again.

Santiago was nowhere to be seen, but he was aquatic. He might have taken to the water with our allies.

What gave me heart palpitations was Thom's absence, but it was too late to worry for him. I would have to trust him to stay alive until I found him again.

Throwing myself into the fray, I knocked Malakhim out of the sky to give Portia and Rixton easier targets. The ones who dodged the punishing strength of my tail, I bit until they crunched like a thin layer of chocolate shell over vanilla ice cream then spit them into the water.

We were holding the island, but the host numbered in the hundreds, and there was no sign of Ezra.

This was his party. He damn well better put in an appearance.

Cole zipped away to strike down a clot of Malakhim attempting to fly with their backs to each other. He didn't have to work hard to send them crashing into the mouth of waiting Diorte. Their tangled wings had all but done the work for him.

A blur of movement below me gave me Miller's ETA. He must have run out of ammo or dropped it off with Rixton and Portia. He sure couldn't use it now. His snake form coiled and sprung, his jaws unhinging to gulp down his prey, weapons and all.

The relentless tide of the opposition pounded us, but we hit back twice as hard, not gaining any ground but not losing any either. The Malakhim took staggering losses, but they kept on coming. We couldn't keep this up forever. At this rate, we would be exhausted when and if Ezra arrived. Hell, we might fall asleep on our feet before he got here.

Please, God, if ever you wanted to prove your existence, now would be a great time.

No miracle manifested, not that I had expected one, which, honestly, might have been the whole problem. Faith. Or a severe lack thereof.

A ripple flowed through the Malakhim, a reordering of ranks, and half of them pivoted to face the rear.

Heart booming in my ears, I prayed even harder, both terrified and relieved this might be the coming of Ezra. The end or the beginning, I couldn't tell yet.

But as a yowling chorus rose, thousands of cats hissing and screaming, and other war cries besides, I was left more confused than ever.

What the actual hell?

Then I saw them, and I wept with gratitude.

I had no idea how Santiago organized this second wave, but I had no doubt he was the one responsible. He had gathered these allies to us, after all, and despite my hopes we could win this on our own, he was reminding me I didn't have to do this alone.

Burnt-orange bobcats with purple wings. Mothlike fighters with their antennae curled tight to their skulls. Beyond the more familiar spread our newer allies, their feline aspects tagging them as ours.

Tabby stripes, marmalade, tortoiseshell fur. Round ears, pointed ears, folded ears. Tails, nubs, tailless. Claws, nails, talons.

All colors and shapes and sizes, all armed and spoiling for a fight if their pinned-back ears were any indication.

Flying cats versus birdmen.

Life didn't get any weirder than this.

The clash when their frontline met the Malakhim's rearguard was earsplitting with all the caterwauling, but it was music to my ears. The Malakhim compressed in the air, fighting in close quarters, threatening to knock each other down with dueling wings vying for the same airspace.

The tide was turning in our favor. We were *winning*.

But where was Ezra?

The flagging Malakhim screamed their own challenge, a throaty morale boost with no origin I could identify.

That couldn't be good.

As much as I didn't want to eat more people, I let the dragon's instincts rule me, and she had no qualms about filling her belly. I couldn't say for sure it was Conquest goading me. It might have been pure instinct. Either way, the battle spun out, faded, as I threw myself into staying alive.

A burst of dazzling light on the horizon set my heart pounding double time.

He was here.

Ezra was here.

What have I done?

Unbidden, the crystalline voice I recognized as Conquest answered, *"What must be done."*

Unable to let either of them distract me, I kept plowing through the vanguard, stealing glimpses of the coterie from the corner of my eye. They hadn't spotted Ezra yet. Cole would know what the light show meant, assuming Wu hadn't been improvising when he busted us out of the bunker, but the others might not grasp its significance.

Wu.

Damn it.

In the chaos, I had forgotten him. Now that I thought about it, I hadn't seen Kapoor either.

I couldn't very well press pause on the action while I hunted them down, and then, I didn't have to wonder.

Wu had shucked his usual business casual appearance in favor of donning the uniform of the Malakhim, a fancier version, sure, but it stated his allegiance louder and clearer than if he'd worn a *Daddy's Boy* T-shirt with matching pacifier.

That fucking coward had switched sides.

Cole hovered beside me, noticing the same thing and showing about as much surprise as I felt.

I had never wished so hard to be holding a harpoon gun of my own. I would aim that sucker and fire a bolt straight through Wu's treacherous heart. Assuming he had one. It might be safer just to spear him through the head, feed him to a Diorte, and call it a day.

No wonder he made a point of hammering home the fact we couldn't kill him without killing me too. What he had done to me paled in comparison to this epic betrayal. With the enclave safe across the ocean, he must have decided to crawl home to Daddy before things got hard. Did he really think Ezra would let the enclave live now that he knew about them? What a colossal idiot. Or maybe that was just me.

Eager to lead this charge, I could taste his blood in my mouth, and I salivated at the chance for payback.

A blast of pure, white light exploded across my field of vision, and I had to blink away spots.

Wu hadn't changed his position, so the angle of the flare was wrong for him. That must mean ... Ezra was coming. I half expected his father to bail since his son was kind enough to lead the charge for him. But no, he was here. I couldn't see him yet, but I could track him by his glow if he didn't dial it down.

The fighting tapered off as Wu approached, the Malakhim looking to him for guidance, and it cost them. The Cuprina-led contingent closing in behind them showed our enemies no mercy. Wu didn't cross over onto land but stayed above the water, out of range of our allies.

"Conquest," he intoned. "You are a blight on this world."

These guys really loved name-calling. Too bad I wasn't human at the moment. I would have hurled a few choice names back at him. I had to settle for hissing through my very sharp, very blood-stained teeth.

"Come with me." He held out a golden rope that shone with power and reminded me of a juiced-up version of the tether he left tied around Kapoor's ankle. "I give my word your coterie will not be harmed if you cooperate. You can end this without further bloodshed."

The dangerous growl rumbling through Cole was fierce, a promise of violence if Wu tried getting that noose around my neck or anything else.

Honestly, it gave me warm fuzzies. Harpoon guns aside, I would pay good money to watch Cole take a bite out of Wu.

"This is your final warning." His face remained impassive, blank like he had never met me, never fought alongside me. "Come with me, or you will all perish."

"Suck it," Rixton yelled from below us. "You're a fucking liar and a Wonder Woman wannabe. Lasso of Truth? Really? The irony."

The harpoon gun lay buried in the sand. It must have run out of ammo. Ah, well. There went that fantasy.

"What he said," Portia hollered, fury vibrating through her. "Get down here so I can kick your feathery ass."

Wu ignored them and adjusted the loop, allowing the rope to hang at his side. "Father will not be pleased."

"No one cares about your daddy issues." Santiago ran from the direction of the largest structure, his hair and clothes soaked through. "I've been wanting to do this for a long time." He aimed a grenade launcher at Wu. "Boom, baby."

The blast didn't so much as dent Wu, but it did hurl him several yards away, and it knocked the closest Malakhim down with a splash.

I still had to suppress the urge to clap. It was no harpoon gun, but it was a decent substitute.

"I told you it wasn't powerful enough," he griped at Miller. "You should have added more —"

Portia snatched the weapon from him, rested it on her shoulder, and fired again. Wu took her shot in the chest. His altitude dipped as he shook it off, but we had lost the element of surprise, and he was prepared to counter direct hits.

Damn it.

We should have let that tree finish him off when we had the chance.

"This is not good." Portia dropped the weapon and pulled a sword. "Hope you've got a Plan B."

"Do you not see the flying cat brigade?" Santiago growled. "That's our Plan B."

Shock painted her face with comical surprise. "But Luce said —"

"She says a lot of things I ignore," he scoffed. "That's how I've managed to keep her alive this long."

Warming up her arm, blade glistening, she said, "Plan C it is then."

"*Luce.*"

Dragon brain rejected the name until I heard it called again and spotted Death wading into the water. Arms reaching over her head, she called for me again.

Here goes nothing.

With a nod, I blazed a path toward her — and Wu.

Wings, don't fail me now.

I dipped low and managed to wrap her upper body with my tail. She held on tight and started to climb up my body. The added weight wasn't the issue. The problem was I was still new enough to flying to require my tail's assistance. Add to that she was climbing up my back, causing my wings to brush against her, throwing off my rhythm, and costing me precious altitude.

The water shone, mirrorlike beneath me, the waves flecking my belly with crimson foam. We were going to hit the water. I couldn't see any way to correct myself.

Then Cole was there, lifting me, positioning me to finish the climb alone. Once I topped out, I breathed a sigh of relief that Death echoed as she settled between my shoulder blades.

Thank God, Wu hadn't sunk me when he had the chance.

Talk about missing a prime opportunity. He could have captured me there and then, and I couldn't have done a thing about it.

An itty, bitty part of me processed that apparent stroke of luck, and an even ittier, bittier part of me wondered at my fortune.

"We have one chance," she yelled over the noise. "Take me to Ezra."

Wu was the closer target, but she must be thinking the same thing that kept running on a loop through my head.

Kill him, I die.

Kill me, he dies.

What the actual hell was he thinking, standing between his father and me? Before I had to risk my luck or fortune or — dare I think his conscience — a second time, Cole barreled into Wu and sent him spinning aside, clearing us a path. Without looking back, I took it. We shot straight down the gauntlet formed by our allies beating back the Malakhim.

Rising onto her feet, Death dug her toes into my spine. She flung out her arms, and power radiated from her in a creeping wave. Malakhim dropped around us like flies to the cheers of the feline contingent. There was no outrunning Death. Before she had required contact. Now she had transcended, throwing her will at our enemies, battering them out of the sky.

Ahead of us, the impossibly bright center of their army shone upon us. I was outrunning my terror, but it was catching up to me.

I zipped past Ezra, close enough to feel the beat of his wings stir my mane, and Death leapt from my back.

No, no, no.

A scream ripped from my throat, coming out as an agonized roar as she struck him. Leaning in, she gave him a kiss, and his power dimmed a fraction. Ezra wiped his mouth and spat, his glow dialing higher. He struck her across the face for the impertinence, and she plummeted.

Clumsy in this body, I couldn't cut a tight enough circle to beat the nearest Malakhim to her. They caught her between them and pierced her body with their blades. Five, six. Seven of them. Skewering her. Over and over. Malice in their eyes and hate in their hearts. Then they dropped her like garbage.

I dove after her, caught her by some miracle, and spun us away from Ezra. Clutching her in my talons, I sped for land. I shifted when my feet touched dirt, a scream for Thom lodged in my throat, and he came running. I laid her on the ground and took her hand, holding on tight.

"It's going to be okay," I kept repeating. "It's going to be okay."

Janardan emerged from the shallows and ran for us. He dropped to his knees beside Death, and she smiled at him, her teeth bloody.

"It was worth it, my love." He kissed her softly. "To fight on the right side for once."

Her eyes closed, and Thom swore, redoubling his efforts, but nothing he tried brought her around again.

Janardan fell backward a heartbeat later, his eyes wide and unseeing.

Whipping my head toward the Sound, I watched the bodies of her children bob to the surface.

Death was gone, and she had taken her coterie with her.

The dead she had brought to life dropped where they stood. Corpses littered the island, washed up on the shore. Our advantage had been lost. The numbers tipped back in their favor. I had no choice but to leave her with Thom and take to the skies to knock as many Malakhim into the water as possible before they overtook us.

That burst of power must have used up all her reserves. Death had pitched her might against Ezra and failed. How could I hope to best him?

Wild panic fluttered in my breast, a frenzied storm of emotion hammering out a single message.

Run, run, run.

We had kicked a hornet's nest, and the enemy swarmed us.

Run, run, run.

There was nowhere to go.

Run, run, run.

There was nowhere left to hide.

Run, run, run.

I always thought the world — my corner of it at least — would end in Canton, but I saw now that was the best-case scenario. The one where we beat Ezra then Wu and I went on to seal this terrene.

This was as far from the best-case as it got. This was beyond worst-case. This was total failure. This was . . . the end.

I was the last cadre member standing, and I had conveniently placed my entire coterie on an island to make it easier for the Malakhim to pick them off at Ezra's discretion.

After all this, I had failed. I wasn't breaking any cycles. The cycle was breaking me.

CHAPTER SEVENTEEN

Adam kept his face impassive as Death and her coterie passed from this world. Luce hunched over her sister, her heart breaking for a woman she had barely known, and Adam hated himself that much more. He had allowed this to happen. He had known Death would end here, and he had done nothing to stop it. The inaction was critical to his plan. Had he attempted to save her, his father would have known his contrition was an act, and he had come too far to throw it all away for one life. Even one life animating many.

Luce wouldn't forgive him for her sister. She had grown attached to Death, and her mate was a good friend to Cole. They would mourn them, but grieving meant they were still alive, at least for a while longer.

The pretentious light glaring on his periphery dimmed as another body joined the other guards who hovered between him and Ezra.

Once his father would have welcomed him with open arms, now he kept precautions in place.

Father relaxed as the numbers shifted in his favor again, but not enough. As pleased as he was to rub yet another failed coup in Adam's face, he remained on edge. Luce was the wild card in this scenario, and he watched her with an intensity that bordered on obsession, a fixation Adam wished he didn't share.

Father wanted her dead so badly Adam could taste it, and it was sweet.

A smile tickled his lips, but he couldn't allow it to surface.

His father was afraid. Of Luce. Of what she represented.

Change.

The sands of his rule were slipping through his manicured fingers, and he could no more catch each grain than he could prevent this final reckoning. The bill for all his sins had come due, and he would pay it here, now.

"Finish her."

The order broke through Adam's reverie. "Yes, Father."

"Bring me her head." He turned as if to go. "Do this, son, and all is forgiven."

Ezra was that certain he had kicked this dog until he had no bite left. That convinced he had nothing to fear from his offspring. He gave an order, and he expected it to be followed for no greater reason than he wished it done.

He. Turned. His. Back.

The simple act compounded centuries of abuse until the veneer of the dutiful son crackled, fissures spreading across Adam's face until the submissive expression he had arranged on his features before crawling back to his father shattered into fragments too small to ever be realigned.

Adam barked an order in Otillian, the common tongue, and movement stirred on the island.

Father had never lowered himself to master the language, and few of his Malakhim had an ear for it since they were trained to believe the fabrications Ezra spun like silk from a spinneret.

So unconcerned was he, so confident in his victory over Adam, and Luce, he didn't look back.

A missile of black feathers and horns bowled through the regrouping Malakhim in the rearguard and struck Ezra in the spine. Kapoor was wrath incarnate as he wrapped his legs around Ezra's waist and howled with all the anguish of the tortures that had been inflicted upon him.

Faster than even Adam could track, Kapoor produced twin daggers, pressed them to the topmost wing joints fused to Ezra's shoulders, and began to cut.

Ezra screamed when Kapoor sheared his uppermost wings.

Adam closed his eyes and listened to the singular note, the most beautiful sound he had ever heard.

Victory.

The Malakhim froze as one at the cry, pivoting in the air to race to their master's rescue.

Much to Adam's regret, he had no time to watch Kapoor exact his vengeance. If he wanted it complete, he had to defend Kapoor before backup reached them. Adam fought off the winged masses for as long as he could, until his arms burned, and his wings labored to keep him aloft. He heard nothing from behind him, but he couldn't afford to turn and check.

The magnitude of Ezra's charm might have smashed through the command Adam gave Kapoor. He wasn't sure which of their wills would prevail when pitting father against son, and it made him sick to picture the battle waging behind him, to know he had thrown Kapoor into the fire again and abandoned him to burn alone. Yards might separate them, but it might as well have been miles for all the good it did him.

The worst mistake Kapoor ever made was deciding Adam was his friend. It was an honor he wasn't worthy of, a claim he should have rebuked, a death sentence for the other man. But Adam saw the value in Kapoor, nurtured that relationship, and turned him toward his own goals.

Luce was right. He was a bastard.

But he wouldn't be one for much longer.

A loud splash jerked Adam toward the water.

Kapoor was down. Blood smeared his face. His wings twisted behind him. A slash opened his abdomen.

Three of Ezra's wings drifted on the current around Kapoor, all of them uppermost wings, the strongest ones, the largest ones, the ones that kept charun like them airborne. Ezra was gravely wounded, but ego and pride kept him from grasping the full extent of the damage.

Or, he thought again as his father barreled toward him, it was rage that blinded him to everything but the thirst for retribution.

At last his father understood how parched the throat grew when one thing alone could quench you. He wished his father was less dangerous, less capable. He wished he could rip the final wings from his back and toss him to the earth to wander as a man. But that was idiocy. Left to his own devices, Ezra would find new ways to enthrall the weak-minded until he amassed another army of blindly loyal followers. That was his gift.

No, he had to die. That was the only way for them to be certain.

Adam might have set up the dominos, but his father had knocked them down, setting off a chain reaction that had been centuries in the making. He could have prevented this reckoning, so many times in so many ways, but mercy — like Otillian — wasn't a language his father understood.

What Adam had helped Ezra forget over the long centuries was the nature of the magic in the blades he had entrusted to the janitor to aid him in his duties. Their power, the reason they killed charun, was they turned their victims mortal. Not for long. A few minutes or hours, depending on their strength. Just long enough to mortally wound them and then hunt them to ground.

Adam knew this because he had forged the blades himself from the precious metal he harvested from several previous incarnations of Death. Each time he killed one, he collected the metal from her *rukav* and bided his time until he had enough, until he had learned enough, to create the twin daggers.

As gifts.

For his father.

And then, after his father was done being amused by them, Adam let enough time pass before he proposed allowing a trusted charun to wield them.

The miracle was not that his father allowed it. He viewed himself as invulnerable, after all. The true miracle was that Kapoor hadn't stabbed Adam through the heart decades ago. He should have. Adam deserved that and more.

Ezra slammed into Adam, the force clacked his teeth together, and he tasted copper. But he didn't have to squint. The light had drained from his father like a switch flipped. Only rage made him incandescent now.

"You dare?" Crimson spittle flew from his lips. "You would choose this whore over your own blood?"

There was no point in taking offense. All women were whores to his father. Including his own mother. Adam had wondered, for a time, if he begrudged the fairer sex their ability to reproduce, to create life. Ezra might be able to control who and what they birthed into the world, but he was reliant on them to give him Malakhim, and that contrasted sharply with the legend he had woven around himself.

"I'm choosing my blood." Adam unsheathed a short dagger from his hip. "With you dead, my descendants will know peace.

Finally. They will thrive." He spun it on his palm. "They will never know the woman who birthed their line, because you killed her out of spite, but I remember. I will never forget her." He slid the blade between Ezra's ribs and wished he relished the moment of shock, but he mostly felt the bruises forming from Cole shoving him out of Luce's path and the aches and pains that came from battle. "Her death sealed our fates."

"I can't," Ezra murmured, confusion tightening his features. "Die."

Wu twisted the blade, and blood poured over his hand. The light went out of his father's eyes, and he didn't recognize the man without his charm. In death, he was rendered ordinary. Ezra would have hated that.

"Yes." He let go of his father's body. "You can."

Ezra plummeted, but the Malakhim didn't let him hit the water. They swarmed him, attempting to protect him, but it was too late. He was dead and gone.

Adam had been wrong. Revenge didn't taste sweet. It tasted like the copper in his mouth and the bile in his throat. It didn't heal him, mend him, or otherwise repair his tattered spirit. It gave him . . . relief. But the well of his soul had gone dry too long ago to dredge up more than that.

No wonder Luce's eyes held pity when she looked at him. She had seen the truth of him, the frayed edges hidden beneath the slick veneer, and known on an instinctive level there was nothing left in him to give.

Adam was burnt out, a cinder, while Cole had roared his defiance and fought her every step of the way until she won him over with the raging tempest of her soul. He almost hoped their mate bond was strong enough to end Cole's life after the terrenes were sealed. He wouldn't want to live on without her. Adam knew from personal experience.

He searched for Kapoor, but he couldn't find a body among the hundreds already chumming the waters.

When he was spent, he returned to the shore to face his judgement.

CHAPTER EIGHTEEN

———⊷◉⊶———

Good thing the enemy was retreating, our allies in hot pursuit. I hadn't budged since Ezra dropped like a rock from the sky, a comet extinguishing as it landed in the arms of its fellows. I couldn't seem to get my arms or legs to work. I couldn't get my brain to work either.

Shock.

This was shock.

I had grown so numb that I was just as stunned to find myself dumbfounded as by what I had witnessed.

Ezra was dead.

Dead.

Wu would have gone after him if that wasn't the case. He had come this far. He would have finished it.

Guess this meant he wasn't a traitor, depending whose side you were on.

God, I was so tired of questioning his loyalties. I couldn't keep up with his switchback maneuvering.

After all the talk and prep work, all the months of recruiting, all the cutting of ties, I didn't have to lift a finger. I never even met Ezra. He would forever be a glint on a horizon, a figure spied across a battlefield, a person unknown.

For all that I had fought and bled and cried to reach this point, victory rang hollow. I hadn't fulfilled some epic destiny. Ezra's blood didn't coat my hands. More than ever, I felt like the tool Wu had fashioned me to be. This must have been his plan all along. He wanted top billing, claiming his father's final moments for himself. It's not that I was eager to kill anyone, but I had done nothing any cadre member couldn't have done before or after me. At least not yet.

The reason for cultivating me had never been clearer.

Killing his father hadn't been the issue. He just proved that. With the enclave's help, he could have rallied enough charun to defeat the Malakhim or at least cripple them until he was ready to make his move.

My sole purpose in this war was to play martyr. No wonder Wu hadn't fessed up to my role sooner. If Kapoor hadn't told me, I'm not sure Wu would have until the last possible second. How he would have explained it then, I have no clue, and it didn't matter anyway. Not now.

I was breaking Cole's heart. He just didn't feel the cracks spreading yet.

The coterie would be furious, their hearts dented too, but they would live.

They would all *live*.

The temporary reprieve bogged me down until I couldn't have budged even if my limbs had been feeling cooperative. Guilt hit hard and fast soon after.

Death had given her life, the lives of her mate and their children, to spare mine. So had Kapoor. So had countless others. Our allies arrived when I had given up hope. Their loyalty and sacrifices would not be forgotten.

All I could do was pray Wu had a plan to protect my people. After. I wouldn't sacrifice them. I had lost too much to give up more.

I hit my knees and retched until I emptied my stomach. As much as I wanted to shy away from the tender caress of Cole's fingers down my spine, I was too spent. I accepted his comfort, hating myself for that weakness the whole time.

I plopped down on my butt once I was certain I was done. As if it mattered one bit if I got vomit on me when I was drenched in blood and other things. The smell might even be an improvement. That thought sent me into a laughing fit, and I flopped onto my back to stare up at the gloriously Malakhim-free sky.

"She's off her rocker." Santiago limped into view. "She finally cracked."

"She's relieved," Miller rasped, leaning on Maggie for support. "It's over. We won."

Phoebe landed nearby, shed her dragon skin, and curled against my side, her arm around my waist.

"What a story this will make." Thom plopped down beside me. "The two-souled demon who saved the world from angels."

"We're charun," I corrected him primly. "Not demons."

He laughed softly and leaned against my other side, happy to have lured me out of my hysterics.

"Wu is coming this way." Santiago tightened his grip on a sword he had taken off one of the bodies. "Can I kill him now?"

"Not yet." With great and terrible reluctance, I nudged Phoebe aside and shoved upright to face him. But I didn't get to my feet. I was too damn tired. "Are you here to double-cross me too? Triple-cross? Quadruple-cross? You'll have to forgive me. I can't keep up."

"I didn't expect gratitude," he began.

"Good," Maggie spat. "You won't find any here."

The barbed tone was far more Portia than Maggie, but my friend maintained her control over her body.

"I arranged for a meeting with Father," he started again.

"That's why you left Kapoor tied out," I realized. "He didn't know where you had gone."

And had Wu confessed, Kapoor would have fought him to join him. The urge to hunt was too strong.

"I promised Ezra I would deliver you to him." Wu kept going in an almost apologetic tone. "You had fortified the island. You had rallied the allies best suited to aid you. This was as ideal a situation as any. I convinced Father he could lead his forces to certain victory and crush the legend you were creating in his fist."

"How did you kill him?" I drew my knees to my chest and hooked my arms around them to anchor me. It was that or fall backward and risk not getting up again. "You never explained that part of your plan, and I figured that meant you didn't have one. I expected us to wing it."

Wing it.

Because he had so many.

God, Luce. Hold it together.

"Cole isn't the first to consider there might be other uses for the metals each member of the cadre produces. The individual properties are specific to each incarnation, a quirk we discovered some time ago." He glossed over the whole experimentation angle being how they came to make these scientific breakthroughs. "Death produces the least of all the cadre. It's theorized that since she reanimates her children, which puts her in total control of them, she requires less to bind them to her."

That much made sense at least. "Okay."

"I collected the metal over a period of ascensions, from multiple incarnations, and then I forged a blade. When it proved successful, I made it a twin, and then I destroyed all my research so it couldn't be done again. Not without resources enough to subdue and harvest from cadre, and the list of people outside our organization capable of such a feat were too few to worry me."

"I'll go out on a limb and say those were the black daggers Kapoor was wielding when he took down Ezra." The action happened too far away for me to discern any details that made them special, but they did the trick. There was no disputing that. "Are the blades poisoned?"

"The metal doesn't kill charun. Not in the way you mean. It isn't poison, and it doesn't drop them the way Death's gift works when she wields it. It turns the immortal mortal. It makes charun as easy to kill as a human."

The implications sank in, and I grasped what he wasn't saying, what he wouldn't dare speak in front of Cole and the others, who thought the worst was over.

Two blades. Two sacrifices. Two very hard to kill charun.

He meant for us each to take one to the seal where we entered this world and take our lives with them.

The span of years he had plotted and planned for this boggled the mind. I was too human in my thinking to encompass that much time devoted to revenge. He had looked at his life and understood there was no point in searching for love again and that procreation was too dangerous. His father wouldn't let him choose his own mate, and he would rather cut down his grandchildren than claim them.

"Are you sure he's dead?" Miller sat to relieve Maggie of her burden. "The Malakhim carried him away."

"They don't understand death." Wu shook his head. "Not in relation to him."

Their god had fallen, and they had no frame of reference for what that meant. Ezra had trained the ability to think as individuals out of them until they were a united whole. No doubt they would follow whatever protocol matched this scenario closest, and then they would sit and stare at one another until help came to give them fresh purpose.

Had they not killed so many with their boundless hatred, I might have pitied them.

"But he is dead," Santiago pressed, as eager as the rest of us for confirmation. "It's over."

"He's dead," Wu confirmed, and then he slid his gaze to me. "But it's not over yet."

"All that's left is to seal the terrenes." Portia picked up the thread, sounding as relieved as the others to have what they expected to be the largest hurdle overcome. "Luce has to return to Canton for that, right? To the seal in Cypress Swamp?"

"Yes."

"What about you?" I had never asked him where his people breached. "Where do you go?"

"We entered this terrene over what is now Beijing." He kept his gaze locked with mine. "It will take me fifteen to twenty hours to reach it."

I gazed out at the frothing water, washing red onto the shore, and knew I would have to place one last call to the NSB if I wanted to avoid an incident too big for them to sweep under the rug. "What about the knives?"

"I was hoping you could request your allies search for them." He dipped his chin. "And Kapoor."

"I can do that." I made to stand, but I didn't get far.

Santiago put a hand on my shoulder and offered, "I'll do it."

"Thank you." I covered his fingers with mine for a brief second. "For saving us."

"Don't make a big deal out of this," he grumbled, snatching his hand back.

He walked into the water, wading out to his waist before he dove.

The celebratory vibe I had envisioned for this moment never manifested. It was hard to consider this a win after so much loss. "How long until the Malakhim report Ezra's death to his superiors?"

"Hours," Wu said with certainty. "Only Father and I can operate the seal within this terrene. Without us, the Malakhim will be forced to wait for contact from the other side. There are two check-ins each day, and we're four or five hours from the second."

The militant policing of their border with us drove home the critical need for destroying the seal. All of this would have been for nothing if their people marched through the breach and replaced Ezra before we got into position. This was a one-shot deal for us, and we had already pulled the trigger.

"How long will it take your people to mobilize?" I was guessing not long if they checked in like clockwork to ensure their prize terrene remained under their control. "Does your father have a successor?"

Once upon a time, Wu would have been expected to step in. He was marked as a traitor now. The Malakhim would be sure that news carried to the right ears. Within hours, there would be a bounty on his head, I was sure. Hunting him down would be the first order of business for Ezra's replacement.

"They will be ready to breach this terrene within twenty-four hours of notification. There are protocols in place that will take no time to activate. Our people are keen to hold this world, and there is no hope of charun from the lower terrenes breaching any higher."

That fit with what Sariah had told us from the get-go. I hadn't believed her then, but I did now.

Thanks to Kimora's death, I no longer had to wonder how she knew so much about the higher terrenes. She must have overtaken a Malakhim at one point, though I doubt her mark had belonged to Ezra. True Malakhim were too set in their ways to accept anything less than death before dishonor, and it didn't get worse than a Malakhim agreeing to a bargain. My guess was she rooted out one of the Malakhim lite, possibly through her connection to Kimora, and used his knowledge gained from infiltrating Ezra's ranks to make the call.

Wu wasn't the only one who played the long game. She had learned the art at her mother's knee. But she would be a future problem for the coterie, not for me.

"We have no time to waste," he said, and I could tell he meant it. "Our window of opportunity is already closing."

All hope that I could take an extra day — hell, an extra hour — to say my goodbyes evaporated like mist.

I had already said them anyway, right? Many times. I had been tossing *I love yous* at people like confetti at a parade. Everyone I loved knew what they meant to me. How many people got that closure? How many were allowed to put their affairs in order before they go? I was lucky.

Yeah.

Lucky.

Water splashed, and I puzzled over Santiago returning so quickly. "That was fast."

"What can I say?" He held up his hands, a knife in each, the blood washed off them. "I'm good."

The expected response would be a derisive snort, so I put in the effort. "Not that good."

"Fine." He threw them at my feet, and they stuck in the soft earth. The hilts glinted oddly, the metal alive with black iridescence. "The Diorte attempted to retrieve Kapoor after he hit the water. They couldn't find him, but they salvaged these. They were on their way to present them to you as a token of his bravery."

With so many predators in the water, and so much prey falling from the sky, I had a grim certainty where Kapoor had ended up, and so must Wu. He shut his eyes, and moisture dampened his lashes, tears he wouldn't let fall. The news had gut-punched him. He was lucky I didn't too.

"I'm sorry," I told him, aware he was the closest thing Kapoor had to a friend. "He was a good man."

"No, he wasn't." Wu sobered before I worked up to a full eulogy. "He wanted to be, but good men can't enact change on this scale without stepping over the line. He and I left that line behind a long time ago." He knelt and chose his blade without revealing the magnitude of what it meant. "I'll call you when I'm in position."

His wings flared, and he touched the sky before I could decide what to say to him.

Good thing too. I didn't want our parting words to be in anger, and that's all I had left. It was the fuel I was burning to see me through to the end, and he was a motherload of kindling.

"We should move out too." I palmed the remaining dagger, wary of its heft, and got to my feet. "Canton is about four and a half or five hours away."

Doing the math gave me a much-needed morale boost. If we hurried, the coterie could steal another four or five hours together before we had to move into position.

"I'm hungry," Rixton announced. "Saving the world ought to taste like pizza. Extra pepperoni. Extra mushrooms. Extra sausage. Extra onions. Extra —"

"We get the picture." I rolled my eyes. "Place the order when we get close. We'll eat at the farmhouse together."

One last meal. I couldn't think of a better group of people to share the honor.

"I knew I liked you for a reason, Bou-Bou." He slapped me on the shoulder. "Now that this is over, we need to talk about your career choices."

I was so far removed from the daily grind, I had to stop and remember I was employed by the NSB's charun taskforce. They hadn't fired me. I hadn't quit. I just stopped going to work when the heat got turned up too high for me to pretend any longer.

Try as I might, I couldn't fake caring. In a few hours, none of it would matter. That didn't mean I could get away without answering. "Are you asking for a promotion or for me to accept a demotion?"

"Um, hello? Picking up the badge again in Canton is a promotion." He preened. "What else would you call being partnered with me?"

"Other, less flattering words come to mind."

"Poor thing." He clucked his tongue. "Clearly you sustained brain trauma during the fight."

"No one hit me in the head."

"See what I mean? You're obviously delusional."

Unable to stop a laugh from escaping, I shook my head. "Let's go home."

When Air Cole passed over Canton, I allowed myself to pretend I really was going home to the farmhouse, to my old job, to my old life. That the nightmare had really ended. That we had won. That there was some prize for victory. But then I spotted the charred remains of the police department and lost my grip on the fantasy.

Someone had left a few lights on in the farmhouse, not that it mattered in the grand scheme of things. I wasn't all that worried about running up my utility bills at the moment. Pinching pennies ranked somewhere below actually using my gym membership and returning a DVD rental from a few years back.

Cole touched down, and Phoebe landed beside him. We didn't have to wait long for the others to come up the drive in their rented SUVs. Gathered together, all of us alive and back where it started, I had to admit it was a better homecoming than I ever dared to dream.

And when the front door opened, and the smells of lasagna and freshly baked bread poured out behind Sherry, I couldn't stop the tears from streaming down my face.

"You're here." I beat Rixton to her and hugged her tight. "How are you here?"

"Your friend Wu arranged it." She fluttered her lashes at Rixton over my shoulder. "Unlike some people, who still carry on about dragon-riding nonsense, I got to straddle an angel."

Mouth hanging open, he peeled me away from her. "You did what now?"

"Straddled an angel." She bit her bottom lip then let it pop free. "Rode him for *hours*."

Rixton dove for her, and she screamed at the top of her lungs, pivoting to run, but it was too late. He scooped her up, an arm under her legs and one behind her back and swung her around until she ran out of breath and curled against his chest.

"On the topic of angels," Rixton said. "Where's my baby?"

"Mr. Boudreau offered to babysit since angels don't come with built-in car seats."

Rixton planted a smacking kiss on her nose. "That's why you're the brains of this operation."

"On the topic of babies," I interrupted, extending my hand behind me. "Sherry, there's someone I would like you to meet."

The air shimmered next to me as Phoebe shed her dragon form and her invisibility. Closing her soft fingers around mine, she came to rest her shoulder against mine.

"This is my daughter, Phoebe." I gave her hand a reassuring squeeze. "You may or may not remember her as a baby dragon the size of a corgi."

"Kid, you require no introduction." Sherry laughed, and

it sounded joyful, genuine. "You're the spitting image of your mother."

"Thanks," she said softly. "I'm sorry I chased you down the hall that time."

"You're fine." She waved it off. "They warned me there was a baby dragon in residence. The important thing was I could run faster than you."

Cheeks red, Phoebe ducked her head and leaned into my side.

"What's that?" Sherry reared back, her hand on Rixton's chest. "It feels like . . ."

"A deflated tire?" I supplied. "It's Rixton's boobs."

"I don't have boobs." He squished Sherry against him. "Don't listen to her, Sher-bear. I can explain."

He carried her across the threshold while she pretended to swoon then ambled into the kitchen.

The others streamed in behind them, lured by the scents of homemade food and lots of it.

This was so much better than pizza.

This was *home*.

Cole rested a heavy hand on my shoulder to stop me. "We need to talk."

Phoebe broke away and hustled to catch up to Thom, who walked in with her.

"Can we talk after we eat?" I forced a smile. "Do you hear my stomach?"

Conflict warred in his expression, but he let the matter drop in favor of taking care of his mate.

We entered the kitchen to find Sherry had spent the hours it took us to fly home baking. Food covered every available surface, and two Malakhim lite bustled from stove to fridge carrying out her orders.

Her time in Haven had clearly put her at ease with charun,

and for that I was grateful. It didn't mean she and I were okay, but it meant maybe she wouldn't mind if Rixton kept a hand in after I was gone. Which, honestly, we both knew he would be unable to resist.

Now that he knew charun existed, he wouldn't forget just because the world was safe. For the time being. The opposite was likely true. The NSB had formed its taskforce with the purpose of concealing charun activity from humans. While I had to hand it to them — they did perform a public service in hunting down predatory charun with a taste for human flesh — their primary focus was in covering their own asses.

With ease, I could picture Rixton forming his own team, perhaps with the members of my coterie, in answer to that. He would want to protect humans, but he would also want to help charun. He could do both, and well. He had the brains and the temperament for it. Not to mention the heart.

I'm not saying he could weave our species together into one societal fabric during his lifetime, but he could make a solid start at integrating the outliers, like the enclave, who were just as much children of this world as any other.

We piled our plates high and sat in a circle on the floor with our legs crossed. We invited the Malakhim lite to join us, but they ate out back at the picnic table to give us time alone together. I was glad. I wanted to soak it all in. The smells, the sounds, the smiles.

Once our bellies were full, we all pitched in and cleaned up so Sherry could relax. That left us with four hours, give or take, and the weight of the deadline pressed in on us all. The others might not grasp the permanence of this final step, but the coterie bond must have fed them bits of my anxiety.

Rixton and Sherry wandered off upstairs, giggling like teenagers, and I hoped they were on their way to defile Santiago's new room. The coterie scattered to avoid witnessing what came next, and I couldn't blame them. Not for the first time, I was grateful to have plain ol' human hearing. There are some things you just don't need to know about your friends.

Portia and Santiago lowered the backseat in one of the SUVs to give them a flat area to set up a game. I couldn't tell what it was from here, but it didn't take long before Portia started cackling. Miller leaned on the open door closest to Portia, laughing with her each time she beat Santiago, and I didn't imagine the hints of Maggie peeking out to watch him.

Thom and Phoebe had climbed a tree near the back of the property. I wasn't sure what they were doing, but she was chattering away, reminding me of her baby dragon self, and he had shifted into his other form to climb onto her lap while she massaged his wings.

Seeing that, my heart swelled until I ran out of room for the feeling. It pushed through my eyes at their corners and dripped down my cheeks. Thom had a long way to go before he could fly again, but I was glad each time I saw his boxy tomcat form. It meant he was healing, and not just physically.

"Happy tears?" Cole walked up behind me, slid his strong arms around my middle.

"Thom is spending more time in his natural form, especially with Phoebe." I didn't point out their location. His senses were keener than mine, and he never let Phoebe out of his sight. "That's good, right?"

"It's very good." He brushed his lips over my nape, exposed by my ponytail. "It means he trusts her."

Trust was a good thing. A very good thing. They would all need to lean on each other after I was gone.

"Want to go for a walk?" I linked my fingers with his where they spanned my abdomen.

"I could walk," he said, a tease in his voice that caused me to glance over my shoulder and narrow my eyes on him.

"Why are your eyes twinkling?" I took a healthy step forward, but he didn't release me. "What are you thinking?"

"I'll show you." He led me into the woods, away from the others. "Want to go for a swim?"

The invitation took me by surprise. "That's not what I expected you to ask."

"We could go skinny dipping."

"That is definitely more of what I had in mind."

"You just want to get me naked."

"Um, yeah?" I ran a hand down his arm. "I should examine you anyway. We just survived an epic battle. Who knows what injuries you sustained without knowing? You could be dying, and we wouldn't know unless you took off all your clothes and let me thoroughly examine you."

Cole pretended to consider this. "It would be a shame to die after everything."

Decision made, he scooped me up in his arms. It reminded me of the way Rixton carried Sherry, and that made me smile. When Cole did romantic gestures, he did them well. With my head cushioned against his chest, I swung my feet as he took us deeper into the woods, past our tent, to where the ravine dropped off into the manmade pool where Maggie and I used to swim as kids.

"Hold your nose."

Busy snuggling my mate, I struggled to clear my thoughts. "What?"

"Your nose." He stepped to the edge. "Hold it."

"Cole." I started kicking. "Don't you dare."

"Suit yourself."

The crazy man stepped right off the edge, and we fell straight into the water with a percussive splash.

I came up *howling*.

Cole came up belly-laughing.

Clearly, I had created a monster. All those times I wished for him to enjoy his life to the fullest, I hadn't envisioned this playful side of him. With the burden of Ezra removed, he acted freer, lighter. Hope lifted the edges of his mouth, and plans for our future spun out behind his eyes. I recognized a daydreamer when I saw one. I hated I would star in those fantasies when I was about to retire. Permanently.

"You're evil." I rested my hands on his shoulders and dunked him. "*Evil.*"

Heavy as he was, Cole sank like a stone. Concern tugged on my heart when he didn't bob to the surface immediately, and I turned to search for him in the water, spotting him seconds before he pounced, plunging us both into darkness.

Beneath the water, his lips met mine. I was too busy devouring him to notice when he managed to get me free of my pants, but I cried out when he sheathed himself in me with one long stroke as we broke the surface.

Wrapping my legs around his waist, I clutched his shoulders, murmuring nonsense in his ear, and when I came, I saw stars I wasn't entirely sure could be blamed on the oxygen deprivation.

Cole followed me over, a growl in his throat, his arms cinching around me.

Face buried in his neck, I couldn't have asked for a better send-off than this.

CHAPTER NINEETEN

———————

Cypress Swamp wasn't far from the farmhouse. We left an hour before our deadline to ensure we got into position before Wu made his call. The entire coterie joined us, and it took both airboats to get us all on the water. It felt like overkill, and it felt comforting, and it felt like the worst possible scenario given what was about to happen. At least they wouldn't see. They would be up here, and I would be down there. Suspended in that odd bubble where time ran slower and the fabric of the world frayed along its edges.

"Wu better hurry." I hadn't put down my phone since Thom killed the engine. "That window he mentioned is about to slam shut."

Cole joined me, and I didn't have time to finish smiling at him before he closed his hand around my throat. It didn't hurt, but it wasn't done with affection. It's not like he had decided to kiss me or get kinky with me in front of the others. This was more . . . restraining.

Uh oh.

Scanning for Thom or Miller, I spotted the others congregating on the secondary boat to give Cole a moment alone with me.

Traitors.

Meltwater eyes bored into mine. "Did you think I wouldn't figure it out?"

"Um."

"The god killer daggers were the final clue," he said with quiet anger vibrating in his voice. "There's no reason why each of you would need one unless you were both meant to use them on a creature that couldn't be killed with ordinary weapons or without great difficulty. With Ezra defeated, and Sariah in the wind, that only left . . ."

"Us," I finished for him.

"I'm not surprised he put you up to this, or that your sense of duty overrode your common sense, but how could you not discuss this with me? I'm your mate. Doesn't that mean anything to you?"

"You wouldn't have let me go through with it," I whispered. "You would have fought me every step of the way."

"Instead you stole my chance to save you. You accepted this was your fate."

All along I had been a wolf in sheep's clothing, so why not also be a sacrificial lamb?

"You're a fighter." Cole's grip didn't tighten, but it didn't loosen either. "Why not fight this?"

"There's too much at stake. An entire world. Filled with humans and charun I love." I gazed into Cole's eyes, but his were as cold as his dragon's ice. "The only way I get through this is if I know it makes you all safe."

"The cost is too high," he rumbled, tremors shivering in his fingers. "Damn you, it's too high."

Saying *goodbye* would have been so much easier if I hadn't had to say a word.

"I'm glad you're all here." I hadn't intended to do this in front of them, but here we go. "I have a gift for you."

The Otillian words Wu had given me as a last favor cut my tongue when I spoke them. I tasted blood, but I kept going, forcing out the complex phrases until I reached the end.

The rose gold metal binding them all snapped in half and hit the metal deck in a deafening clatter.

"You're free," I announced into the silence.

Miller staggered, panic brightening his eyes, but Maggie held his hand, and he clutched her arm like an anchor in the storm of his unleashing.

The crimes of his youth were just that — youthful offenses. Along the way, he had matured, honed his instincts. He no longer required Conquest to leash him. He did fine on his own. If his control hadn't been perfected by his lifetimes spent in service to her, then he wouldn't be able to manifest his half form so well. He would have destroyed the world the first time he shifted, and that would have been that. He might not have faith in himself, but I believed in him.

Cole stared at his wrists where the rose gold bands that had bound him for so long usually rested, at the valleys of scar tissue that hadn't yet healed enough to cover a lifetime of his attempts to break free, like he couldn't believe what I had done.

I had given him what he had wanted for centuries, and betrayal pinched the corners of his mouth.

"We saved your world for you," Santiago growled, "and now you cut us loose. Is that it?"

"You're free." I threw up my hands. "You're safe."

"You had no right to do this without asking us," Miller said quietly. "How could you?"

"Luce followed her conscience," Thom murmured. "Did you expect less of her?"

The heated argument that broke out among them was not the gratitude I had expected. Far from it. From the looks on their faces, a knife through the heart would have hurt less. As much as I wished I could undo it, for their sakes, that was the reason I had done it in the first place. *For their sakes.*

Let them spend the rest of their long lives pissed off at me. As long as they were still breathing, I could do this. Let them hate me for freeing them, hate me for leaving them. Hate was better than hurt.

From a great distance, through the ringing in my ears, I heard my phone.

"We're in place," Santiago answered in a clipped tone after prying it from my numb fingers. "Waiting on you."

"Tell him to start counting." Cole broke his reverie. "We need five minutes."

Santiago relayed the information, unable to look at me, and I swallowed hard against Cole's palm, which he had yet to lower.

Unsure what he had planned until this moment, until me granting him his freedom wrecked his equilibrium, he released me. There was no warmth in his voice, no emotion whatsoever. He set a timer on his phone and shoved it into his pocket. "Let's go."

The shame of disappointing him, of hurting him and the coterie, propelled me into the water without another word. Maggie cried out, wresting control of her body from Portia, but it was too late. I understood now, how she must have felt waking with Portia inside her. A denizen of a new world where all her options had been stripped away, her fate predetermined by someone else's choices.

I didn't require help this time finding the seal. Its presence shivered over my skin, drawing me deeper and deeper until my lungs burned from the pressure and my gut twisted in a wrenching tug seconds before my feet touched sediment. Breath exploded out of me, and I sucked in . . . whatever filled this place. I didn't care so long as I could function.

When I opened my eyes, Cole stood beside me, his expression somehow grimmer than before, calculations running fast behind his eyes, lending him an air of distraction. But he was here. That's what mattered. That he remained with me until the end.

He held up two fingers, indicating the amount of time I had left before Wu took his irrevocable step toward achieving his ultimate triumph. The phone hung from his fingers, his grip so tight it should have crushed the device.

Cole gave me a nod, and I positioned myself over the seal, careful not to disturb it. Then I took the dagger from the loop on my belt and placed the tip at my heart.

Two minutes ought to have lasted longer.

They passed in a blink.

When the timer on his phone hit zero, I expected him to wrestle the blade from my hand or knock it pinwheeling away, but he did neither. He watched, gears whirring in his head. Part of me wondered if he was in shock. The rest figured it must be denial.

Closing my eyes, I began mouthing the Lord's Prayer in the same cadence as Aunt Nancy taught me as I pulled the sharpened metal toward me as hard as I could, blocking out the resistance in my body, in my mind. Focused on sheathing the blade in my chest, I didn't grasp what the difference in sensation ripping through my body meant.

Breath hitching, I flung open my eyes and sought out Cole, desperate to warn him, but it was too late.

Conquest shot up my throat on a soundless battle cry, smashing through Luce Boudreau and shattering our bond forever.

CHAPTER TWENTY

———

Adam stood in ankle-deep turquoise water in Five Flower Lake in the Sichuan Province. He balanced on the rotting trunk of a fallen tree, one of dozens crisscrossing the lakebed, and indulged in a tranquil moment of admiring the ancient forest while breathing the crisp air. Despite what the place meant to him, and his kind, he had always found peace here.

"You told me it was beautiful," Knox said from behind him. "I didn't understand until now."

"I wish you were seeing it for the first time in happier times." Adam faced his descendant, his favorite if he had to choose one, and regretted heaping more death on his head. "You should come back one day."

"These are happier times." Knox crouched at the water's edge, stared at his reflection. No, beyond it, to a place Adam couldn't follow, his thoughts a million miles away. "The war is over."

"You know as well as I do it's far from over." Adam tilted his head back, examined the expanse of blue sky and its stippling of white clouds. "This is the next step, not the last."

"We have all the backup we need. Luce raised a formidable force, and most saw no action. They'll be eager to contribute." Knox grunted when he stood, his left leg still bothering him after a break decades ago. "We'll keep the peace, even if that means hunting down every last Malakhim and spit-roasting them."

"They're automatons." He borrowed the description from Luce because it fit them. "You can't blame them for following orders. It's all they know." He flexed his toes. "Your best bet is to allow our people to continue their infiltration. Over time, they can redirect the Malakhim's focus. They'll be lost once their way home ceases to exist."

That was the golden carrot Ezra had dangled in front of their faces.

Serve me, and one day I will send you home.

The fools believed he meant to their home terrene, which most had never seen. What he meant was one day he fully expected them to die in his service, and they would pass on to the next world, one where only souls could journey. But they believed him, believed in him, and there would be no deprogramming them.

"They killed her," Knox rasped. "They're no more lost than I am."

The truth, that a Drosera had worn his daughter's face the last time they saw her, he no longer recalled. His mind had blanked it, all of it, back to the moment Kimora was held captive by the Malakhim.

Adam didn't have the heart to remind Knox of the truth, and he wasn't certain he would listen in any case. He wasn't convinced Knox could absorb the series of actual events that led to her death. The man was traumatized, barely functioning, but he had wanted to be here for this moment. For her. To give her death meaning.

Adam always pictured sharing this with Farhan, but in his heart, he knew that was never a possibility. Farhan was always going to die, and so was he. The odds of them dying together had always been slim. Now they were nonexistent.

His friend was dead, and he never thanked him. He never apologized. For any of it. For all of it.

Knox wasn't the only one of them shattered by loss, but he was the only one who stood any chance of recovery. Knox had the enclave. His people would support him, nurture him, and help him heal. If he let them. Adam hadn't had that network. He'd had two grief-stricken little girls to raise and a father to hate.

"It's time." Knox checked his phone. "You don't want to cut it too close."

"I'll call Luce when I'm in position." He lingered, but Knox made no move to embrace him, and he didn't expect it. No matter who had killed his daughter, Knox would forever blame Adam for failing her first and foremost. Right behind himself. "Take care of the others."

Once Knox would have snapped out a confirmation, but he didn't so much as nod.

The enclave wouldn't require his ironclad control to protect them in this new world, bought with so much blood, but they would struggle to adapt without him. Adam could only hope he would see that, and duty would, as it always had in the past, sway him to remain with his people.

Without another word, Adam took flight. He allowed himself one lazy circle around the perimeter of the placid lake. He raced his reflection as he had when he was a child, trailed his big toe in the cool water behind him, spreading ripples across the surface. But all too soon he reached Knox again, and he knew it was time to go.

"Wait."

Convinced he had imagined the reprieve, Adam hovered above the felled tree where he began. "Yes?"

"Get your dumb ass down here." Tears glittered in Knox's eyes. "Did you really think I would let you go without saying goodbye?"

Aware he was undeserving, but thankful someone cared enough to be here, Adam lit beside his descendant. "Yes?"

Knox lurched toward him, wrapped his arms around him, and wept into his shirt.

"Shhh." Adam stroked Knox's back. "It's all right."

"I shouldn't have blamed you." He gusted out a shaky exhale. "I wish you didn't have to do this. I don't want to lose you too."

The childlike tone turned Adam's resolve brittle. "I'm sorry I have to leave you too."

"I'll stay with the enclave," Knox vowed. "Your sacrifice won't be forgotten."

Their embrace ended, and Knox wiped his face dry. Adam didn't bother. Father was dead. There was no one left to punish him for the crime of feeling.

This time when Adam took flight, he didn't dawdle. He shot for the sun, blasting past the lowest clouds. The atmosphere thinned, and his lungs protested, but then he punched through a membrane that turned the air thick but breathable.

A waystation gleamed ahead, its white gold shine blinding in the sun. The ornate platform was meant to support two soldiers as they each gave their reports. One Malakhim would return to the host with news, while the other returned through the seal.

Usually a host would be swarming the area, but Ezra had summoned every man to him, and the chaos of his death had prevented them from returning. Soon the shock would wane, and they would understand immediate action was called for in order to stabilize their masters' hold on this terrene. Protocol would kick in, and they would report the events of the past twenty-four hours and usher in a new era. Unless he stopped them first.

Adam touched down, settled his wings against his spine, and

ignored the wet footprints he left as he pulled out his phone and dialed Luce.

"We're in place," Santiago answered in a clipped tone. "Waiting on you."

A pang resonated through him. He wouldn't hear Luce's voice again, wouldn't get to offer any apologies, and he supposed it was just as well. He doubted she would accept them. She had her orders, and she didn't need him to throw them in her face.

"I'm in position," he said softly. "Five minutes."

The call ended, and Adam broke the phone in two to protect the sensitive information it contained.

Spreading his wings as far as they could reach, he closed his eyes and enjoyed the cool air rustling through his feathers.

The time came, and he didn't hesitate. He palmed the dagger, set the tip against his chest, and drove it into his heart with enough force the handguard dented his skin.

Death wouldn't take long, so he forced himself to smear his life's blood on his hand and press it against the seal. Forehead resting against it, he shivered as his vision edged to grays and then to black.

Adam hit his knees, and an odd giddiness filled him knowing he would never rise.

It was over.

All of it.

At last.

He focused on breathing around the bright pain slicing through him and counted out his remaining time with each sluggish heartbeat.

One.

Two.

Three.

Four . . .

"Zachariah," a soft voice breathed in his ear. "What have you done?"

Dead.

He was dead.

He must be to hear that voice, that name, after so many centuries.

"Rebekah." A new pain, an exquisite ache, spread through his chest. "You're here."

"Shhh." Phantom fingers slid through his hair. "Where else would I be?"

Adam opened his eyes on nothing but pure, white light, and panic seized him in its fist. "*Father.*"

"No, love." Rebekah laughed, actually laughed. "He can't touch us now."

More than anything in his long life, he wished that were true. "Where are you?"

"I'm here." Her delicate hand slid into his. "I've always been right here."

He let her help him to his feet, and he stood up weightless. The sensation tingled through him, rejuvenating him, and he turned his head to where Rebekah's voice emanated from the blinding light.

Out of the corner of his eye, he noticed a men's dress shoe. But she stepped back before he saw more than the leg it attached to, cutting off his line of sight, preventing him from seeing more.

"Look forward," she murmured. "Not backward."

Lifting her hand to his mouth, he kissed her knuckles, and then he followed her home.

CHAPTER TWENTY-ONE

———◆———

Pain sharper than I had ever known cleaved my chest, but removing the blade would only kill us quicker.

Foolish girl.

She had done this, ended us, and for what? This world? Its people?

We stood suspended by the palm he wrapped around our throat. Under different circumstances, I might have purred to find Nicodemus's hands on me of his own free will again. It had been so long since he touched me without an order behind it, I found I missed the novelty of a willing partner. Not that Nicodemus had ever been that for me. For Luce, on the other hand ... He had been all too pliant in her arms.

And still the little fool had tossed him away, tossed *us* away.

No sound permeated this place, the seal too tight for even noise to escape, but we didn't have to hear him to read the grief welling up in him as our blood trickled into the peculiar atmosphere. As much as I didn't want to die, I thrilled at striking this final blow, at witnessing his end.

No, I didn't want to die, but I would take what was mine with me.

"You mourn," I mouthed, ignoring the fire blazing through my sternum.

"My mate is dead," he answered just as silently. "Of course I mourn her."

Luce Boudreau.

The woman who thawed an ice dragon's heart.

Good riddance.

"You are mine, and you always will be." I rested our hand on his chest, over his madly thumping heart. "When I die, I will take you with me. We will be together throughout eternity. I will have it no other way."

A calmness smoothed the hard lines of his features, a promise he knew more than I did.

"Luce set us free. The coterie bond is gone." He glanced down at the bangle encircling our wrist. "Your own power suppresses our mate bond." He tightened his grip. "I will survive."

"Bastard." I curled our lip in a snarl. "You cannot leash me with my own power."

"Goodbye, Conquest."

"Ah, but you don't see Conquest. You see your darling Luce. Your chosen mate. The mother you wished for our daughter."

Nicodemus said nothing, but raw emotion pooled in his eyes, more than he had shown since the death of his family, his people.

Luce meant that much to him. She meant *everything* to him. She was what *I* should have been to him. All our centuries together, and he grieved for her, who he had known for the blink of an eye?

Fury sent our hand seeking the blade's hilt, and we tightened our grip. This was all I had left.

Adam Wu must be dead or on his way to dying, as some cord

within us pulled taut thinking of him. The worthless bastard was taking us with him, and we could do nothing to stay. As hard as we fought against the pull, we were losing the battle, our limbs growing heavier, our thoughts spinning wider and slower.

Nicodemus should be fading. He should be wilting, paling, faltering. Not standing there, watching life drain out of our eyes. But he stood tall, firm.

And hope, that most worthless and pointless of all emotions, radiated from him in waves.

Seconds.

I had seconds.

Precious few of them.

And the strength for one more act, to prove to him that he would belong to me for all time, that no wishes would be granted here.

We raised the dagger, and his mouth formed a shout just as mute as our laughter when we yanked the blade free, then plunged it back into our chest, over and over until our vision blurred, and the dark night of eternity swept over us.

CHAPTER TWENTY-TWO

———◆———

Cole breached the surface and sucked down enough oxygen to shout, "Over here."

Santiago, already in the water, eased Luce out of his arms in less than a second. He raced with her limp form to the nearest airboat where Thom had laid out his medical equipment in accordance with the plan the coterie had hatched behind her back. Even prepped and waiting, Thom might not be able to pull off a miracle, but they had to try.

Cole reached the deck of the airboat a minute later and hauled himself over its edge. Water poured off him as he crawled to Luce, took her cool hand in his and pressed her palm against his cheek.

"Move." Thom shoved him aside. "I need room to work."

He knew that, knew he was in the way, but he couldn't pry his hands away from her.

"Come sit with me." Maggie wrapped an arm around his shoulders, or tried to, and guided him onto the bench. "She's beat the odds before. She can do it again."

"I can't lose her."

He hadn't meant to say it, to voice his greatest fear, and now it hung in the air over his head.

She was dead.

Dead.

Thom had to bring her back.

She couldn't be gone. Not forever. Not his Luce.

"Shhh." Maggie rubbed his back in comforting circles. "I know."

The way she kept repeating the soothing noises broke through enough for him to realize he had been sitting there, chanting the phrase like a prayer.

I can't lose her. I can't lose her. I can't lose her.

"Talk to me." Maggie kept her voice low and soothing. "How did it go down there?"

"Everything went as planned."

Luce wasn't the only devious member of the coterie. As soon as they pieced together what she meant to do, they began to work on ways to get around the cost of the sacrifice using what they had gleaned from Wu and Luce over the past few days.

Desperation had almost driven Cole to Wu to beg for more information, any tidbit that might shift the balance in her favor, but Wu had gone too far. There would be no pleading for answers from him.

They had to pray that Thom's skills and his extensive study of the human body since Luce came back into their lives was enough to revive her.

Six minutes.

That was it.

That was all.

Six minutes until her brain began dying.

How many of those had he spent getting her here? How many remained? How many —?

"Conquest surfaced on command?" Maggie coaxed, attempting to keep the conversation going.

"Yes." He cleared his throat. "Luce made the sacrifice. She plunged the blade into her heart." He shut his eyes, and he saw it. Over and over again. The dagger in her hand, then the dagger in her chest. "I summoned Conquest before Luce died, and she appeared." He mashed his lips together. "I antagonized her until she lost her temper and finished the job."

The coterie had hashed out a script designed to force Conquest's hand, and he stuck to it.

It never would have worked if she hadn't felt Wu's life draining, dragging hers into the void after him. Still, his role had nearly broken him. Allowing Conquest her final, petty revenge to end the cycle and make Luce's sacrifice count would haunt him until the end of his days.

"Then you did your best." Her breath hitched before she got it under control again. "You did everything you could to save her."

Fury surged through him, igniting his temper, and he snapped, "I could have —"

"Killed Wu before it got this far? That would have killed her too." Santiago joined them, willing to protect Maggie for Portia's sake. "Killed Ezra before it got this far? That would have been impossible without Kapoor's god killer daggers, which Wu did a damn fine job of keeping secret."

"Stop." Cole put his head in his hands when it became too heavy to hold up on his own. "Just . . . stop."

For once, Santiago did as he was told.

The next five minutes were a flurry of activity Cole couldn't bear to watch as Thom and Miller worked in tandem to revive Luce.

It was a gamble. All of it. Wu claimed she was Conquest's soul in a human body. But Luce was her own person. When the bangles suppressed Conquest, Luce remained. That had to mean she had her own soul.

It had to.

Had to.

Merging with Conquest had brought the corpse Wu had stolen for his experiment back to life, so Cole had every reason to believe that when Conquest's soul dimmed, it would do the opposite and kill Luce.

But he had to try.

He had to.

Had to.

The mate bond had been silent for a while thanks to the bangles. Now it was gone.

The hollow ache in him resonated through his bones, a clawing hand ready to seize his soul and haul him down with Luce. Maybe he had been wrong. Maybe he hadn't escaped death. Maybe he had only prolonged it. At least this way her father would have a body to bury, even if the thought of her entombed in earth . . .

A sob hitched in his chest, but he was wound too tight to release it. It clogged his throat, made it impossible to breathe. The edges of his vision blackened, the world folding in on itself, on him. He slid from his seat, hit his knees, and toppled onto the deck.

CHAPTER TWENTY-THREE

————◦◊◦————

"Fuckity fuck fuck fuck," Santiago bellowed. "Thom, he's down."

Santiago figured this would happen, but had anyone listened to him? Nope. They followed the dumbass course of action he vetoed until he went hoarse and then it blew up in all their faces.

"Is he breathing?" Thom shouted, still working on Luce. "Does he have a pulse?"

"Do I look like a medic?" Santiago grumbled on his way to kneel beside Cole. "He's alive."

Barely.

"Idiot." Santiago slapped his cheek. "You survived Conquest, and you're going to give up now?"

A slender hand encircled his wrist and stopped him from striking Cole again.

"Leave him alone." Phoebe shoved him onto his ass then curled up against her father's side. "Leave us both alone."

Hating to sound like he cared, he figured someone had to point out the obvious. "You were supposed to stay at the farmhouse with the Rixtons."

"I'm not an idiot," she said thickly, throwing the word back in his face. "I could tell something was wrong."

"Damn invisible dragons sneaking around every damn where like it's their damn world, and we're just living in it." Damn, damn, damn. "Just tell us if he stops breathing, okay?"

Silent tears flowed down her cheeks. "Okay."

Portia was staring a hole through him from the second airboat. "What?" He leapt onto its deck. "I left them alone like the kid asked."

Tears glimmered on her lashes before she hurled herself at him like a missile and struck center mass.

"We're going to lose them both," she cried against his shoulder. "What will we do without Cole and Luce?"

Lip curling, he couldn't decide where to put his hands, if he ought to shove her away or break free and run. A good push would send her into the water, which would be hilarious, and get her off him. Two birds, one stone. But he could also hop back on the other boat to avoid becoming a casualty of the emotional wreck that was Portia in meltdown.

She gazed up at him, eyes red and watering, and he sighed, allowing his arms to encircle her.

"We'll survive." Snot slid down her face like fat slugs crawling out of her nostrils. "I'm not Cole, and I'm sure as hell not Luce, but I know how to access coterie funds, how to secure us jobs, how to purchase real estate. We can survive this." A cold spot formed in the middle of his chest. "You're free. We're all free. We don't even have to stick together. I can set us up individually or whatever."

He didn't see the slap coming, but he felt it. The red-hot imprint of her hand throbbed along his jaw. Running his tongue along the edge of his teeth, he was pretty sure she had knocked one loose.

Eyes puffy and red, she snarled, "You are *not* abandoning us."

"You crazy —" He bit his lip when he registered her expression. Taking a deep breath, he tried again. "I just finished saying I could take care of us. We haven't been free in … forever. Excuse me if I figured some of us were still nursing escape and/or revenge fantasies involving Conquest."

"I don't feel Maggie at all," she said quietly. "She's retreated so far." She flicked her gaze up at him. "Can a friend die of a broken heart? The way a mate does? I've never lost one as close to me as Maggie is to Luce." Her chin dropped. "I don't know what will happen to me if she dies." More tears fell. "I feel like a real piece of shit for even mentioning it."

Santiago took a moment to picture life without Portia, and yeah. He could imagine it ripping out your heart, stomping it to mush. Hard to survive with a boot print on one of your vital organs. Not that he would ever tell her that.

"Maggie will be fine," he said, primed to leap back if she swung again, but she stepped into him and rested her head on his shoulder, "because Luce is going to live."

"Aww." She smeared snot across her face when she wiped it on his sleeve. "You're lying to comfort me."

"Yeah, yeah." He cringed at the damp fabric resting warm and slimy against his arm. "I'm a real hero."

CHAPTER TWENTY-FOUR

───◆───

Everything ached, and I was dying. Death couldn't hurt this much. For all the talk about fighting to live, I was ready to plunge over the edge into the abyss if it meant this pain eased.

"Can you hear me?"

Shock ricocheted through me, and I had to wet my lips a few times to get out his name. "Thom?"

Gentle fingers brushed across my chest, exposed to the balmy night air, and I almost threw up from the pressure.

"Hold on," Thom ordered. "I'm doing my best, but you have to pitch in too."

Pitching in sounded like so much work. Hadn't I done enough? Hadn't I earned my rest?

"Mom," a young voice sobbed nearby. "He won't wake up. Daddy won't wake up."

Daddy.

My fuzzy thoughts pointed like an arrow straight to Edward Boudreau, but I was an only child.

Child.

Phoebe.

Cole.

She meant Cole.

Cole wouldn't wake up?

The lids I couldn't heave open seconds ago lifted with tortoise speed, and I let my head fall to the side. "Cole." I twitched my fingers, too weak to move my hand, let alone my arm. *"Cole."*

"He fainted when your heart stopped," Miller explained, leaning over me. "He hasn't come to since."

"Cole."

"Hold still and listen to me." Thom replaced Miller. "You're the tether holding him here. You must live if you want him to survive." He brushed his fingers across my cheek. "Rest, Luce. The best thing you can do for him is to take care of yourself."

Eyes falling shut, I reserved my strength. "Conquest?"

"I don't scent her on you." Thom pricked my arm, and my thoughts spun slower. "You'll have to search within yourself to know the truth. Later."

"Sleep." Miller stroked my hair. "We'll take care of Cole."

Loopy from whatever Thom had pumped into me, I slurred, "I'm 'live, right?"

"Yes." Miller chuckled softly. "Thank all the gods and goddesses, yours included."

"Pretty sure ... my god ... exists," I mumbled. "Think I saw him ... a minute ... ago."

For a few seconds there, I had seen beyond the dark to the brightest, whitest light imaginable.

My gut told me if I had walked into it, I would have found Uncle Harold and Aunt Nancy waiting for me. I swear I smelled her chocolate chip cookies, a lure guaranteed to set my feet on the path to eternity. I took one step, despite my best efforts to ignore the promise of happiness everlasting.

But the pain had anchored me to my body, the weight of an elephant herd doing yoga on my chest.

A second pinch on my upper arm shooed the elephants away, and I relaxed into the weightless darkness.

CHAPTER TWENTY-FIVE

―――――•◆•―――――

Warmth cocooned me, and I snuggled deeper into its source. Well, as deep as one can snuggle into a boulder. Happy to keep my eyes closed, I ran my fingers across the defined muscles in Cole's chest, sucking in a breath when mine began to ache from the effort of raising my arm.

"Are you all right?" he rumbled from above me, where his chin rested on the crown of my head.

"I think so." I touched an itchy spot beneath my collarbone, brushed my fingers over scratchy gauze, and froze. "Oh crap." I flung open my eyes. "I'm alive."

"Yes." He leaned forward, kissed my forehead. "You are."

Vague memories of Phoebe wailing for him surfaced next, and my pulse decided to go for a run. I looked him over, but I found no obvious injuries. A few new scars marked his body, but they were well on their way to being healed and nothing I wouldn't expect to find after Hart Island. "Are you all right?"

"I'm as okay as you are." A smile tugged on his lips. "Conquest died, and I survived."

Relief flooded me in a giddy rush that pushed out actual giggles. God, I sounded like an idiot. And I didn't care. Not one whit.

"Did you get injured after?" I lowered my arm when the skin began to pull. "I remember Thom saying . . . something. You were hurt, right?"

"I survived Conquest." His rough fingertips traced my cheekbones. "You almost killed me."

A moment passed where I was certain my heart had stopped in my chest. "What?"

"You're my mate." A new light shone in his eyes. "You almost died, and you almost took me with you."

"Why are you smiling?" I would have shoved upright, but I hurt too much. "Those are two very bad almosts."

"You're my mate," he repeated, rolling onto his back. "That makes me happy."

"Men are weird," I huffed. "Charun males are even weirder."

"All this time I thought I belonged to her, body and soul."

Cuddling him, I waited to hear what he said next.

"She assumed the characteristics of a Convallarian, and I thought . . . I never accepted the mate bond, but she mated me all the same. This proves the only hold she had over me was her own. I'm truly free of her, Luce."

"I'm glad." I pressed a kiss to his side. "You deserve to make your own choices."

"You're the choice I made."

And it had nearly killed him. God forbid charun do one thing that wasn't life or death.

"If Conquest is dead," I wondered, "what does that make me?"

"Human," Thom said from the doorway. "As near as I can tell."

"Human," I echoed, dumbfounded. "How?"

"Wu brought Conquest's host back to life with his healing

magic," Thom explained. "He used the body to create a cage to hold her soul, reanimating you in the process."

"I remember this story." Wu had explained the impossibility of it all to me, and it still gave me the creeps to hear my origin story. "Where does the surprise plot twist come in?"

"We theorized Conquest was a partition in your brain. This proves you were two souls inhabiting one body."

"I'm not charun at all?" I was just getting used to the idea, damn it. "I've lost my dragon?"

"We don't know," he admitted. "The dragon appeared to be a biological function rather than directly tied into Conquest's consciousness, but with her gone . . ."

An unexpected pang rocked me. "The dragon might be too."

Might was too kind a word considering they could sniff out Conquest from a mile away. They would have been the first to notice if any part of her lingered in me, including a whiff of Convallarian.

"I'm sorry, Luce." Thom backed away to give us privacy, and I let him go without a fuss. Clearly, the loss of my wings had struck a nerve. "Often what we wish for isn't what we expect when we receive it."

I had wanted to be human, and now I was.

Reaching deep inside myself, I pulled on the space where the cold place always waited, but frost didn't fill my mouth, and my breath didn't fog. I took stock of myself and came up short. The tension riding me these last few months was gone. There was no push and pull in my thoughts, no tug of war in my gut. I was, perhaps for the first time in my life, at peace.

Weird.

The theory I was mortal had merit according to my catalog of aches and pains. "How long was I out?"

"Six days," Cole rasped softly.

Almost a week and the world hadn't collapsed around me or fallen on top of my head while I slept. "Where is Dad?"

"Downstairs with Phoebe. He's teaching her to play poker."

"The Rixtons?"

"They're back home, with Nettie. I'll call them, let them know you're awake."

Exhausted from the effort of sitting upright, I reclined back onto my pillows. "I can't believe the farmhouse is still standing."

"It's seen better days, but it's structurally sound." He hesitated. "It can be repaired."

"I'm going to buy it from Dad." I fiddled with the sheets to avoid his reaction. "It's been on my mind for a while now, but I didn't want to think that far ahead." I reached for his hand. "I loved growing up here. I bet Phoebe would too. There are plenty of rooms for the coterie . . ." I remembered then, that they were free. "Thom is here to watch over me, but where are the others? Have they . . . ?" I swallowed. "Did they . . . ?"

"Leave?" Maggie strolled in with a cinnamon roll on a paper plate and a paper cup that smelled like coffee. "What do you think?"

Stupid tears filled my eyes, but I couldn't blink my vision clear. "Mags."

"Portia too," she reminded me. "Here. Eat. You'll feel better."

Santiago swaggered in behind her and announced, "I'm taking your old room."

"What?"

"Your old room," he said, stealing the sugary treat. "It's mine now, much like your breakfast."

No surprise there. He had basically moved himself in weeks ago. Still, he could have asked first.

"We figured you could take the master suite." Miller carried another plate with an undefiled roll that he passed to me. "Your dad's old room is twice the size of yours, and you'll need the extra space if you're going to share a bed with Cole."

"Um, yeah." Heat sizzled in my cheeks at the frank assessment. "I would like to share a bed with Cole."

Soft laughter rumbled through him, and he clasped hands with me, but he didn't say a word.

Until Miller got me thinking about it, I hadn't noticed we weren't in my room. This was the master suite, but not how I remembered it. The walls had been given fresh paint in a soothing blue color, and the air smelled like lemons from where the coterie had polished the wood trim and scrubbed the floor. The bed was new too. Dad had slept on a full-size mattress. This was a king at least. More like a king and a half.

"We've begun moving our things in." Miller toyed with a fidget spinner. Must be a new habit. Back in the day, Maggie had a drawer full of them, all confiscated from students. "We assumed you wouldn't mind, but we understand you're building your own family now."

"You guys are my family." I goggled at him. "Of course you're welcome to stay here. Do you really have to ask? I'm glad you want to stick around." I plucked at my sheets. "I wasn't sure if . . . "

"We're coterie," Portia said. "We've been together for so long it would feel weird going our separate ways." She winked. "It's not like we can go back home, so we need to get serious about making a new one here. Together."

The reminder of how I ended up on bedrest made me shiver. "How do we know it worked?"

"I examined the breach site myself." Santiago leaned against the doorframe. "I used the coordinates I've logged a dozen times, but there's nothing there. Just sediment. The lower seal is gone."

A grimmer thought occurred to me. "How do we check on the upper seal?"

"Knox made the journey with Wu," Miller said. "He waited until it was done, checked the seal, and returned with Wu's body for the enclave to bury." He lowered his head. "They've moved into Haven. They're finally home, just like Wu wanted."

"I don't much traffic in miracles, but I'm still here." I placed a hand over my heart. "Are we sure . . . ?"

"I examined the body." Thom sat at the foot of the bed. "He died in service to his people."

That was a pretty way of saying Wu had sacrificed everything he had and some things he didn't in order to take revenge on his father. I hoped, in the end, it had just as much to do with preserving the legacy of his wife's memory through their children as it did getting in the last blow.

I wish I could have been there with him, but Knox would have been the greater comfort. Whatever Wu and I shared beyond our resonance got tangled in lies, guilt, and betrayals. What he had with Knox was simpler. Though, with Kimora's death, it became more complicated.

I surprised myself by saying, "I would like to visit his grave."

There was no excuse for what he had done to me, but I wouldn't exist without him. I would have remained on a slab in the morgue if he hadn't chosen me as a vessel for Conquest to fill. Try as I might, I couldn't deny him thanks for that much if for nothing else.

"I'll take you," Cole promised. "We can pay our respects together."

"I would like that." I exhaled through my lips. "Making peace with him feels like a good start."

Forgiveness would come easier now that we had survived, somewhat intact. From there . . . who knows?

With Wu and Kapoor gone, I no longer had an "in" with the NSB. I had reported directly to Wu, and we had been set on pursuing his goals, and since they paralleled mine, I hadn't put up much of a fight. Rixton might have a point. I needed to sit and think, now that I had the luxury of time, on what I wanted to do with the rest of my life.

Learning Wu's remains had already been interred made me question how the cleanup had gone on Hart Island in my absence.

"We burned Death and Janardan's remains and scattered them across the water," Cole told me. "It's what they would have wanted."

Days ago, I thought I had said all my goodbyes, but I had missed so many. Attending funerals wasn't my favorite leisure activity, but they brought much needed closure. I had missed the Trudeaus' funerals. Wu, Kapoor, Death, and Janardan had also been laid to rest while I recovered. I'm not certain a flowery ceremony would have made any difference in how I grieved for them, but I wish I had gotten a chance to pay my last respects.

Now that I thought about it, no one had mentioned Kapoor. "Did the Diorte locate Kapoor's remains?"

"No." Miller frowned. "The larger corpses were hauled out into the ocean, where the Diorte spent their final days." That must include the bodies of Death's younger and more unusual children. "The smaller ones . . ."

"They're fish food," Santiago spelled it out for me. "The enclave decided to dedicate a bench to Kapoor in their communal cemetery."

"I'm glad." I picked at my cinnamon bun. "It's good that his sacrifices will be remembered as well."

"Let me take that." Maggie set the snack on the bedside table I hadn't noticed, also a new addition to the space. "You can eat it when you wake up, if you're feeling hungry then."

"When I wake up?" I barely swallowed a yawn. "Who says I'm going back to bed?"

The truth was I didn't have the strength to leave it, so it's not like it was a long trip to lean back.

"I do." She helped me settle and covered me with a blanket. "Sleep." She kissed me on the forehead. "We'll figure out the rest later."

"Okay," I mumbled, eyes drooping, and rolled over to nestle against Cole.

CHAPTER TWENTY-SIX

An uneasy stillness pervaded the house when I woke, and it set my teeth on edge for reasons I couldn't pinpoint. I held still and strained to pick up movement in the rooms next to this one or downstairs, but I heard nothing.

Ezra was dead. Wu was dead. Kapoor was dead. My sisters — all dead.

The coterie ought to be safe. I ought to be safe. We had earned our quiet retirement from the grueling climb to the pinnacle. Residual adrenaline must be to blame, shocking me awake at the slightest provocation. PTSD for the post-apocalypse. I'd take it. Struggling to cope meant I was alive.

Unable to shake my worry, I swung my legs over the side of the bed and padded onto the landing. I ducked my head in my old room, but Santiago wasn't there. I didn't enter, too afraid of boobytraps, but I didn't trust its emptiness. It didn't have to mean anything other than the guys had gone into town to pick up more food or supplies, but the ball of dread wringing out my gut warned it meant something.

I tiptoed downstairs, wincing each time the stairs creaked, and I almost laughed at how much it reminded me of being a teen and attempting to sneak out past Dad's room without waking him. The impulse caught in my throat when I walked into a scene straight out of my top five worst memories.

Cole sat in Dad's chair, tension knotting his shoulders, and Sariah stood behind him, a god killer dagger in her hand, its edge resting against his throat.

Not so long ago, her father, Thanases, had held an identical pose behind Cole while her mother lounged on his lap. But Sariah knew Cole better than War ever had, and she didn't risk a more dramatic entrance.

"Auntie, so glad you could join us. The boys were just giving me an update on your health."

"As you can see, reports of my death have been greatly exaggerated."

"I'm glad to hear it." She kept the dagger poised below his Adam's apple. "You know how I worry."

"I do." I clenched my hand on the bottom rail for support. "Family, right?"

"Right." She leaned down, pressed her cheek to Cole's. "And since we're all family here, I'm giving you the opportunity to ally with me before I start picking off your coterie, one by one."

Heady with déjà vu, I took my time answering. I had lived this scenario once before already, and it ended with Maggie bleeding out on the lawn. What would it cost me this time? Who would it cost me?

Without turning my head, I scanned the room to ensure I grasped the entirety of the situation.

Cole sat front and center, her showpiece on clear display. Thom stood across from them. Portia shielded Santiago, who fiddled with his phone behind her back, no doubt attempting to reach any allies we might still have in the area, and Miller shielded Portia for Maggie's sake, which made her fume.

Dad was missing, and so was Phoebe. Thank God. However this resolved, I didn't want them anywhere near it.

That meant it was up to me to buy time until backup arrived and pray they would get here soon.

"Your coterie is dead." I faked Conquest with everything in me. "What do you have to offer?"

"An army."

"I have armies."

"Think what we could accomplish if we combined our forces." Her eyes glittered. "Ezra is dead. His heir is dead. You are the most powerful charun remaining on this terrene, and your coterie is intact."

She had gotten some of her details wrong, but that worked to my benefit, so I was in no hurry to correct her. I was no longer powerful. There was some debate whether I was still charun. I couldn't count on my dragon when it might no longer be a part of me. I was just human. Just Luce. And Cole was dead if she figured that out before I got him free.

"I fought to liberate this terrene, not enslave it."

"How can you trust humans to care for themselves?" Her laughter mocked me. "They require oversight."

"No."

"Have you thought about what will happen in the absence of Ezra?" Her fingers tightened on the blade. "You've cleared the way for any charun with enough might and resources to claim his crown. The vacuum must be filled. Why not by you? You care for these mortals. You would tend them better than anyone else."

"And where does that leave you? While I'm busy tending my mortals?"

"I want to rule." She shrugged like it ought to have been obvious. "We can share top billing. You can manage the humans, and I will rein in the charun."

"You want to start a power bid that will ultimately kill hundreds, if not thousands, of those mortals you so generously set aside for me."

She scoffed at the numbers. "Have you seen how fast they breed?"

"This terrene is sealed." I wasn't giving any information away. She had to know we had been successful, or else she wouldn't have come out of hiding. "Once you control all the charun, then what?"

"Then I rule them."

"Have you ever successfully ruled anything?" I let my gaze slide to either side of her, illustrating how she stood alone. "The coterie you inherited from your mother is dead. That doesn't speak highly to me of your leadership abilities."

"That's not fair." A quick flash of crimson rouged her cheeks. "You killed them."

"And you didn't stop me. As I recall, you ran."

"You're cadre."

"You've told me time and time again that I'm not." I clucked my tongue. "All I'm hearing from you, my darling niece, are excuses."

Teeth grinding, Sariah fumed. "What would an alliance cost?"

"More than you can afford." I held her gaze. "You as good as killed my uncle. Do you really think you can offer me anything that would make up for that? Any hope we had of an alliance died with him." I forced the wobble out of my legs. "Your allies will scatter. You can't hold onto them. You're not cadre, and you have no coterie. The war has been won, and your side lost."

"Have you forgotten?" She drew the dagger across Cole's throat in a shallow cut, and blood welled along its edge. "I have one last bargaining chip. You would do anything for him. You've proven that. Join me, lend your forces to mine, and I will release him. I'll even give you my word that I will never threaten him or the rest of your coterie again."

"Your word means nothing to me."

Teeth bared, she pressed her luck, and her weapon. "Do you *want* me to kill him?"

A telltale shimmer in the air behind her plummeted my heart into my toes.

The adolescent dragon who appeared behind Sariah had to hunch to avoid hitting the ceiling, but that didn't slow her down. Phoebe struck, fast and true. She bit Sariah's head clean off her shoulders with a crunch I would be hearing in my nightmares for months. The god killer dagger fell onto Cole's lap, and Sariah's body toppled a few seconds later.

Legs gone to jelly, I sat on the lowest step before I joined her remains on the floor.

"Well," I panted, the pain catching up to me, "that was exciting."

I caught myself glancing at the door, half expecting Kapoor to stride in and complete the evening, but he didn't, and he never would again.

Dad, however, made his entrance wearing the scowl that had launched a thousand groundings during my teen years.

"Phoebe Heaton." He folded his arms over his chest and tapped his foot. "Shift. Now. Then get a mop." He ignored Sariah's headless corpse. "Hurry up, now. All that blood will stain."

His blasé attitude caused me to laugh, and once I started, I couldn't stop. Even when the pain grew to be more than I could handle, I still chuckled like he had told the greatest joke of all time.

"I told you guys she was cracked." Santiago huffed out a sigh. "No one ever listens to me."

"Give her a minute." Miller watched me with increasing worry. "She's just releasing steam."

The coterie engaged in a heated argument over human coping mechanisms and how maniacal laughter couldn't be a good sign I was dealing with the stress of the past few months. For no good reason, that tickled me even more.

After a full sixty seconds passed, and I was still going strong, Thom crossed to me and bit my hand.

After that, I forgot what was so funny.

The darkness was absolute, but the soft mattress comforted me before I broke out in cold chills worrying if Sariah had captured me again. On the heels of that happy thought, I remembered she was dead. I shouldn't have felt sad about that, but I did. Just a little. "Am I dead?"

A soft rumble came from my left. "No."

Well, that was good news. "How long was I out this time?"

Strain filled Cole's voice. "Three weeks."

"Three *weeks*?" I shoved upright. "Whose idea was that?"

"Yours." He flipped on a lamp and studied me in its glow. "Your body required the time to heal."

Careful of the wounds I recalled from my earlier bout of consciousness, I touched my chest and found delicate scar tissue crisscrossing the area over my heart. "What did I miss?"

"Your father grounded Phoebe for killing Sariah. She's got another week left on restriction. Maggie recruited Miller to help her claim your old room, since it's the second largest in the house. She reasoned there are two of them but only one Santiago, so it's only fair they get more space."

A laugh escaped me, and I was pleased when it didn't hurt. "Business as usual, huh?"

"More than you know." He picked up his phone and hit a button. "She's awake."

After he ended the call, I waited to be filled in on the rest of the news, but he didn't enlighten me.

Rixton burst into the room whistling a jaunty tune with a garment bag slung over his shoulder. "Hey, Bou-Bou."

"I'm recovered enough to kick your ass if you don't stop calling me that."

"Good." He hung it on the curtain valance and grinned. "Then you're well enough to go to work."

"Work?" I goggled at him. "Did the NSB make contact?"

"We made contact with Kapoor's replacement." Cole helped me into a sitting position and then joined me. "He fired you."

"That happens when you take a leave of absence without informing the boss." I massaged my nape, relief and embarrassment mingling. "Guess I'll have to start job hunting."

"No need," Rixton informed me. "I found you gainful employment while you were lazing about."

He pulled down the zipper to reveal ... a Canton Police Department uniform.

"Rixton ..." I didn't know what to say. "How?"

"I might be retired," Dad said from the doorway, "but I know the new chief." He winked. "I put in a good word for you. You can start whenever you're ready."

"I ..." I shook my head as if to clear it. "I never thought this far ahead."

"You don't have to come back if the badge isn't what you want." Rixton sat at the foot of the bed. "You've done enough protecting and serving to last a lifetime. You can always retire and let Cole be your sugar daddy."

"As much fun as that sounds —" and it was genuinely tempting, "— I can't just sit on my hands for the rest of my life."

"Good." Santiago passed me a tablet. "Read this."

The top story in the local paper gushed about a recent housing boom and rental shortage.

"What does it mean?" I passed it back to him. "What am I missing here?"

"Your new neighbors? They're charun. All of them." Santiago smirked when my mouth fell open. "Word spread about your heroics. Your allies want to live close to the woman who saved the world. They've bought up every piece of property they can within a twenty-five-mile radius of your farmhouse. I expect that area will continue to widen over time as more real estate becomes available."

"Canton is on its way to becoming a different type of nexus." Miller smiled as he joined the others. "You're going to have your hands full, Luce."

"We're starting a taskforce of our own," Rixton informed me. "Nothing official, but unofficially? It's going to kick ass. With so many charun in town, we're going to need to allocate resources to helping them acclimate to their new world order. Think MIB, except blue or red. I have cool-toned skin. I look better in those colors."

"Sounds like you have this all worked out." I gave Dad another glance. "What about you?"

"Your friend Wu bought this place from me and transferred the title into your name."

Wu had promised to cut a check for the farmhouse to fund Dad's retirement after I allowed it to be used as a temporary sanctuary for the enclave, but I didn't know he went through with it, or that he had given it to me.

"Oh" was the best response I could articulate.

"With the proceeds, I decided to buy a smaller house in town." He cleared his throat. "With Miranda."

"Does it have a pool?" I joked, but Dad flushed. "It does, doesn't it? Let me guess — it's saltwater."

People would think he was cradle robbing, but I doubted he cared. I sure wasn't going to say anything, especially since the reverse was true. Dad deserved all the happiness his heart could hold, and if that happiness came with a tail ... well ... I wouldn't begrudge him that either.

Examining each face around the gathering, I was missing one person. "Where is Phoebe?"

"She's shopping for school clothes with Miranda," Cole told me. "She wants to enroll, get the full human experience the way you did."

"School wasn't a picnic for me." I shrugged it off but navigating high school had frustrated me no end. "The whole Wild Child thing." I hated spilling my guts with Dad standing there. "She might do better enrolling under your name and leaving me off the paperwork."

"That's for her to decide." He threaded our fingers and brought my hand to his lips. "Something tells me she's already made up her mind."

"How do we explain the resemblance?" I fidgeted with the hem of my shirt. "Several of my teachers are still at the school."

"She isn't catching on." Santiago cackled. "He never said she was enrolling at *your* school."

"She would need documentation to prove she's a resident before she can register outside this district." I was the first to admit my head was still fuzzy, but Santiago was making it harder on me than it had to be. As usual. "Unless she's going private?"

"She'll enroll in Jackson." Cole took pity on me and filled in the blanks. "We have investment properties there. We can use one of those addresses for the school. She didn't want to go private. She wants to have the full experience."

"How will she . . . ?" I palmed my forehead. "Wings."

Human kids her age either begged their parents for a lift to school to avoid the bus or daydreamed about the day they received their driver's license for the same reason. Phoebe would never have to learn how cramped, smelly, and miserable a bus ride could be thanks to her wings and invisibility.

"It sounds like you guys have worked everything out." I cocked an eyebrow at the gathering. "It doesn't seem like I'm needed here. Maybe I should continue napping my life away."

More footsteps rang out in the hall, and Sherry appeared with Nettie in her arms.

"You can't nap your life away." She crossed to us and dumped my godchild in my arms. "I need some alone time with my husband, and I just volunteered you since you're the reason he's been MIA."

"Uh." I held the baby with as much fear as a live hand grenade. "You're leaving her? With me?"

"Yep." She hooked a finger in Rixton's beltloop and hauled him to her. "You've been falling down on the job, G-mom. Now you have to make up for lost time."

"Rixton?" I fed a plea into my expression. "Do something."

Wiggling his eyebrows at Sherry, he chuckled. "Don't worry, I'm about to."

"Back in two hours." She waved to me. "Thanks in advance."

Rixton held up twin peace signs. "Make that four."

After backing from the room, he spun on the threshold and chased after her. Their footsteps pounded down the stairs, and their laughter filled the old house as they raced to the front door.

"I'll take her." Maggie swooped in to steal the baby. "They're so cute at this age."

"They're cute at all ages," Portia countered. "Look at the dimple in her chin."

One thing bothered me. "How did they know to be here?"

Unless my eyes were playing tricks on me, I spied a diaper bag just inside the door to my room. Sherry had come prepared to leave Nettie with me. Something smelled fishy around here.

"I might have helped you along," Thom admitted. "It's not healthy for you to remain in a healing fugue longer than necessary."

The worry pinching his brow made me want to squirm. "Are you saying I didn't want to wake up?"

"He's saying you've endured trauma that can't be healed with sleep and salve," Miller said gently. "You've suffered many losses and had no time to mourn them. Emotional pain can manifest as physical exhaustion. Your spirit needed time to heal as much as your body, but it's easy to get lost in a place where you don't feel the pain you're meant to be recovering from."

"Ah." I got it now. "Thom gathered you all here and gave me a hit of something to wake me."

Miller nodded, and so did Thom, but the latter still appeared unhappy.

"I'm going to take some long overdue advice," I announced to all of them. "I'm going to start therapy. Kapoor swears by it." I hesitated. "He swore by it."

"Lots of cops in therapy." Dad smiled, his relief tangible. "I can grab you a referral easy."

"I'd like that." I noticed Thom had yet to relax. "I'm not okay yet, but I'll get there."

That eased the tension in his shoulders and smoothed the creases from his forehead.

Eager to test my sea legs after lazing about for so long, I stood close enough I could fall back on the bed rather than jam my tailbone on the floor if I wobbled. When I had no trouble getting around, other than the sweat beading my forehead, I shooed everyone out while I pulled on clothes.

Cole remained, and I didn't mind his gaze roving over me one bit. Even if his interest ran more toward clinical than I would like.

Once I had on clean undies, sweats, and a tee, I found myself standing in front of the garment bag Rixton left me. "Where do we go from here?"

"Anywhere." He pressed a kiss to the side of my throat. "Our futures are wide open."

Leaning back against him, I let my eyes close as the possibilities unfurled before me, a road with so many forks I couldn't choose a single one to walk. For the first time in what felt like forever, I could do anything, go anywhere. I was well and truly free. We all were.

Limitless potential swirled in the air, and I sucked it down, eager for a taste of what was to come, content that whatever path I chose, the others would walk alongside me.

"I like the sound of that." I rubbed my thumb over the gleaming badge pinned above the breast pocket of the uniform shirt. "I like it a lot." I turned in his arms and patted his cheek. "Almost as much as I like you."

"You love me." He tickled my sides until I squirmed. "Admit it."

"I do love you." I brushed my lips over his. "So much I'll give you a head start."

Confusion gave way to understanding, and his next kiss blistered my mouth. "Count to ten."

"Five," I countered. "You don't need help to win."

After grunting his agreement, Cole took the stairs with a slight uptick in his usual gait.

I couldn't have stopped the smile curving my lips any more than I could halt the sun in its tracks. I might not feel up to playing prey to his predator at the moment, running was a no-go until I could stand without losing my breath, but that didn't mean I couldn't stalk him.

As much as I wanted to believe I had honed my tracking skills, I suspected he let me find him.

Just as I suspected I let him ravish me in our tent piled high with pillows, hopes, and dreams.

EPILOGUE

Farhan cracked open his eyes on a moonlit beach. Water frothed around his ears, soaking his back, but his skin pulled tight with sunburn, and dehydration cracked his lips.

"We got a live one." A young boy leaned over him, grinning. "His eyes are open and everything."

A woman with cascading blonde hair, tiny shells braided into its length, appeared beside the boy.

"You are right." She patted the top of his head. "You did well, Ian."

"Where am I?" Farhan rasped. "Who are you?"

The dress she wore shimmered like abalone, and the wind snapped the damp hem against her ankles.

"I am Tatiana." She knelt beside him, her fingers cool on his skin. "I am called Queen of the Seas."

"There is no sea queen." No intel existed on a Tatiana of that renown. He would know. It was his job to know. No, it had been his job. With both his bosses dead, he wasn't certain of his current employment status. "How did I get here?"

"We are aware of your organization." Her smile bared teeth as white as pearls. "We have taken great pains to avoid its notice." The boy returned and passed her a waterskin she dribbled over Kapoor's lips. "As to how you got here, we fished you out of the water."

The sweetness of the water left him parched for more, which she provided.

"A pod of Diorte passed through," she continued, "and we assumed you were a carcass they left in their wake. They normally do not feed when they cull, as the purpose is to die. That made you a peculiarity, and I dislike those so close to my home." She cut him off when he started coughing. "I sent scouts. They reported you were alive and brought you here to recover."

"How long ago?"

"Many weeks."

"You left me to bake in the sand for weeks?"

"You were in the infirmary for most of it." Chiming laughter broke free of her scale-encrusted chest. "Once you had recovered enough, we brought you here, where you could wake on land rather than underwater."

"I appreciate that." Farhan shoved into a seated position. "Your infirmary is underwater?"

That would explain why it felt like his brain was sloshing.

"I can't tell you all my secrets." She joined him on the sand, pulled her knees to her chest, and braced her chin on the forearms she draped over her legs. "Unless you tell me yours first."

Decades of ingrained service to the NSB, to his taskforce, firmed his lips.

"It's all right." She touched his cheek. "I was only teasing. Trust isn't so easily earned — or given."

"Thank you for saving me." He accepted the waterskin and took a few careful sips. "I thought I wanted to die. I was prepared for it. I expected it to happen."

"You were part of the battle," she mused. "I suspected as much given the severity of your wounds. We were not involved, but we observed."

Censure honed his voice into a blade. "You saw it going down and didn't pitch in?"

"No one asked us to, which is, I'm afraid, the downside of devoting your life to secrecy. No one knew we existed to ask us, and since it took some watching to grasp what was happening, it was too late for us to do more than fish survivors such as yourself from the water in the hopes we could revive them."

Farhan grunted, awarding her the point. Better to avoid the battle than fight on the wrong side.

Tatiana flexed her toes, thick with webbing, in the damp sand. "What's your name?"

Farhan parted his lips, but nothing passed them.

"Let me guess." She chuckled. "Amnesia?"

"Something like that."

"Well, I can't return you to the world if you don't so much as know your own name. Would you like to join us? You're welcome to stay until you've fully recovered."

He whipped his head toward her. "What?"

"If kindness shocks you, I'm glad you don't remember your life." She stood and offered him her hand. "Come with me. There's food in the gathering hut. You must be starving. The infirmary pumps in nutrients, but let's say no one has ever asked for their recipe."

Admitting kindness only ever preceded punishment would have ruined the moment. "I could eat."

"You need a name." She kept hold of him, guiding him in her wake. "How about Asees?" She pulled on him when he dragged behind. "It means blessing." She glanced back at him. "You are blessed to have survived, don't you agree?"

Blessed was the most ironic name anyone could have assigned him, but he didn't have the heart to tell her so. "Yes."

At the gathering hut, he met more of her people and a few survivors like himself. He noticed she didn't linger with them but remained by his side. He wasn't sure what it meant. Maybe nothing. But hers was the first kind hand to touch him in memory, and he couldn't believe she didn't want something in return.

"You're suspicious." She served him a platter filled with seafood then joined him at his table. "I respect that. After all, nothing is free."

Relief swirled through him. "Exactly."

Tapping a finger against her bottom lip, she said, "The price for you to remain here among us is . . ."

Farhan braced himself for a kill order or equally unsavory task to perform. That's all he was good for, all he had ever been good for, and the fact she looked at him and saw it curdled his gut.

" . . . you must tend the nets twice a day to ensure no dolphins get caught in them."

He waited for the rest. There had to be more. Mines floating in the water that would explode if he bumped them. Sharks trained like German Shepherds to attack anyone who ventured too close. Poison dart fish, killer algae, polluted water — something. There had to be a catch.

"Oh, Asees." She stroked his hair. "There is no trick, no trap. I will teach you myself."

The gentle caress of her soft fingertips threatened to break some undefinable thing in his chest.

"All will be well." She pressed her lips to his cheek. "I swear it."

Capturing her hand, he dared to remember how it felt to want. "Is there a sea king by any chance?"

Laughter filled her eyes and spilled over her lips, and he was helpless not to join in.

Maybe he had died. Maybe this was his own version of Heaven. Maybe he would wake in a hospital bed to find it was all a dream.

Whatever it was, however long it lasted, Asees was grateful for the blank slate and the kindness of beautiful strangers.

"Bou-Bou," Rixton called. "Take a look at this."

I left the human witness behind, bathed in the strobing light from our patrol car, to examine the massive crater left in the asphalt by an as yet to be identified charun. Elongated dirt clods filled the bottom. Eight or nine of them. Each one a perfect match for the others.

"What is that?" I leaned over the edge. "It almost looks like ..."

A furious cry rent the still night, and I jerked my head around in time to spot what appeared to be an iguana on steroids. Make that a winged iguana on steroids. I didn't see where it came from, but it was divebombing us quicker than we could decide on a course of action and react.

"Get in the car," I yelled at the woman. "Get back in your car."

The witness got in, all right. She also cranked it and sped off in the direction of town.

"This is going to end up in the papers," I grumbled. "Just you wait."

I could picture the headline now: *Wild Child Boudreau Fends Off Flying Lizard of Unusual Size.*

The frantic charun landed in the middle of the road and stamped its front legs. The resulting percussive blast almost shook me off my feet.

"It's a mini earthquake machine," Rixton yelled. "How freaking awesome is that?"

"It would be more freaking awesome if it wasn't trying to kill us."

"It's not trying to kill us," he shouted. "It's protecting its nest."

The dirt clods were ... eggs?

"It can't nest in the middle of the road." I reached for my decidedly *not* department-issued Taser. "I'm going to stun it. Get the net ready."

Sprinting for the nest, guaranteeing the mother would follow, I waited until the last second then pivoted, took aim, and shot her in the chest. Electricity buzzed through her, and she dropped out of the air into a twitching heap on the pavement.

"Any day now." I pocketed the weapon and craned my neck for my absent partner. *"Rixton."*

"Incoming." He cast a weighted net over the creature. "Got her."

"This is not what I imagined when you proposed we start our own taskforce," I panted. "This isn't police work. It's game warden work."

We performed captures, relocations, and all manner of services to keep humans as blissfully ignorant of their charun neighbors as possible. Most of them had the sense not to get caught out, but a few kept otherworldly pets that got lost, got stolen, got free of their cages. This had to be one of those.

"Admit it." Rixton gave her a shot of tranquilizer that sent her off to beddy-bye. "You love it."

"You can collect the eggs." I knelt beside the creature, lifted the net, and applied restraints, careful not to hurt its wings. "I got them last time."

We had fished those out of the swamp, and they resembled a clot of frog eggs. The parents were attacking folks out hunting gators. Given how infamous I had made Cypress Swamp, we had to act fast before the word spread and people swarmed the area in search of more cryptids.

A small part of me wondered if I hadn't made a mistake in

deciding to settle in my hometown. Traveling with the coterie had opened my eyes, taught me to relish the anonymity of new towns where no one looked at me and thought *Swamp Thing*. But out there, no one looked at me and thought *that's Edward Boudreau's girl* either.

While Rixton performed the delicate work of packing the eggs into a foam-lined cooler, I set out orange traffic cones to mark the hole so that motorists wouldn't drive into the pit before it could be filled, on our dime. Good thing White Horse turned a hefty profit. Making incidents like this one disappear wasn't cheap.

"Done," Rixton called. "Let's crate momma and get moving."

About to do just that, I jolted when Phoebe materialized beside me.

"I made an A on my exam." She waved the paper in front of my nose. "And I made a friend. She invited me to try out for the dance team."

"That's great." I would have hugged her if she held still long enough. "Have you told your dad yet?"

"Nope." Paper clutched to her chest, she waved to Rixton. "I spotted you on my way home and stopped to show you first."

"We're wrapping things up here." I gestured toward the White Horse SUV Rixton and I had confiscated for our side jobs. "Want to grab a pizza to celebrate?"

"Can I have froyo after?" She put the screws to me. "I'll sneak out your usual."

The ban at Hannigan's was still in effect, so I was forced to use my kid as a froyo double agent. "Fine."

"Can we call Dad?"

"Sure thing, kiddo." I shooed her. "Go wait in the SUV."

Rixton and I finished loading the sedated charun and her eggs in the back, but he caught me by the arm before I climbed in with Phoebe. I didn't feel any dissonance or resonance these days. The former I could live without, but the latter ... I missed. More than I ever thought possible. Almost as much as I missed my inner dragon.

"What's up?"

"You didn't hear this from me," he whispered to thwart Phoebe's super hearing, "but your kid's got a hickey on her neck."

"*What?*"

He caught my chin between his thumb and finger before I could whip my head toward her.

"She's a sophomore in high school," he reminded me. "It happens."

"I didn't know she had a boyfriend."

"I can't imagine why she would keep that to herself. It's not like her father will hunt down her sweetie and chomp him in half."

"I ... " As much as I wanted to defend Cole, I couldn't fudge this. "Yeah. He will."

"Ask Sherry for tips on using makeup to conceal the evidence. Phoebe will thank you for it."

"I'll do that." And when Nettie turned old enough to have boys leaving marks on his daughter, I would remind him of this moment. "Care to join us?"

"Nah." He jingled his keys. "It sounds like this should be a family dinner."

"You are family." I shoved him. "Sure I can't tempt you?"

"Uh, no." He walked toward the driver's side laughing. "Cole is about to find out his little girl ain't little no more. I don't want to be at the same table, in the same restaurant, or in the same town when that happens."

"Chicken."

"Bawk-bawk."

"*Grrr.*"

"That was scarier when you had a dragon to back it up."

Since Thom gave me a clean bill of health, I had been too afraid to reach for my inner dragon, terrified I would come up empty. A smidgen of hope was better than a dollop of truth. But I felt around in me, checking out the corners where Conquest used to hide, and found a kernel of potential.

The world spun around me, and my vision brightened to a vivid crimson.

"How is this possible?" Rixton craned his neck to look up, *way up*, at me. "I thought you were ..."

The growl I made came out reptilian and ancient, much more impressive than my first attempt.

"Don't get your scales in a bunch." He backed toward the SUV. "I was joking about the scary thing. You're plenty scary. Look, I'm shaking in my boots. Terrified. I might even wet my pants."

"Mom?"

Craning my neck, I locked onto Phoebe as she slid out of the SUV.

"Are you ... ?" She linked her fingers at her navel. "Are you still you?"

Before answering, I took full stock of myself and trilled at her.

I was still me. Just me with an inner dragon who must have required those weeks of healing to recover too. What that made me — human or charun — didn't matter. I was Luce Boudreau, and I was exactly who I was meant to be.